The Winchester Goose
At the court of Henry VIII

Judith Arnopp

Best wishes,
Judith x

Acknowledgements.

My heartfelt thanks go out to everyone who helped with the creation of this novel. To my writing group, Cwrtnewydd Scribblers for listening and critiquing. To my husband John for reading, encouraging and believing. To my editors Helen Spring and Cas Peace for taming my punctuation and to my university professor, Janet Burton, for introducing me to medieval women all those years ago.

The Winchester Goose

The Wincestrian goose
Bred on the bank in time of popery
When Venus there maintain'd her mystery
(Ben Jonson – Underwoods 1692 folio)

Prologue – Joanie Toogood - Southwark Stews

Although she follows me, I can tell she wishes she wasn't here. She lifts her skirts above the foulness of the alleyway and her feet slip in the mire, the hem of her gown all besmirched with mud. She is pale, glancing anxiously from side to side, her lips colourless as she shivers and sweats, and her hands are trembling as if she has the plague.

We pass my friend, Bertha, who is sitting on her threshold with her skirts hitched, airing her blue-veined legs. I wave 'good day' to her but she doesn't respond for, just as she sees me, her man comes lurching round the corner, sozzled with drink although it is not yet noon. Every day he pisses all Bertha's hard earned pennies up the wall.

As his wife sets her beefy fists squarely on her hips and lashes him with her tongue, the lady beside me whips her eyes from the raucous disaster of their marriage. She turns her head so fast that I glimpse her yellow hair tucked beneath the veil of her hood. "I cannot be responsible for the things you see here, my dear," I say gently.

The way she averts her eye, raises her nose and flinches away from the stench of my world tells me a lot about her. She shies away from unpleasantness and would rather not see the half-naked starvelings peering from the shadows. Their hunger is an affront, their bare feet an insult, yet it was she who asked me to lead her here. It isn't my fault if she doesn't like what she finds.

We pass a stranger, a shady fellow up to no good. He melts away into the shadows, not wanting to be seen. When I stop suddenly, the lady does likewise and I point a finger along the route she is to take. "See there, past the midden where the pigs are rooting? It's up that stairway behind the inn that you must go. The Cock's Inn it's called, my dear."

She doesn't see the joke. She is an innocent, kept 'nice' by her mother. My own mother did nothing to protect her daughters from the world, but she made sure we learned enough to follow where she led.

"Be careful on those rickety steps," I call after her. "My room is the one right at the end."

I wonder what she will make of the musty chamber, where one corner of the shingle leaks when the rain is blown in from the west. My sisters and I have grown accustomed to damp in that corner and catch the worst of the drips in a bowl, for water always comes in handy. Things've been a lot worse, mind, before our luck began to change. Once, the place was caked with grime and the blankets on our narrow bed were thin and moth-eaten, but I've a thicker counterpane now.

In winter the bitter blast still manages to find a way through the broken shutter but we do well enough and are grateful to have a room at all. It is better than a ditch and provides us what comfort it can. But my fine, pretty lady will not have seen anywhere like it before, of that I am certain.

"Go on up, my dear, that's where you'll find him." I urge her onward, knowing Francis will have thrown off his cloak and be growing impatient. As I watch her sidling past the pigs, tiptoeing through the mire, I snort at her gullibility but then, as she places her foot on the lowest step, to my surprise I feel a twinge of conscience.

I bite my lower lip, wondering if I should call her back. What will she say to him? What would any woman say on finding her husband sprawled on a whore's bed on a dull July morning?

But she is gone, already climbing gingerly up the unsteady stairs, her gloved hand reaching out to push open the chamber door. I hold my breath and listen for the rumpus that will follow for it promises to be as good as any bawdy play. Instead, I hear a scream so grisly that it turns my skin to gooseflesh. The hair stands up on my scalp and, for a few moments, I find I cannot move.

Then, all of a sudden, I am wrenching up my skirts to fly across the yard and scramble up the steps behind her. Just as I reach the top, she stumbles backwards across the threshold with her hands held to her face.

Her eyes are wide open, her mouth like an ugly scar as she gropes blindly at my arms, scrabbles at me, babbling nonsense. I am afraid of such madness and cannot bear to let her touch me.

Crossing myself in the old way, I wrench away from her clutching hands so violently that she loses her footing. Her ankle turns on the top step and I see her face open like a flower as she realises she is going to fall. Before I can stop her, she tumbles backwards, her body bouncing loosely from stair to stair.

I dare not look down and it takes a few moments for me to find the courage to peer at the bundle of fine linen and velvet that is sprawled in the mud. She is lying very still and her face is white, her eyes closed but I think I can just see her chest rising

3

and falling. I don't know whether to run and help her or venture indoors to see what trouble awaits me there.

There is no sound from within and I glance one more time at her prone body before, with my heart hammering like a drum, I hold my breath and push open the door.

Isabella Bourne – 1540

For a long time I thought I was the fairer of the two but as she grew, my sister Eve blossomed into such prettiness that I soon found myself cast into her shade. I am older than her by a year and a half, my hair is a shade darker, my skin less luminous and beside hers, my eyes lack vitality. If that wasn't bad enough, her pretty looks are complimented by a charming wit and ready laughter. But whenever I am in company, I fumble in vain for something even passably entertaining to say.

One of my most unpleasant memories is of an aunt consoling my mother by saying that plainer girls make better housewives. I have no inclination to be a housewife. I want a place at court, as lady-in-waiting to the Queen, where I might have the chance of catching a suitor rich enough to employ a housekeeper and a string of household servants. Our family may be of the middling sort now, but our bloodline is unparalleled. In the privacy of our parlour I have heard my father say more than once that our lineage is superior to that of the King, and it is common knowledge that if my grandfather had only sided with Lancaster at Bosworth, instead of York, then our dynasty might still be riding high. As it is, we creep and scramble a wearisome way back up the ladder of fortune.

You may think from my words that bitterness mars the love I bear my sister, but she is too loveable to dislike. I may wish I were the favourite daughter instead of a foil for her beauty, but I love her all the same. She is the other half of me, the better half, and sometimes I think she is the cleverer half also. She certainly seems to get what she wants.

I can hear her laughter now, bubbling along the corridor, her footsteps skittering lightly on the slate floor. She bursts into the room, her skirts sweeping the rushes, her cap slipping from her hair.

"There you are, Isabella. Did you hear the news, the wonderful news?"

I put down my needle, her happiness lifting my spirits long before I glean its cause.

"No, what news is this?"

She grasps my wrists and pulls me to my feet, spinning me round, forcing me to join her in a dizzy dance.

"We are summoned to court, you and I. We are to go together to meet the new Queen. I know she will invite us to join her household, I just know it."

There is a small twinge of disappointment that, as the elder sister, I will not be going to court alone. Without Eve beside me I may have managed to shine a little brighter, but I push the bitterness away and return her joy, squeeze her hands and join her in a merry jig.

We are still turning in joyous circles when a footstep sounds on the threshold and we look up to find our mother watching us. As serene as always, she glides into the solar and takes her place at the hearth, her hair carefully covered with a cap, her hands folded neatly before her, perfectly poised, perfectly elegant. "I see you have heard the tidings."

Ignoring etiquette, Eve launches herself into her lap and I watch a little enviously as Mother's hands slide about my sister's waist. Eve is as irresistible as a spoonful of golden honey.

"Will we have new gowns?"

"Oh yes, and shoes and sleeves. You must both do us proud, the Bournes are as good as any family at court. But remember, both of you, modesty is a woman's greatest virtue and once lost it can never be regained, so guard your honour above all things."

I stand a little apart, a flush upon my cheek, wondering if I should ever be given the heady choice of behaving immodestly. I've barely spoken to a man outside the sphere of our family. While Eve launches into a discussion of the latest dances and the best place to purchase a velvet coif, I wander to the casement and look out across the courtyard gardens and let her chatter dwindle away.

A little later, when Father and our young brother, Tom, join us I notice straight away that he is unusually quiet. I know that he would like to keep us forever babies and worries about Eve and I leaving the security of Bourne Manor. Even here in the countryside we have heard tales about the goings on at the Royal court.

Father no longer attends the King, not if he can help it. Since Queen Anne's beheading he has managed to remain safely at home, reading the Scriptures, praying for religious peace, trying to be impartial in a world that forces a man to choose between God and his King.

Father believes that for all her brittle ways Queen Anne did not deserve to die, and he refuses to give credence to the lies that were spread about her.

The men accused alongside her were his friends and, once or twice, he even talked with the Queen herself on liturgical matters. To him, her sharp intelligence was of more importance than her beauty or her quick, ready laughter and he believes that, given the chance, she would have made a good consort for Henry.

Of course, a favoured Queen championing the Lutheran cause would have served my father and his friends well, but it was not to be. Once she lost the King's interest, her influence waned too and when his eye fell upon another she was killed for no greater crime than failing to provide the country with an heir. Although we could not show it, my family were sorry at her death and her rapid replacement with the King's favourite was like salt rubbed into a sore place.

No one expected Jane Seymour to keep the King entranced for very long and everyone acknowledges her childbed death to be a happier way for a Queen to die than on the scaffold. Now people talk of Queen Jane as if she were some wondrous phoenix who sacrificed herself in giving life to the Tudor prince. But Father, and I suspect others like him, see her as just another sad little pawn in the rich game of Kings.

Father says King Henry is surrounded by ingratiating, self-seeking fools, and those who adhere to the old ways try to oust those who champion the new. Thus the power at the King's court tips back and forth like a child's see-saw with Henry in the middle, the pivot upon which they all swing. As one side rises, so the other falls. We all know the danger.

"You must not fall foul of King Henry," Father tells me. "It is best that you try to be invisible and not attract his attention." He glances from my plain, attentive face to where Eve is stitching at the fireside, her forehead painted with the flame's rosy glow. "And keep your sister invisible too," he adds sadly, although we both know that Eve's vitality draws all men's eyes, wherever she goes.

It will not be easy to keep her safe.

7

For the next few weeks I feel as if I am spinning on a great wheel, for each day passes so quickly I can scarce catch my breath. But then suddenly the wheel stops, and I am no longer engaged in trimming frocks and sewing petticoats. Instead, I am dazed to find myself sinking into a curtsey before King Henry and his new Queen. Eve is crouched beside me. I can hear her short, excited breath as her corset stabs into her belly, just as mine is doing.

We remain prostrate, waiting for the invitation to rise; our skirts are spread around us, our heads meekly lowered. I hear the King's impatient sigh and suspect he is bored, itching to hunt or dine. When the Queen speaks, her voice is so guttural that I do not at first recognise the sound as conversation. She has to repeat her request and I realise she is bidding us to rise.

Diminished by the astonishing figure of our King, Queen Anna, lately arrived in England from Cleves, smiles down upon us. She is as unlike the other women of the court as can be. Her clothes are heavy, covering every part of her flesh and leaving only her face and hands visible. Beside the light gowns and snowy bosoms of the court ladies she appears drab and matronly, even to me. My eyes sweep over her, taking in her plain face and the strange clothes that seem to encase her as if she were a parcel never, ever to be unwrapped. Not even by a King.

When I tear my gaze from her clothes my spirits lift a little, for her cheeks are dimpling in welcome and her eyes are twinkling, full of kindness. With a rush of relief I know I have nothing to fear, not from this Queen, and I return her smiles in full measure.

The other women, as bright as butterflies about a fat moth, titter behind their hands as the Queen

8

beckons us forward and begins to force her hesitant tongue around our unfamiliar language. I suddenly wish that I knew a few words of German, that I might put her at her ease. I can imagine how friendless she must feel in this foreign country, this alien court and this huge, draughty palace. With great daring I open my mouth, venturing to speak and willing her to recognise me a potential friend but, as usual, Eve forestalls me.

She takes a step forward, oblivious to the indrawn breaths of outrage from the other ladies. "Oh, Your Majesty," Eve says boldly, "what a pretty thing."

I glance at the King, who narrows his eyes as he assesses the exchange between them, assesses Eve who is supposed to have remained invisible. Queen Anna blinks at my sister for a moment, and then puts a hand to her neck and clasps the jewelled cross that Eve has admired. Her cheeks are redder than they were before and when she speaks her voice is husky with emotion.

"Thank you. My mother gave it to me just before I left Düsseldorf."

She blinks back tears and Eve, with a look of pure compassion, reaches out to cover the Queen's hand with her own. The shocked intake of breath from the watching courtiers is louder this time but the friendship between Eve and the Queen is sealed, leaving me on the outside.

I soon come to realise how lucky I am to be an ordinary girl. For all the fine jewels and pomp, it is hard to be a Queen. There is no respite for Anna and each minute is filled with duty and spectacle, allowing no time for privacy.

Apart from Mother Loew and a handful of lesser women, Anna's household has been sent home to Cleves to make way for English girls who, like us, are eager for advancement. Lady Rochford is there. I know my father's opinions of her and let my eyes trail across her features, her indrawn mouth, her fleeting glance. She has served at court for a long time and has been a member of Henry's Queens' household since her youth. It was her time with Anne Boleyn that made Jane notorious, for the whole court was shocked when she so narrowly escaped the Tower herself by giving evidence against the Queen and her own husband, Queen Anne's brother, Thomas Boleyn.

At home we were forbidden to speak of such things but gossip finds a way of reaching even the most protected ears. As I let my eyes trickle across her closed face, I wonder how she finds the strength of will to rise above the mutterings against her. How can a woman accuse her husband of intrigue, treason and incest and ever sleep at night again? I shudder with repulsion.

Anne Basset and Catherine Carey, who are standing beside Jane Rochford, see where my thoughts are wandering and wink at me. Eve and I played with them once or twice when we were children and I can tell, even before we are introduced, that very little has changed. They are both still vivaciously ambitious, vying with one another in both dress and manners. I flush a little and return their smile, wondering if our childhood friendship will be resumed. I have never yet had the chance to behave like a young girl; perhaps in their company I can put aside my seriousness and grow more frivolous, more like Eve. Perhaps the young women here may even come to like me a little.

There is no peace for Queen Anna. Several times a day, ladies come to help her dress, maids fetch and carry, messengers come to and fro so that her rooms constantly buzz with attendants. When she prays, when she sleeps and even when she uses the close stool, a group of women remain on call should she have need of them. The only time she is ever to be left unattended is when the King chooses to visit. Then we must glide soundlessly from their presence. But so far, during my time with her, he has come not at all.

The gossips whisper that he came for the first few weeks but she does not please him, he finds her appearance repellent, the style of her clothes unattractive. Like most men he cannot see through the superficiality of her plain face to the warm, human heart that beats within.

Poor Anna, I wish I could help her. I know she is troubled by the conundrum of providing the King with an heir, but she confides in no one. It seems to me that the King does all he can to avoid her bed and, when for the third night in a row he does not attend her, Eve tries to offer her some comfort.

"Perhaps the King is ailing, Madam," she says. "I expect his leg is troubling him again."

The Queen, vulnerable in her high-necked nightgown, her thick red-brown braids hanging from her ears, assumes a cheerful expression and turns her attention to her yappy little dog. She takes him into her bed to sleep beside her upon the richly embroidered counterpane, but as I bend to pick up her soiled linen, the smile slides from her face and her eyes grow sombre again.

In truth, she lacks the skills to entertain a man like the King. She does not play an instrument and has neither the ready wit of Anne Boleyn, nor the soothing nature of Queen Jane. Poor Anna is awkward, making so many blunders each day that the courtiers begin to turn away from her and her advisors frantically try to force her into some semblance of the sort of woman Henry requires. But we all suspect it is an impossible task. We all know what Henry really wants.

The Queen's lack of womanly wiles sorely tries the patience of the King's secretary, Master Cromwell. As the man responsible for championing the marriage, he is the one who will bear the brunt of the King's displeasure. He visits my mistress daily, advising her on how to deport herself and, in matters too delicate for him to broach, he employs the aid of her closest confidantes. Her senior women put their heads together to decide who is best suited to instruct the Queen on the wifely duty of which she surely has no knowledge.

Francis Wareham

I am just turned fifteen on the day my mother's laundry maid accuses me of fathering her brat. Of course, I try to deny it but when she produces a child with a knot of flaming hair just like my own, no one believes me. Father takes a rod to my back, each red-hot stroke deepening my sense of injustice, my hatred toward him, and my anger at the world, but I squeeze my eyes tight and refuse to give in to boyish tears.

After that day my mother does not look at me again. Instead, she maintains a pained, pious expression that would try the patience of a saint. The girl, Kate, is a pretty thing but she won't talk to me either. She does nothing but weep on the day she is sent away in shame. I have no idea what they plan to do with her child and do not think of it again.

A few years later Father catches me in the scullery kissing a kitchen wench and without delay draws out his instrument to abuse me again. As the thin tip of his switch cuts into my bare buttocks I bite my lip and decide I've had enough. I resolve to seek my fortune elsewhere and at midnight I rise from my bed, fumbling for my cloak in the dark. Before I leave I break his rod across my knee and leave the two halves on his desk. Then I saddle his favourite horse and ride away, determined to never return.

I do not look back. My brother, Theobald, is welcome to my share of the inheritance for I am determined upon a life of adventure. Maybe I will become a pirate and sail upon the sea, gleaning riches from the weak and the foolish. With my childhood

13

behind me I ride into the night, spurred on by a bravado that cannot last.

There are a hundred miles or more of rough road between my father's manor and London Town, but at first travelling is easy. I live well enough for a day or two, sinking my teeth into the pasties I'd had the foresight to steal from Mother's kitchen. I soon discover that a wink and a winsome smile go a long way with country wives, and I manage to glean other bits and pieces to sustain me along the way.

Thankfully, the weather is mild; it hasn't rained for weeks, so the road is firm and I am in high spirits and make goodly progress.

I am eager to reach my destination, lured by the gold-paved streets and the tales I've heard of the merry whores who line Bankside on the outskirts of the town.

London is a place of fortune, a city of learning and advancement. I spare not a thought for the reports of burnings and beheadings, for I am a green boy and think that such things can never touch me. Even in the countryside we know that a man's thoughts are no longer his own, but my own opinions can have no impact upon the wider world.

Before I am even half way there, a gang of thieves sneak upon my campfire, wave a dagger beneath my chin while they steal my breakfast, and ride away on my father's horse. I curse them roundly as they gallop off, more livid at my own carelessness than their dishonesty, but it teaches me a lesson and thereafter I become more wary of strangers.

The journey is far tougher on foot and by the time I limp beneath the Bishop's Gate, I no longer look like the son of a gentleman. People barge me in the street and look down their noses at my filthy doublet and the clumps of mud on my boots.

By luck, when I chance upon an inn and stumble into the yard to beg a pot of ale, I am greeted by a plump matron whom I later discover is named Marion. When I tell her my sorry tale she takes pity on me. I am glad for her motherly, gap-toothed smile and her big sorry eyes.

She makes much of me, plying me with food and drink, and I soon discover there is nothing Mary-like about her at all. Having buried several husbands she has long forgot what it means to be chaste and, within an hour of sluicing my head in her horse trough, I am warming my feet at her hearth. As she leans over to ease my boots from my stinking feet, I peek down her bodice to the generous curve of her bosom. She gives me just the sort of sly smile that a man like me cannot resist, and although she has thirty years to my seventeen, I cannot stop my hands from reaching out for her.

Marion is a merry sort, happy to begin and end the day in a cheerful bedtime romp but, between times, I have to learn to toe the line and treat her like a worthy woman before her meagre staff. She is reluctant to lose the respect of the underlings and so I follow her will, happy to remain her favourite, working in her kitchen, sampling her baking by day and the charms of her body by night.

I am there a week or so but then, one market day when I think she has gone for the morning, she comes back unexpectedly and catches me servicing her kitchen wench in a niche below the stairs.

Stars spin in the blackness of my inner eye as her broom comes down hard upon my head. My companion throws her apron over her face and flees, but I am too stunned to run and so suffer the full brunt of Marion's anger. Her blows are hard and painfully accurate.

So, without a penny to my name or a cloak for my back, I leave the comforts of Marion's hearth and, hunching my shoulders against the rain, I wander the filthy streets, looking to find myself another comfortable berth. I have nowhere to go and as a stranger in the city, I am vulnerable and a little afraid, although I would never admit that to anyone.

"It's about time I saw a bit of London Town," I comfort myself, for apart from Marion's kitchen and the mysteries of her bedchamber, I've seen very little yet of the city.

I already miss Marion. She was generous with her affection and, more to the point, believed in keeping up a man's pecker by feeding him well. When I think of her plump pasties and steaming stews, a part of me regrets sampling the tart, untested pleasures of the kitchen wench. As I turn toward the outskirts of the city I smile ruefully, for I know myself well enough to admit that if there is one thing I will never be able to resist, it is temptation.

Night is drawing in when, close by the chapel on London Bridge, I spy a bundle of straw in a doorway and settle down upon it to watch the down-and-outs and the desperate pass by. Hoping they will not notice me in the darkness of the doorstep, I burrow into the straw, wrap my arms about myself and rest my head against the stone wall, imagining instead the warm cushion of Marion's bosom.

Hours pass, the thinning crowd dwindles to nothing and peace settles. Above me, a bright moon hangs in a web of stars while below, the Thames, a stinking river of turds, slips slowly through the slumbering city.

I am dreaming when a sharp blow in the ribs tears me from sleep. I give a great cry as I am yanked from my nest and thrown into the gutter. I grunt as my attacker's boot sinks into my belly again and, gasping,

I roll away, scramble to my feet and run, his obscenities dying away as the space between us increases. My feet slither on the slickness of the cobbles and once I am sure I am no longer followed, I slow my pace, tuck my balled fists beneath my armpits and shamble onward, cold, miserable and alone.

I should have realised that pile of piss-ridden straw was somebody's home, for nothing in this city is free. Hunching my shoulders against the chill, I cross the bridge into the place I now know to be Southwark.

The darkness and unfamiliar territory transform me from a brave adventurer into a frightened boy and I dart from doorway to doorway, keeping to the shadows, desperate to lay myself down to rest. My thoughts turn to my mother. At first, the way is full of drunks and I know there are thieves on every street, murderers in each dark alley. I keep my head down and for the first time I wish myself back home. My head is still lowered when I turn a corner and suddenly run up hard against someone sheltering in the shadow of the wall.

"'Allo, my dear." A lanthorn lights a kind and comely face and, in the motherly manner that I crave, she takes my elbow and leads me from the main street into the foulness of an alleyway. At first I am afraid, knowing that my vulnerability in this wicked city screams aloud. I must look to be easy pickings but, with my money already gone, all that remains for a villain to take from me is my life.

Theft and murder, however, does not seem to be on this villain's agenda and I soon realise that she is engaging me in a sort of rough courtship.

"Wassa fine fella like you doing wandrin' about at this time o' night?" Her eyes sweep across my body, a smile lifting one side of her mouth and a dimple flickering in her cheek. Then, as the moon slips from behind a cloud and reveals my frozen features, she draws back and raises an eyebrow. "'Ere, does your mother know you're out?"

Her teasing reduces me further. It is years since I have felt or behaved like an infant. I am almost eighteen years old but there is something about her that unmans me and, to my dismay, I feel my chin begin to wobble although I fight to keep it firm.

"Hey." Her voice is soft as she reaches out and runs a finger along my cheek, trapping a tear that has escaped my control. A waft of her exotic perfume swims about my head. "Aw, bless you, me dear. You come along with Joanie, I've a place nearby where I can offer you comfort."

At the rear of a shabby inn, she takes my hand and leads me up rickety stairs to a room that is devoid of furniture apart from a narrow bed and a washstand. The fire has gone out but as if by sorcery, she kneels and the flame leaps beneath her hand, immediately imbuing the room with a comforting glow. Then she turns and comes toward me, begins to loosen my doublet and pushes me into the only chair. Into my fist she pushes a pot of ale, the handle of which is warmer than my fingers, and I clutch it as if my whole life depends upon its solidity.

After I have filled my belly Joan kneels before me, opens her bodice and guides my hand beneath her shift, making my whole body tremble. I feel like an untried boy again, although I've pleasured more girls than I can count. Then, without a word she begins to untie my cod-piece.

I am flat on my back in her bed. She smiles as she straddles me, her great breasts swaying in the light of the fire, her mouth open, her eyes enjoying my astounded pleasure, my rigid disbelief in her mastery. The smile on my face is that of an idiot for I am discovering that Joanie is the mistress of love. She

18

shows me things that I have never dreamed of and the memory of my previous encounters, the fumblings with servants and the courteous couplings I enjoyed with Marion, all dwindle away. They were nothing.

My head is filled with Joan, I can think no further than the lascivious lapping of her tongue, the spread of her white thighs, the bounce of her cherry tipped dugs and the relentless grip of her quaint.

I am lost in Joan.

I am Joan.

"You can't stay here, I have to work." She softens the harsh words by finding me a job as a pot boy in The Cock's Inn close by her room. I tell myself she wants to keep me close so that I can visit her often but I soon learn that the romance is over and now she takes a hard-earned penny for every favour.

Trapped in the torture of calf love, each time I visit her I beg to be allowed to stay but when she has done with me, she pushes me over the threshold and I am left staring at the scarred panelling of her door. I lurk in the yard, terrified of leaving, and when I see other men climb those stairs to sample her wares, jealousy bites deep.

I block my ears to the sounds of their pleasure but she has no mercy, and when she waves her leman goodbye, she leans over the balustrade so that her breasts tumble into view. She knows how I long for her but, ignoring my anguish, she casts a cock-stirring wink in my direction. I clench my fists, unsure if the person I long to kill is Joan, her fancy men … or myself.

I work hard at The Cock, collecting the pots, scrubbing the pewter with sand until I can see my face in it. When the last customer leaves, I wipe the scarred tables ready for the morning trade and sweep the floor, ignoring the winsome eye of the serving wench.

19

Then, with my wages in my fist, I climb the stairs to hand it over to Joanie. Almost every penny, save that which buys me bread, goes into her pot. Soon she has a new covering on her bed, new sleeves for Sundays and two stools where once there was only one. Joanie, at the peak of her beauty, is popular in her trade and prospers.

Now, I hesitate outside her door before knocking, uncertain if she will let me in or turn me away. My summons provokes a rustle of movement inside and, remembering my manners, I raise a hand to whip off my hat. The door opens slowly and a face appears from behind it, but it is not Joan who greets me.

Her younger sister, Sybil, leans on the threshold and watches me as, like an underling, I fumble with my cap. "I – I was looking for Joan."

Sybil leans forward, grabs my doublet and begins to draw me into the room.

"Joan ain't here, dearie, but Betsy and I can look after you." Betsy, Joan's youngest sister, is draped across the solitary bed, the sanctuary where, only yesterday, I had made love to my Joanie.

"No." I pull away, affronted by their forwardness. "My business is with Joan."

Betsy pulls herself from the pillows and walks, half dressed, toward us. I glimpse a pink nipple, a nest of dark hair lower down. Once, I would have fallen on her, any portal in a storm, but now, felled by love's arrow, I tear my eyes away and fasten my gaze just to the right of her ear.

"You're that country fellow she was telling us about, we know all about you. Sweet on our Joan, ain't cha? She'll be back come mornin', she's making her salutation to the Bishop."

The whores of Southwark pay their rent to the Bishop of Winchester and sport with the clergy hereabouts. Sybil and Betsy fall about at the crude joke but, made prudish by love, I curl my lip in distaste. The thought of my Joan debasing herself with a priest bites deep. My belly curls like a worm with jealousy and I have a wild longing to rescue her, take her back with me to my father's house, seek his forgiveness and resume my life as his dutiful heir.

I try to picture Joan, dressed sombrely in a matron's gown, her hair tamed beneath a white linen cap, but the image is difficult to capture and it fades completely when I try to imagine myself presenting Mother with a Winchester Goose as my future bride.

My happy dream dissolves.

But, I tell myself, that doesn't mean there is no hope of Joan ever becoming my wife. If I can only earn enough to keep her, she can give up whoring. There must be a better way to seek a living. I dislodge Sybil's fingers that are clutching my doublet and, throwing Betsy's arms from around my neck, I clatter down the stairway with their laughter following in my wake. Fumbling for my dignity, I walk briskly toward the bridge to clear my head.

Bankside teems with whores, thieves, villains, dispossessed monks; even the nobles who jostle shoulder to shoulder with the poor are here on shady business. Close by the bridge I lean over to watch the dark brown river pass slowly beneath me.

The water is littered with refuse and branches and as I stare as far into the depths as the murk will allow, the corpse of a sheep, washed down from the hills, crashes suddenly from between the pilings. The roaring torrent forces it to turn in a circle before the river takes it again and it resumes its stately journey. I am suddenly struck by my own likeness to this dead, sodden sheep that bobs helplessly along to wherever the river current cares.

I sigh raggedly and thrust a hand through my hair, as close to desolation as I have ever been. I want Joan with a desperation that will not let me rest and, like a wasp about a honey pot, I persist in the happy dream of wedding her. I know that my days of drifting are over and, for once in my life, I must be decisive.

I must *make* something happen.

A raven shrieks suddenly above me, and I look up to where a gibbet creaks and turns on the wind. Higher up on the parapet, a cadaver's mouth gapes as if in laughter and it seems to me that even the dead lack faith in my ability. A scattering of kites dart and dive down to tear the flesh from the maggot-ridden scalps and I scoff, feeling superior to the so-called friends of the King who are loved no longer.

It is as I turn to leave that I realise with a start of surprise that someone is observing me from an open doorway. An inconspicuous doorway with a nameplate swinging in the wind that is so grimy even the literate cannot read it. I narrow my eyes, wondering what it is about me that he finds so interesting and as I make to move indignantly on, a slight jerk of his head indicates that I should go with him. He turns and disappears into the darkness of his lair while I shift from foot to foot, wondering if I dare follow.

London is a hellhole, a noisy, dirty nightmare peopled with devils and cowards, but such is my wretchedness that I venture after him regardless. I have little left to lose. I sidle along a dark, panelled passage until I come to a door that stands open, lit from within. After a moment's hesitation, I step inside.

The doorway is so low that any man of height is forced to duck his head so that he creeps into the room furtively, as if on nefarious business. I straighten up as soon as I am able and look about me, tugging my doublet down and fumbling with my cap. A miserly flame provides such little light that the corners remain in darkness, making the room appear little more than a cell. I am all too aware of those shadows and everything they may conceal.

He stands with his back to me, one hand resting upon a table with an inkstand and books piled high, rolls of parchment tumbling to the floor. He pulls his gaze from a high-up window, where I can just discern the white streaked sky, and pulls back a stool. He is a small man, slightly stooped and balding, his eyes penetrating and calm. He takes a seat, elbows on the table as he regards me silently, the tips of his fingers pressed together. I notice that his nails are bitten to the quick.

I lick my lips, glance shiftily into the shadows, uncertain if he is honest or otherwise. He has a monkish look, which makes me suspect trickery all the more and my disquiet increases. Since the King closed the monasteries England is peopled with such men, monkish fellows up to their overgrown tonsures in deceit. Outcast wretches seeking a path in an altered world; a world they cannot make fit. He clears his throat and his voice when it comes is surprisingly musical, like a popish chant.

"My name is Nicholas Brennan and I've been watching you," he says and my blood chills as I cast my mind back, mentally retracing my movements, wondering what I've done wrong. I can't recall having broken any laws and so I cough the nervousness from my throat and feign a confidence I do not feel. With a hand to my dagger, I swagger a little, tilt my head and pitch my voice a shade lower than usual.

"Indeed? And may I ask why?"

His eyes slither about the room, as if seeking eavesdroppers, and I remember that in some parts of England there are spies in every hollow.

23

"I am ever on the lookout for a likely man. My master has need of those he can trust." There is a pause before he adds, "And I know your father to be an honest man."

"My father?"

"Oh yes, Master Wareham, we know well who you are. My people have been watching you for some months now. You keep intriguing company. A whoremonger is never taken seriously. He can come and go, both in court circles and lowly, with no questions asked. Such a man could serve my master well."

I scowl and decide I do not like this fellow. A whoremonger indeed! But before I can remonstrate with him, he pinions me with his icy stare, compelling me to do as he wishes.

"And who is your master?" I ask, trying to sound as if the answer to my question concerns me not at all. "What does he do?"

"His name need not concern you, but my master strives for a better England and attempts to lead the headstrong King along a new and learned path, young sir." He leans closer, the stench of his rancid breath forcing me to avert my nose. "My master is a powerful man. He is the King's servant, but you will not hear his name from my lips."

"How can you ask me to serve a man I do not know? Perhaps he works against the King. I should never do that. I am an honest fellow."

"I'm glad to hear it." Master Brennan fixes me with pale, cold eyes that seem to burn right through my bravado. He clears his throat. "You have my word that we work only in the King's interest and for the good of England. In these days it is hard for a man to know whom to trust, the King more than anyone is vulnerable to spies and betrayal. We serve King Henry and work only to bring down his enemies … and …"

24

He tosses a purse into my lap, a fat purse that clinks with good fortune. "We pay our servants well."

My fingers clutch involuntarily at the coin and I realise that with an income such as this, I can marry where I will.

Isabella Bourne - 1540

It is late April and things are no better for Queen Anna. I feel for her but she shuns any show of pity so completely that an outsider would not recognise her fear. She prays almost constantly and when I overhear her in conversation with the ambassador from Cleves, although I cannot understand her words, the tremor of terror is stark in her voice.

We are all aware of her predicament. The King is clearly displeased with her and has ceased to pretend otherwise; outside of ceremonial matters he pays her no notice at all. Everyone at court is afraid, not knowing what will happen, and there are those who question whether the King will resort to the axe to rid himself of yet another unwanted queen. It is as if a great blade is wavering above us while we watch warily, uncertain where it will fall, each one of us dreading its descent.

Master Cromwell's eyes dart warily about the hall. As the man who brought Anna of Cleves to the King's notice, he must be quivering with fear, although he hides it well. King Henry scowls openly. He doesn't trouble to disguise his displeasure and why should he? His courtiers exist to please only him.

After supper, while he ignores his wife, his piggy eyes seek out and fasten on the dancing maidens. I do not dance but hover close to Queen Anna, inwardly despising those silly women who compete shamelessly for royal approval. I cannot understand why anyone would vie for Henry's favour. His reputation as either lover or husband is scarcely commendable, and he is far from the handsome prince that my mother recalls from the days of Queen Caterina of Aragon.

Mother says that when she was young, every girl at court was in love with the King, for in those days he was congenial and handsome, his favour valued more than rubies. Even today, in his slashed and padded jewelled doublet, his bandaged leg concealed beneath tight white hose and his cod-piece so prominent it draws every eye, he still cuts quite a figure. He is every inch a King but my unmaidenly imagination can see all too clearly the horror he must present once divested of his grandiose robes. These days his hair shows streaks of grey among the red and he has become grossly fat, his eyes sunken in a podgy face and his mouth reduced to a slash of bitterness. He is tight-lipped and mean and Anna has my sympathy.

If I were Henry's Queen I would be glad for him to seek comfort in the beds of other women, but Anna is too well-schooled in royal duty. She is failing and she knows she must provide an heir. It is imperative that she does so but I don't believe that for Anna, it is really all about duty. I think that, as well as wishing to please the King and secure her place in his heart, she yearns for a child, someone of her own to love, someone who will return her love in full measure.

We all want someone we can rely on, someone to trust, but trust is a scarce commodity in this court where everyone peers over their shoulder, scared to speak, afraid of contradicting some new royal edict. A son would make Anna safe, and if she could just grow a royal prince in her belly, she would become as favoured as Jane Seymour and we could all breathe easily again.

As it is, she trembles and prays. We all tremble, waiting for the storm to break, knowing that if the

Queen falls then the rest of us may come tumbling down with her.

The music is starting up again, filling the hall with false merriment. The pipers are red-faced, their cheeks blowing, feet tapping and the flaming torches and candles catch the gold thread in the tapestries and reflect the sumptuous jewels of the company. It is a shimmering, glittering mêlée but I keep to the shadows, concealing myself behind the other, more scintillating women of the court. I wish that Eve would do the same. But, as I knew she would, my sister Eve draws the eye of all the young men and some of the older courtiers too; those that should know better.

She dances so well and so frequently that I wonder she does not drop. Her face glows, her skirts wheel around her and her eyes shine as she turns about the floor. Such inbred grace ensures that she has just as many partners as Katherine Howard, the latest of that family to come to court. All eyes are upon her, and her uncle, the Duke of Norfolk, watches her too. He and his friends, Suffolk and Stephen Gardiner, lounge in a darkened corner to watch her sport before the King.

Katherine is the newest appointed lady-in-waiting and although she is first cousin to Anne Boleyn, she seems untainted by any shame. I watch her flirting with the young men and feel a twist of disdain at such laxity, although her behaviour is no more blatant than Eve's.

Eve and Katherine are two of a kind, beautiful, bright and irresistible. I sigh as I watch my sister being led onto the floor for the fourth dance in a row and wonder, if I were so blessed, whether perhaps it would go to my head too. Maybe, given half a chance, I too would preen myself like a peacock and flaunt my charms as if they were on sale.

Pressing my lips together, I resolve to have a word with Eve and remind her of Mother's warning to preserve her honour but, even as I watch, a gentleman approaches and bends low over her hand. He is tall, not a young man, but his robes are of the best quality and I recognise an elegance of the first degree. Her fingers flutter in his as he raises them to his lips and when he straightens up, he stays at her side, whispering in her ear. She tosses back her hair, leans against a pillar and looks up at him through her lashes.

I am not sure if I should intervene.

One of the Queen's ladies, Blanche, is beside me, watching the dancing, and I touch her arm, discreetly asking if she knows the gentleman's name. Blanche peers short-sightedly across the room, raises her brows and tells me he is Sir Anthony Greywater, a widower lately endowed with extensive lands in Wales. I can see she is impressed, and with growing interest I watch my sister flirt with him for a while longer, comforting myself that Father can only approve of attentions coming from a man of his standing. I decide to do nothing.

As the music starts up again the Queen crooks her finger and I hurry to her side. "Bella, could you fetch my wrap for me, there is a chill about my shoulders."

I bob a curtsey and weave my way through the throng. Although I hurry along the corridors and up the twisting back stair, it takes me some time to reach the Queen's apartments. The guards at the door recognise me and put up their pikes to let me pass.

"Oh, Fritz," I cry in dismay, and the silly dog gets up and stretches, his legs and tail stiff while he shows me his pink tongue. The Queen's wrap, that he has made his cosy bed, is scattered with tiny white

29

hairs and I am forced to spend some time picking them off, praying she won't notice and hoping she won't scold me for my tardy return. I flick some rosewater on it to mask the odour of dog and hurry back to the hall.

The first thing I see on my return is Sir Anthony standing alone, watching the dancing from the shadows. My eyes swivel to where Eve blossoms beneath the attentions of another man, another stranger.

This one is younger, less elegantly dressed and less courtly of manner but undoubtedly very, very handsome in a roguish, flamboyant sort of way. Even my attention is taken by the smooth, youthful contours of his face. Many eyes are drawn by their laughter as they twirl and hop in the dance, and people are putting their heads together, whispering behind their hands. I bite my lip, suppressing the desire to force my way onto the floor and drag her away. I watch them, my lips compressed like an old, disapproving maid while my cheeks flame with a curious mixture of shame and envy.

"What would Father say?" I demand much later in the privacy of our room. "Flirting like that before the whole court ... before the King himself!"

She flips back her hair and preens before the small mirror, cutting a jig before the fire, the movement of her small, tight breasts discernible through the thin material of her nightgown.

"Are you my mother, Bella? I had thought you were my sister ... and my friend." She pouts, knowing that her pursed lips and downcast eyes only add to her prettiness, but I refuse to be so easily seduced.

"I don't want to spoil your fun, Eve, but you must be more reserved. It was bad enough the way you were flirting with Sir Anthony, and he is a good man who will not cross the boundaries of respectability. You know very well that Father would condemn the way you were behaving with ... with that other young man. Were our father as harsh as most you would receive a good whipping and face a ration of bread and water."

Eve hugs herself and swirls about the room. "Master Wareham," she murmurs. "His name is Francis Wareham. He is so handsome, don't you think, Bella?"

She bounces onto the mattress, slipping beneath the covers beside me and putting her cold feet on my legs, making me squeal and pull away. I fold my arms across my meagre chest and scowl at her, but she remains unperturbed.

"I do believe you are jealous, Bella, which one is it you fancy for yourself? Sir Anthony Greywater ... or Master Wareham?"

She slurs the latter's name so that it rolls off her tongue as if it were a naughty word.

"Don't be ridiculous. Why should I be jealous? I've had partners aplenty."

But in truth, I am a little piqued for when I do have dance partners, they are mostly old, some of them barely able to mark time with the music. Eve laughs at me and ignoring my coldness, snuggles into my shoulder.

"Did you see Katherine Howard dancing before the King? I wonder what she hopes to gain. Anyone would have thought him the handsomest man in the room when, in truth, she could have the pick of them. I'd not favour an old goat like Henry over the likes of Thomas Culpepper."

"Eve! The King's youth and vigour are unequalled. He is still very handsome," I say pointedly, lowering my voice to a whisper. "Besides, it is not safe to suggest otherwise." I have told Eve

31

more than once that she must guard her tongue, for there are court spies in every corner.

"There is only you to hear me and anyway, all the court secretly agrees. The King we saw this evening is a travesty of his former self. He is an old man and it would be better for all concerned were he to realise that fact …"

She yawns suddenly, the truth of her words echoing in my head like a bell, ringing out in a terrible foreboding of disaster.

Joan Toogood – Southwark

I have never set foot outside the stews until the day I cross the bridge, the better to see Anne Boleyn go up river for her coronation. There is a great crowd gathered to see the pageant and the river is full of boats, the air ringing with bells and the sounds of the revel. I don't see much of the Queen, just the fall of long dark hair and a fleeting glimpse of her forehead, but at least I can go home and tell my sisters that I've seen an honest-to-goodness Queen. Over the years that follow I retell the story so often that they are sick of hearing it, but it is a golden day for me and I can't forget it. "It was a proper spectacle," I say, "and I'll not live to see another queen crowned." I little realise that she who has climbed so high will rapidly fall so far.

Years later, after the dark days of Anne's sorry end are over, the bells of London ring out for our new Queen, Jane, and peal again even louder when she breaks the King's curse and births a bonny little prince. They say that King Henry is cock-a-hoop over his longed-for heir, but a few weeks later, when the childbed sickness takes her and the Queen's death knell is rung, we shake our heads in sorrow for the poor, motherless little boy.

Queens, so many Queens and so many disappointments, it's a wonder the King can stand it. Those who are foolhardy enough to whisper such things say that Old Harry is cursed and will never keep a wife. They mutter of a wrathful God seeking vengeance on the house of Tudor that has brought down the church. But I say nothing. I just button my lip and lift my skirts for my punters. I know my place.

It is just a year or two later that we learn another Queen is on her way, a royal princess this time, coming all the way from Cleves, wherever that may be. So I hide the badge of my trade beneath a borrowed cloak and elbow a way across the teeming bridge into the city again. There, I stand shoulder to shoulder with the good, decent folk of London Town and watch the Princess from Cleves ride into the city.

She is a far cry from the other Anne. This one's face is red with cold, her hands barely able to clutch her mount's reins, but she manages a frozen smile, a glimmer of royal snot at her nostril. Children and women throw winter greenery in the path of her horse, their hearty cheers welcoming her hither, every one of us wishing her better success than her predecessors. As the procession moves through the crowd, I push to the front and see how young and sturdy she is. I feel a gleam of hope for England's future. This one looks to be a good girl, a fine sturdy breeder of princes, if ever I saw one.

Not that it concerns me, of course. I turn away from the pomp and, wrapping the borrowed cloak about me, hurry back to my side of the river. I have work to do. I shouldn't be loitering, dreaming of princesses and high gleaming towers.

I know my place.

My sisters are at home. Sybil is stirring a thin gruel over the fire while Betsy runs a lack toothed comb through her hair, teasing the ends into curls about her finger.

"Did ye see 'er?"

I throw off my cloak, sink onto a fireside stool, and stretch out my toes to the meagre flames.

"'Course I did."

"Is she as fine looking as they say?"

34

"She was pinched with cold, the poor mite, and her eyes ringed with fatigue, but I imagine she will scrub up well enough."

Sybil thrusts a bowl into my hands and I greedily suck the thin liquid between my lips. Darkness is falling, it is time for me and my sisters to go out into the cold and ply our trade.

I was no more than six when I first saw my mother serviced by one of her 'gentlemen'. He had her over the board, his great hairy arse drumming back and forth so hard that the table legs shifted in the floor rushes. I stood and watched with my thumb in my mouth, no more troubled than if I was witnessing a wedding. In fact, it wasn't until I was twelve and expected to earn my own keep that I saw anything remarkable in it at all.

She picks my first customer well. He is growing old, his cock soft and more willing than able. He sits me on his knee and lets me play with the tasselled girdle of his cassock. When I take exception to his exploring hands, my mother, who is sitting opposite, casts a scowl at me and although I wriggle and pout, I fight him no more.

He lays me down and presses against me and there follows a deal of shoving and a lot of grunting. When he slumps suddenly, as soon as I am able I scramble from beneath him and run to my mother's side. As we walk briskly through the alleyways toward home, I am full of doubt and want to cry but my mother does not speak or offer comfort. I learn later that because of the things the priest did to me, I am no longer a maid, but I have no idea what that really means.

After the initial squeamishness has passed, I no longer mind the old gentleman and once Mum hands me a shiny gold coin at the week's end, I begin to see the reason for it all. The older men favour me and my visitors are mainly clerkly types with trembling hands and nervous ways. My path in life is set and I become grateful to the men that put food in my belly and provide me with the means to buy a pretty new cap once in a while.

Soon I learn that the more I please them, the more reward I get and, as a consequence, Joanie Toogood becomes a favourite. Sometimes, when I go home in the early hours and fall into bed where my younger sisters sleep the sleep of the innocent, I am so tired that Mother lets me stay there 'til late afternoon.

I laugh at those who prate of love and I scorn the idea of matches made in heaven; there are far too many devoted husbands among my customers to pull the wool over my eyes. I know a man keeps his brains in his cod-piece, and no sooner are they out of their wives' sight than they are casting about for a willing whore.

I have never experienced tender feelings and never expect to. Men are soft, too easily distracted and too quick to utter mistruths, or at least that's what the men who keep company with me are like. I couldn't count the number of wives I've wronged, but what am I to do? A girl has to make a living.

My mother does not live out my twelfth year, and I am still a novice when I find myself in charge of my sisters. I know the future will be hard for us. Sybil is not yet ten and Betsy younger still. For two years I work double hard to keep them from my fate, but we all know the day will come. There is naught to do to stop it.

It's been a hard night. I am soothing my nether regions in a bowl of warm water while Betsy scrapes together a meagre meal. Sybil squats beside me, pouring fresh water between my thighs. Her hair straggles about her worried face, her fine eyes bright with held back tears.

"You do the work of four gels, Joanie," she says. "It ain't right."

"You want to eat, don't cha? Want clothes on your back?"

She nods and I see her throat working as she tries to give voice to the words she would rather not speak.

"I am old enough now, Joanie, maybe it's time."

On the day I encounter Francis Wareham for the first time, Sybil has been working for two years, and Betsy for six months. Our youngest sister takes to the life like a duck to water and seems to enjoy it too. Her cheer is not feigned like mine and Sybil's and, for her, whoredom is a vocation, not a chore. She works her way happily along the Bankside, greeting her gentlemen, young and old, as if she were a Goddess smiling upon worshippers. Sybil and I would think ourselves blessed if we could enjoy our trade as much.

But with the three of us working, our hardship eases a little. The Toogood sisters become well known as girls who will guarantee a good time. We are sought after and often times, if the money is right, we work together, earning as much in an hour as we could in a whole day of working alone. It is after such a romp, when I am enjoying a rare evening off, that I bump into a boy, lost, hungry and cold, and in want of mothering.

"Poor mite," I say, seeing his tears and his frozen cheeks. I take him home with me.

There is something about the lost look of this young'n that persuades me to let him stay 'til morning. He has nowhere else to go; he's green and unspoiled and, for once, I take some pleasure in the act. In the days that follow, some deep-rooted instinct to nurture prompts me to help him find employment as a pot-boy in The Cock Inn.

After that he is always hanging around, putting off my other customers, and I have to be cruel, try to ward him off, scared to find myself in straights again.

I soon realise that poor little Francis is one of those men who yearns only to crawl back into his mother's womb and feel the comfort only infancy offers. And, since the woman that bred him now scorns him, he seeks that lack in me.

Part of me thinks it ridiculous the way he clings to me, suckling like a piglet, as if he is trying to claw a way inside or consume every part of me. I lie beneath him, astounded at his energy and when I've finally had enough of his rutting, I call him, 'my baby' and 'little one'. Playfully, I pat his bottom until he cries out, his fingers digging deep into my flesh as if he would turn himself inside out to gain the thing he seeks. Poor Francis doesn't realise he will never rediscover the thing he is looking for. None of us can go backwards; we must all plod on toward the end.

Afterwards, when he has done, he is too shy to look at me. He ties up his piece, leaves a coin upon my washstand and creeps away. I smile at the empty chair, more touched by him than I care to admit. Francis Wareham is a disquieting fellow and there is something about him that is hard to forget. He doesn't go far but hovers on the brink of my life until, after almost a year of mooning around me, he is suddenly gone, disappeared from Southwark as if he had never been there.

To my surprise, I miss him a lot and ask around, but no one has seen him; it is as if he has melted away and, knowing his tendency to melancholy, I worry that he has cast himself into the stinking river or been thrown into Clink.

London is rife with rumour that the King has not taken to his new German wife. Rumour follows rumour and there is talk of imprisonment, death, and divorce. The memory of the Boleyn, ending her short reign on the scaffold, flickers at the back of every mind.

There are whispers of a new fancy in the King's life and we all know that what King Henry fancies, he usually gets. I remember the strained, white face of the woman from Cleves and would not be in her shoes, not for all the wealth in the world. I'd sooner be Joan Toogood the whore, than Anna, the unloved Queen.

The streets are all but empty and I have had a quiet night. I turn away from the thoroughfare and begin to work my way back toward home, when I hear a step behind me. It is dark and although I know the alleyway like the back of my hand, I feel a shimmy of fear and quicken my step.

The man behind me hastens his step, too.

At the far end of the alley I see a glimmer from a friendly window and my feet fair fly through the filth, hurrying for the sanctuary of home. But, just as I reach the entrance to the courtyard at the rear of The Cock, ready to climb the stairway to my room, a hand falls upon my shoulder, all but scaring me out of my hide.

"Joanie? Don't you know me?" His smile is wide. He whips off his cap, a fine thing of velvet with a jewel and a feather.

"Francis?" I sweep my eyes up and down, taking in the smart, crimson-slashed doublet, the jewelled hilt of his sword. He has obviously found good fortune.

"Well," I say, "don't you look fine, my dear? Too good for the likes of me now, I warrant."

"Never," he says. "I'll never be too good for Joanie Toogood."

His wide grin is seductive and I smile back at him, glad to see he has found some wit in his absence. Then, just as hot as ever, he sweeps me into his arms for a kiss.

Francis is the only man I don't mind kissing. I turn my face away from the mouths of other men, shove their noses against my paps and let them wipe their drool on those instead. But Francis' mouth is sweet, his lips soft, the abrasion of his cheek is gentle. He smells of youth and vigour. I could grow fond of him … if I gave myself leave.

Sybil and Betsy squawk loudly when I throw them out of our room, demanding privacy. As their cries dwindle away I turn toward Francis, who throws off his cloak and pulls me close, his hands roving all over my body, into my bodice. He frees my dugs so he can kneel and suckle like a starving child, and I groan at the rasp of his tongue. Thus encouraged, he wastes no further time and rucks up my skirts, burrows between my legs, his hardness seeking sanctuary. He loves me, good and hard, for ten minutes or so while I hang from his neck, my head back, eyes closed. And then it is over … before I am ready to stop.

While I gasp for breath, balanced on the cusp of pleasure, wanting to pull him back into me and make him finish, he sits up and fumbles for a cup.

"Did you miss me?" he asks.

I look at him, my lips parted, my cheeks hot with the flush of frustration. No man has ever brought me so close to peaking before and my quaint is throbbing, but I can't tell him that.

He has a newfound confidence, a sense of manliness that was missing before. My Francis has not only grown up, he has been taking lessons. I narrow

40

my eye and wonder where he has been practising …
and who with.

"I never noticed you were gone," I lie. "And
wherever did you come by such fancy clothes?"

"I've a job of work now," he says proudly. "A
gentlemen's post with a tidy pay."

As my lust subsides I raise a cynical eyebrow at
his boasting.

"Why, of all the men in London Town, did they
pick you?"

I am recovering quickly now and remember I
must not let him sense my affection. He has thrown
off his shirt and his skin glows in the firelight, the leap
of the flame shadowing the muscles of his torso. I'd
like him to love me again, slower this time, giving my
abused body the time to differentiate between work
and pleasure. I want to relish the freshness of him.

I roll over onto my back, let my breasts fall free
and, as I hoped, his eyes fasten upon them. My teats
tighten, wanting his mouth, but he is not yet hungry. I
know that as the night progresses he will want to feed
from my trough again.

"It is all hush-hush, so tell no one about it, Joan.
Not even your sisters. My master says I am the only
man for the job."

He bounces beside me on the mattress and
fiddles with a strand of my hair, running the coarse
curl through his fingers as if it is a fine ribbon. There
is something different about Master Wareham, he has
seen and done things that have changed him. He is
growing up, moving away from me, and I feel a
squirm of jealously at his new life and the new people
in it.

I watch him, loving every inch of him, the
auburn curl of his hair, the movement of his jaw as he
speaks. I know there have been other women and,
suddenly afraid that he will forget about me, I throw

off caution and open my arms to him. After a single moment's hesitation he falls back into them, laying his head on my bosom as if he were a bairn.

"What sort of a job, my dear? Who do you work for? You can tell me." I stroke his hair from his forehead, my touch as gentle as thistledown. He wriggles beside me, puts his mouth upon my naked skin and a jolt of pleasure stabs me. His tongue is hot, wet and probing, his voice muffled.

"No, hush, I cannot say. Only that it is a position close to the court and the pay is so good I will soon be able to take a wife."

He fastens his lips upon my nipple.

"Good boy," I say. "Oh, what a very… good … boy."

And at my words he suckles harder, making me whimper. His leg slides up mine, his hardness thrust against my hip, and something shifts within my belly. I feel myself sinking into him. My legs part and I urge him to mount me. For the first time I want a man; this man, just this one, Francis Wareham, Gentleman of Court.

Isabella Bourne- June 1540

The court is atwitter with the news that the King has granted lands to Katherine Howard, raising her from a poor relation of Norfolk's to a woman of some status. She is flaunting about the palace in a necklace that none of us has seen her wear before. It can only be a gift from the King. We all know it and so does the Queen, although she gives no inkling that she suspects any ill-doing.

In our bed at night Eve whispers that Katherine has surely lain with the King. "She has been bought with property and trinkets," she whispers, her face flushed with excitement. "She is no better than a strumpet."

I nudge her sharply in the ribs.

"Shush, for Heaven's sake. To speak against his favourites is to speak against the King himself. He is too pious a man to flaunt his mistress beneath the Queen's nose."

Eve snorts inelegantly and pulls the blankets up to her chin.

"What about Boleyn and Jane Seymour? He flirted with them beneath the noses of his wives. Haven't you seen his eyes fastened on Katherine when she dances? I've noticed he pays particular attention to her breasts."

"You can hardly miss them," I reply, with a small tinge of regret at my own scant paps. Eve wriggles like a restless puppy beside me.

"I just know they are lovers, I can always tell. I wonder what will happen if she gets with child."

Katherine would not be the first to be deflowered by Henry. The King has other bastards and rumour has it that Katherine's own cousin, Mary

43

Boleyn's eldest child, was sired by the King. But it is curious that, of all his bastards, he acknowledges only Henry Fitzroy and consequently he is treated like a prince. More so, indeed, than Mary and Elizabeth, whose status waxes and wanes with the King's fancy. His other bastards are left to make what way in life they can.

I pull my attention from royal scandal to concentrate on the present. "It is wrong to gossip, Eve, especially about the King's affairs. It is best to keep your eyes open and your lips sealed."

"Oh, I can say anything to you, Bella. I know I can trust you."

She sighs and I feel her relax into the pillow, her breath slowing. I shift on the mattress and slip an arm about her, relishing her warmth. In many ways, for all her apparent sophistication, Eve is naïve. She may be well-versed in how to attract a man but she knows little else. As she settles down to sleep, I listen to her regular breathing and acknowledge to myself that every bit of scandal she utters is undoubtedly true. My eyelids begin to flutter, my thoughts swirling into dreams.

In the morning I am torn from sleep by a banging on the chamber door. With my heart thumping, I slither from bed to tiptoe, shivering and barefoot, to see who calls so early.

"Father!"

I pull back the bolts and throw open the door, allowing our parents to sweep into the room. They have just ridden in and when Father embraces me, leaving a chilly kiss on each cheek in the French manner, the cold from his garments seeps through my thin nightrail. Mother clasps me tight before turning to where Eve is still gently snoring.

My sister always sleeps deep and would probably slumber through the Apocalypse. I jump on the bed and shake her awake and she wriggles, shrugging my hand away and uttering a foul word. I gasp and look up, red-cheeked, at my mother who allows no discomposure to show.

It is not the same with Father.

"Eve!" His outrage penetrates even my sister's dreaming ear and she springs up in bed, blinking wildly as she struggles to gather her senses. Her plump, pink face is still marked by the creases of the pillow and her hair stands on end. I can see that she half believes herself to still be asleep and dreaming.

"Mother? Father?" She stumbles from bed, clumsily embracing them both, her sleepy prettiness making them forget to scold her. As I watch them I realise that Mother is fairly twitching with news and I am touched by the sudden sense that something is about to change. Although I don't know why, I am suddenly afraid, aware of our vulnerability. We are all victim to the whims of our elders.

"Why are you here?" I ask. "You should have sent word and I would have made sure we were ready to greet you."

"You used to like surprises."

Mother is drawing off her gloves and slipping from her warm mantle. She straightens her hood and perches on a fireside stool. "When you are dressed we will talk, the news concerns us all. My lord, why don't you discover if our rooms are ready while the girls are dressing, we will meet with you in an hour."

Father does as he is bid and while Eve and I help each other to dress, Mother gives us the news from home. Bess, the gardener's daughter, has married and now has a son, and Father's favourite hound has birthed a litter of pups. Her words evoke the scents of home and I am filled with a sudden longing to be back

45

at Bourne Hall, playing with Bess and my little brother Tom in the garden, forever a child, and as far from the uncertainties of the royal court as I can be.

Mother gets up and begins to wander about the room, picking up trinkets from our dresser and putting them down again, flicking through our clothes press, checking that our maid is keeping our gowns in order. Eve's hair crackles and snaps beneath my hand as I brush it and then she does mine, tucking it up and pushing it beneath my cap.

Mother looks us over.

"You will do very well," she says. "Come, let us meet with Father now."

***

"No! Sir Anthony Greywater does not please me!"

I stand aghast as Eve rejects Sir Anthony's offer of marriage. Mother shifts in her seat, her lips pressed tight together, her eyes a warning to anyone other than Eve that disobedience in not an option. The suit is to be put before the King and if he sanctions it, then it will go ahead, whether Eve likes it or not.

I watch my sister stick out her chin, my father's exasperation threatening to overspill, my mother's temper increasing. Eve is not yet fifteen, perhaps she is too young for marriage, although many girls marry sooner.

"Eve," I intervene with great daring, hoping to defray a family argument and save her from disgrace. "Sir Anthony will make a splendid husband. His fortunes are rising high and Blanche says he has built a house on the old abbey lands he was given Apparently, the medicinal gardens are now a wonderful pleasance. You will not find better."

"Yes, I *can* find better, Bella. Sir Anthony does not please me. Perhaps he could be persuaded to marry you instead, you are the oldest after all and it is right that you should be the first one wed."

We are all shocked into silence. My cheeks flame with disgrace. In all honesty, she is correct and I should be the first to be married but I am not so reduced as to accept her cast-offs. I am not yet seventeen and hardly an old maid, but I swallow the insult and try to reply gently.

"But he has asked for you, Eve. Think of your position. You will be a married woman with a wonderful home and Sir Anthony has the King's favour. It could mean a permanent position here at court."

Mother and Father are watching, letting me do my best to persuade her.

"I know." Eve's head is down, her face slack. I do not understand such reluctance.

"Think of the new gowns you will have." I try to encourage a smile but although she tries, her mouth goes out of shape and I know that she is close to tears. I lick my lips, searching for a more persuasive tack but, just as I open my mouth to speak, the bell chimes for Matins and Father steps forward.

"Sir Anthony has asked to see you today and when he calls here this afternoon I expect him to find a willing and worthy bride."

I have never seen my father so ill at ease. He hates confrontation of any kind and has raised all three of his children with kid gloves. Behind us Mother makes a sudden movement, but when I look up she pretends she is brushing something from her skirts and avoids my eye. Eve's head is lowered and I see a tear fall onto her lap. There is nothing to be done about it. If Father says they are to marry, then Eve will have to comply.

And so, this afternoon we stroll slowly about the garden. Sir Anthony plucks a rose and Eve accepts it with a delicate mew of thanks. She is strangely mute, not herself at all and I find myself forced to fill the awkward silences with a constant chatter that does not come easily to me. All the time I pretend gaiety I am aware that it is not me he wishes to listen to. He lures Eve away from me a little and I hear the earnest pleading in his voice.

"I have to visit my estates for a week or two," he says, "but when I return I hope our suit can be finalised and we can marry before the season turns."

Eve opens and closes her mouth but does not speak. She lowers her head again, a scarlet blush upon her face. Taking her silence as modesty, Sir Anthony offers her his arm and we stroll on again, listening as he admires the roses and compares them with those that grow in his own gardens.

I watch him from beneath my lashes and cannot see what there is to dislike. In truth, he is past the first flush of youth but he bears himself nobly and seems considerate and kind. Any woman should be glad of his attention, yet Eve is not satisfied and thinks she can do better. She is quiet for days, almost sulky and none of us can reach her. The only person she responds to is the Queen, whom she dare not ignore.

Then, one night after supper, I leave the hall in search of the Queen's Book of Hours that she has left in the chapel. On my return, skimming silently along the corridor, I spy a couple in the shadow of the stairs. I stand watching, holding my breath, intrigued and disturbed by his eager hands upon her body.

How must that feel? I ask myself, my limbs growing weak as I watch the silent mummery of their passion. I am an innocent but even I, a girl of just seventeen who has as yet never been kissed, can recognise unquenchable desire when I see it.

His arms are wound tightly about her, her bosom flattened against his chest while his lips feast hungrily upon her throat. Something turns over in my stomach as he pulls off her veil and she throws back her head, her hair tumbling to her waist, catching the light of the torches, so that it writhes like a living thing.

My hand is already covering my mouth when the woman turns into the light and I see it is Eve and Francis Wareham. From the heat of their clinch I can tell it is not their first encounter.

Only then do I begin to understand.

Francis Wareham

Nicholas Brennan arranges for my invitation to court, where I am instructed to mingle with the Queen's ladies and watch her behaviour, making note of who comes and goes. I am also told to keep close watch that Norfolk, Suffolk and Gardiner do not get too close to the King. It does not take me long to guess that my anonymous master can only be Cromwell, although I am not to report to him; all my findings must go through Master Brennan.

Norfolk and Suffolk, who are of the old nobility, despise Cromwell for his low beginnings and his proximity to the King. I confess, I too have no great love for him but I am wise enough to lick the hand that feeds me. So I watch them, make notes of who they speak to and take what pleasure I can from it.

Since I cannot enter the Queen's private chambers without invitation, I watch her at functions, note the way she slurps her soup through terror-frozen lips. She is as plain as a pikestaff, her clothes stiff and uncompromising, and it pains me to keep my eyes on her when they long to feast upon the fair countenances of her ladies.

There are two women in particular who stand out like doves among a field of crows, and I am not flattering myself when I say that they, in turn, are not blind to my charms. Katherine Howard and another girl I do not know, outshine the others tenfold.

Katherine is niece to the Duke of Norfolk and I suspect that her uncle has set her as a decoy to lure the King from the Queen's bed. But whatever her mission, if indeed she is aware of one, she is a minx – a cock-stirrer of the first degree.

I watch the heavy lidded eyes of the King follow her as she teases him, twirling in the dance. She lifts her skirts a little too high, exposing her neat ankles, before sinking into a curtsey so low that the King is in danger of tipping from his seat to see into her heaving bodice. Her breasts are prominent and although she lacks the fine matronly assets of my Joan, her neckline is cut so low and so tight that they seem to writhe in a dance of their own.

One evening when I am watching her, secretly relishing her breezy disrespect for modesty, I realise that the King's eyes are not, as expected, upon her but fastened rather unpleasantly upon myself. A chill dowses me like icy water. I whip off my cap and bow my knee, but the King's expression does not falter. His eyes are narrowed and he does not smile.

I have displeased His Majesty and he has marked me out as a jade; a thing that will not please Master Cromwell. I am supposed to remain invisible and not draw either the displeasure of the King or the notice of my master's enemies. A quick glance confirms that Master Cromwell is watching me also. I feel his cold, lizard-like eyes upon me and dare not return his stare for we are supposed to be strangers … which of course we are, having never exchanged a word. Thereafter, mindful of my duty and the disposition of the King, I keep my gaze firmly on the opposite side of the room from Katherine Howard.

A burst of laughter draws my attention to another pair of girls, one plain, the other fair, who are diverting the Queen from the attention the King is paying to the little Howard piece. As they take their places on the floor and prepare to dance, the court gentlemen separate, allowing me a perfect view. The prettiest one throws back her head, her trickling laughter lifting the corners of my own mouth. I lean on a pillar, lift my cup to my lips and transfer my interest from Katherine to her.

She is light of foot. Beneath the confines of her hood her fair hair runs like water, her bosom bouncing lightly as she hops and leaps in the dance. Her charms are subtler than Katherine Howard's. This one is delicate, like no woman I have ever yet known, her breeding is unmistakeable, a lady of the first degree. My taste buds begin to tingle.

Slowly, I pass around the shadowy contours of the room, positioning myself carefully where she will surely pass by. As I go, I garner snatches of conversation from the courtiers. Without seeming to, I watch her a little longer, drawn to her flushed face and glowing eyes and when the music ceases, there is laughter and the exchange of thanks.

She is about to pass right by me and with great daring, I make to step from the shadows. But a tall stranger intercepts us and bows over her hand. I fall back and watch as that old fool, Greywater, offers her his stuttering attentions.

As I ponder this sweeting's name I forget to keep an eye on Norfolk, or the Queen. Is she an Alys, or perhaps a Jane?

She knows she is watched and tosses her head, lets the light of the torches play upon her throat as she flicks back her hair with a dainty hand. After a while she lowers her chin and casts about the room beneath her lashes to discover who it is that watches. Across the crowded hall our eyes meet and we both become very still, as if in mutual recognition.

When the music begins again, I leap into action, surprising myself by stepping forward, making my bow. I am not usually one for dancing but when I take her hand, I am filled with a lightness that affects even my clod-hopping feet. We exchange no words but I swear, as I lead her in the dance, there is a flash of fire each time our fingers touch. She is blushing like an unclothed maid and when the steps of the dance draw us close enough, I can feel her trembling, taste her desire, and I know she is sensing mine.

I move in closer than modesty allows and Sir Anthony Greywater looks on impotently as, before the oblivious eyes of the King's court, I sink in my hook and begin slowly to reel her in.

It is two days before I have the opportunity to steal my first kiss. During a revel I notice her slip from the hall and as soon as I am able, I follow and accidentally encounter her on a shadowy stairway. Coming to a stop before her, I put a hand to my heart as if overwhelmed with the coincidence of us meeting there. She looks down, her cheeks pleasingly clothed in pink as, careful not to alarm her, I execute a sweeping bow. Then, rising slowly, my eyes lick up her body, pausing at her bodice before fastening upon her face. We have no need of words.

I lay a light hand on each shoulder and draw her close to place a chaste kiss upon her forehead, like the blessing of a priest. She trembles beneath my touch like a feather in a draft, and I know she lusts for me. It is apparent in her wide eyes, her red-bitten lips, her shallow breathing and the way her eyelids flutter closed as my face comes close to hers for our first gossamer-light kiss.

I give myself another week before I hump her.

Isabella Bourne - 1540

I cannot but feel a little sneaking admiration as I watch Eve manipulate our parents. Secure in the knowledge that she is irresistible, she always gets her way. It is like the opening of a scene in a play when she slowly opens the door and walks to the fireside as if in great agony, her hands clutched to her stomach, her head lowered, her bottom lip a'tremble.

Father is warming his backside before the flames, he looks at her from the corner of his eye, aware that he is being coerced but defenceless against such lethal female weapons. Many parents would chastise a daughter who dared to refuse a suitor, but neither Eve nor I have ever yet suffered a real beating and I don't expect Father to resort to it now. He is a gentleman and a philosopher not a bully; a man who solves problems with words rather than violence.

Mother, on the other hand, is clutching and twisting her hands in her lap. If one of them were to strike out at Eve, it would be her. She finds it hard to watch her daughter throw herself away on a nobody, but she knows Father is not the sort of man to impose his will on Eve. He clears his throat and frowns, trying to look stern, as if he is in control.

"You put me in great difficulty, Eve," he says weakly. Eve cleverly makes no reply, but lets a single tear drop upon her writhing fingers. She looks up at him, pretty, vulnerable and tragic as she demolishes her father's resolve. "Sir Anthony has quite set his hopes on you. He has excellent connections, such a match would serve us very well indeed … and he is a splendid fellow."

Eve is spurred into response. "He is old!" she cries, and I raise my brows for Sir Anthony is in his prime, no more than thirty-five. "I cannot love him, Father, please, find a way to free me from this …this arrangement. I have not even been properly consulted."

A rustle of movement as Mother leaves her seat to glide across the room and take her place beside her husband. She hisses her disapproval.

"Love has nothing to do with it, Daughter. Not at this stage. When we were first married I was not enamoured of your father either but I soon grew to respect, and then to love him."

"Thank you, my dear." He raises an ironic eyebrow in Mother's direction and I smother a smile. Mother was lucky, her father chose well for her and I think she has been happy. All the same, in our position it is better not to let your heart light upon a man of your own choosing. It is not a woman's place and we all must trust in our fathers to arrange a good match.

Eve is being ridiculous. I for one would welcome a suitor as fine as Sir Anthony. I rather fancy a fine household and although I can never hope for such a good match, I can easily picture myself as mistress of Greywater Place, daintily organising the servants and ordering the meals.

Father sighs, raises his arms and lets them fall helplessly to his side again.

"Oh, for Heaven's sake." He stares into a dark corner, his brow furrowed, and I know that Eve has won. We all know it. He has been easily vanquished but I can see that it costs him dear to be so soundly beaten. "I will think on the matter and see what, if anything, can be done. In the meantime, stay away from Master Wareham. I will speak to him forthwith and see what he has to say for himself."

His severity is feigned and we know it. We dip a curtsey and Eve and I glide demurely from the room, heads lowered, hands clasped in our voluminous sleeves but, as soon as we turn the corner, she grabs my arm, her face alight with victory.

"I have him, Bella. Father will talk Sir Anthony round and I will have my Francis yet."

"Do you mean you haven't had him already?" I snatch my hand away. "Your behaviour the other evening suggested otherwise."

Eve is dismayed at my spite and she slaps at me like a spoiled little girl.

"Oh, you don't understand what love is like. Look at you, all bound up in ropes of decorum. Just wait until someone kisses you, Bella, only then will you know how the blood howls through your veins and your body screams like a wanton to be touched. Piety is for fools, love is the thing."

Her face is pink with excitement, her eyes lit by a wicked, devil's flame. I feel a warm flicker in my belly just listening to her talk of such passion and I can see that she will not heed Father's warning to keep away from Master Wareham. My little sister is running headlong into disaster and I have no idea how to stop her.

Francis Wareham

I watch and wait and listen at doors, storing any tit-bit of gossip or conversation and bearing it back to Nicholas Brennan. "Make sure you are not followed," he warns me, but I shrug off his lack of ease and hurry back to court and all that awaits me there.

The King is disgruntled, his new Queen nervous and edgy, and to the barely disguised joy of Stephen Gardiner, Master Cromwell is visibly nervous. I am pleased that duty draws me so often into the vicinity of the Queen and her ladies for there is one among them who lingers in my thoughts both night and day.

It is not often I am wrong about women, but Evelyn Bourne's virtue is not as easy to conquer as it promised to be. What do I know of ladies? I've humped serving wenches and whores and imagined all women to be the same but it seems I must tread more carefully with this one, if I don't want to be the one caught.

Her father, Edward Bourne, is from a family still struggling to regain its former status after fighting for the wrong side at Bosworth all those years ago. In truth, the Bournes have done well to survive the Tudor regime this long, for both Henry and his father have striven to keep the Plantagenet faction low. The Bournes keep their heads down, breed fine sons and pretty daughters to barter for power and wealth, and work a stealthy way up the ladder.

But it seems that sweet little Evelyn, for all her wanton glances, is a lady in deed as well as word and, although I do all I can, I can only manage to plough her furrow so far. She meets me when she is forbidden and allows me liberties that she shouldn't, but then she pulls away and I find I am driven to distraction. If she wasn't a lady of the Queen's household I'd throw her down and take her in the floor rushes. But she demands a pledge, a betrothal and a ring, and so mad has her half-commitment made me that I find myself agreeing.

Such frustration is too much for a man to bear and whenever I can, I hurry over London Bridge, fight my way through the raucous crowd, casting off the clutching hands of other whores to bang on Joanie's door. There I lose myself in her motherliness and try to forget the virginal, tight laced torment of Evelyn Bourne.

Eve's father grills me, demanding to know my means and my prospects, and all the time I am stood in his stuffy parlour, through the window I can see Eve playing with her little dog in the garden, lifting it in the air so that her wide sleeves fall back to reveal slim, white arms. Arms that I long to feel entwine about my neck, arms that I long to pinch and bite and lick. He says, quite pointedly and politely, that Evelyn comes with a limited dowry and wants to know how I will keep his daughter fed, where will we live? I am out of my depth. I want to hump her, not marry her, but what can I do?

He has me in a cleft stick.

She is laughing now, throwing back her head, baring her long, white neck. Her father is waiting for me to speak but I hesitate to answer for Eve leans forward, her breasts pouting over the edge of her bodice like doves about to burst from captivity. I long to free them, to feel those tight little dugs pressed against my naked chest. My cod-piece strains with lust and my need is so great that I promise anything.

I cannot tell him I am a spy for Master Cromwell, so I make up a story of a private income, the promise of inheritance to come, and hope I can produce the proof of it. Nicholas Brennan will back me up, forge the necessary documentation, I am sure.

It is obvious that he is not in full favour of the match but, like a gentleman, he pumps my hand up and down and begins to talk of dowries and investments. All the while a sweat is building up beneath my collar. I wonder what the hell I have done.

And then, within a week, the Queen and Evelyn Bourne along with her, are sent from court to escape the plague and I am left kicking my heels, wondering how to get close to her again.

Evelyn Bourne – June 1540

Bella and I are still with Queen Anna who must be frantic with worry although she hides it well. The King has sent her household to Richmond for fear of plague that stalks the city every summer, but between you and me, I know of nobody who has seen or heard rumours of the sickness this year.

All the ladies believe it is just the King's ploy to be rid of his wife for a while so that he can continue his dalliance with Katherine Howard. Many people claim to have seen her in the royal barge with the King, sailing across the water to Winchester Palace to be entertained by Bishop Stephen Gardiner. It is common knowledge that his entertainments go that bit further than most, and his friendship with Katherine's uncle, Norfolk, is well known. It is no secret that the King has been courting Katherine Howard for months now, and the gifts he sends her grow daily larger and more difficult to conceal from the Queen.

Dear Anna, she pretends she notices nothing, but I have heard the desperation in her voice when she begs God on her knees to intervene and make the King like her just enough to get her with child.

I wonder what it must be like to be so plain and unlovable. In truth, if she made more of herself she could be pretty enough, in a solid, monotonous sort of way. It is vivacity that she lacks and the King demands that his women be bright and witty.

Even among her ladies her foreign upbringing makes difficulties, for the language barrier means that when we laugh she never sees the joke, and we have to carefully explain what is funny and why. Of course, this quite takes away the humour of the situation although she pretends to understand, smiling in a sort of puzzled way as if it is our sense of fun that is at fault, and not hers.

I like her though and I like her little dog, Fritz. She lets me take him into the gardens to do his business, and when we were still at court, Francis Wareham was always waiting close by to meet me in a garden arbour. Now we are far apart, and I miss him with my whole heart and soul.

Oh, when he is close to me he makes my whole body sing. The sight of his handsome face lighting up at my approach is worth risking the displeasure of Father, Queen Anna, and even the King himself. He is so full of lust for me that within moments of greeting his hands are upon me, his lips working down my neck toward my bosom, so that I am soon breathless with desire.

Once, our embrace became so blistering that my skirts were hoisted high, my leg hooked about his waist as his hands and mouth drove me into a fever of desire. We were so engrossed in one another that it's a mercy we even heard the yelp and the little splash when Fritz slipped into the fountain.

We tore ourselves apart and found Fritz swimming in frenzied circles. Francis had to scramble to reach him and finally hooked him from the water just in time. He looked so funny, his dripping fur clinging to his skinny little rat's body. I scurried back to the palace to rub him briskly on a towel before taking him back to the Queen's presence. Thank God he didn't drown for I would have lost Anna's favour for sure.

Now we are at Richmond, everyone is out of sorts. Not ill, but disgruntled, missing the court festivities and the attention of the King's gentlemen; especially me. I miss Francis so much it feels as if a hole has opened up in my chest and my heart's blood is leaching away.

Oh, God knows when I shall see him again.

Bella doesn't seem to mind it here. She is happy to quietly take refreshments with the Queen, making garments for the poor, chatting about trivial things, but the domesticity of it all is like a heavy weight, it is crushing me. I want to dance, I want to sing, I want to feel the hot glance of Francis Wareham and know that after nightfall, when I sneak from my sleeping sister's side, he will be waiting for me in the shadows.

It is weeks since I felt his lips on mine, the hard, urgent pressure of his body and his exploring hands. I am not sure how much longer I can wait. I feel that when we eventually meet again I will beg him to make me his there and then, and we will be caught humping like dogs in the park. I long for an excuse to return to court, anything to provide the opportunity of meeting with him, but I cannot see that happening, not for a long time.

The gossips are saying that Henry will put Anna aside and marry Katherine Howard, but I'm not sure I believe that, she is his legal wife after all. A man, even a King, may get away with that once in a lifetime but not twice, surely.

But Katherine Howard is more fortunate than I, for when we were sent here to Richmond, the King sent her to Oatlands and they say he visits her every day. So the royal court is split and I would wager my favourite hood that there is more fun to be had with the King's household than there is here. We are like a house of nuns, starved of male company and the lady we serve is like the Queen of sorrows.

I wonder where my Francis is now? Is he with the King or has he followed Katherine's household to Oatlands? I sigh and put down my needlework, close my eyes against the tedium.

"Are you tired?" The Queen smiles kindly on me and I feel a twinge of guilt for my unfaithful thoughts. She is a good woman and a strong one. She puts me in mind of the tales Mother told us of Henry's first Queen, Caterina of Aragon. She lost the King's favour but she kept her head and her dignity, and never once bowed down to his outrageous demands. Her behaviour won everyone's respect and I hope that, should I ever have the misfortune to be faced with a faithless husband, I would prove to be as brave myself. The Queen is waiting for my answer.

"A little," I say and when she smiles I return it in full measure before bending over my stitches again, straining my eyes. It is not long before Queen Anna takes pity on me and claps her hands for refreshments.

"It is growing dark, Eve," she says, "why not take Fritz outside for some air? Bella can accompany you."

Queen Anna is good like that. We both know that it is but an hour since he was exercised yet she allows me to escape into the garden again. Outside the day is still warm and I regret having wasted it in the royal apartments, but we must follow the Queen's wishes and she dislikes the heat of the sun.

"It's so dull here, Bella," I sigh, looking across the gardens to the river. The dog snuffles at the edge of the path, lifts his leg against a shrub. I watch him make a pile of shite on the evenly clipped sward before scraping up the grass with his back legs, leaving bald patches. The gardeners will curse him in the morning.

"Come along, Fritz," I say and he follows Bella and I along the golden gravel walkways.

"The Queen is afraid." Bella tucks her hand into the crook of my arm and we walk slowly, putting off returning indoors for as long as we can. I yawn rather too loudly, for my head feels stuffy after being cooped up indoors. I long for the celebrations we enjoyed when Queen Anna first arrived, days of celebration, the jousts, the picnics on the riverbank, minstrels in the park and the thrill of chasing deer in the King's wood. Bella plucks a bloom and holds it to her nose.

"You'd think the Queen would be glad to be rid of him. He never visits her and his affection for *you know who* is blatant. He has no shame."

"I expect she remembers Henry's other Queens. No woman has come out of marriage with him unscathed; if it were you, wouldn't you be in fear of imprisonment or worse? I pray nightly that the King will be lenient and just send her home to Cleves in disgrace."

I put a hand to my mouth. "That would be awful, think how people would talk if the King of England found her so unattractive that he sent her back to her brother like a coat that does not fit. She would be ruined and never marry again!"

Bella says nothing as we stand and watch the dying of the light. Although the night promises to be warm, soon it will be time for the torches to be lit. A few weeks ago I would have been growing excited at the thought of the evening banquet and dancing, of seeing Francis again, but now I sigh, for the coming dark means nothing more than a quiet supper, a game of cards and an early night.

"Oh, Bella, I miss Francis so. I have a hollow place just below my heart that only his presence can fill."

My sister laughs unkindly. "You are too hot," she says, "besides, you will both be wed soon and I wager you will tire of him in a month."

I am shocked.

"No, Bella. Never, ever will I tire of him, I will love him until the day I die."

And I believe my words with all my heart.

July 1540 - Richmond

Queen Anna was right to worry. I am looking from the chamber window across the gardens to the river, when I see a company of men disembarking at the wharf. They are obviously from the King's court, their faces solemn and their robes as black as a priest's.

As they draw closer I squint my eyes and recognise my lord of Suffolk and Stephen Gardiner, the Bishop of Winchester. Gardiner is Cromwell's enemy. None of us have set eyes on Cromwell for weeks and strongly suspect that the swinging pendulum of political power is bringing Gardiner up again, while Cromwell descends. Some say that Katherine Howard is Norfolk's bait to snare the King's favour. None of them have a care for what may befall us, closeted as we are with the forsaken Queen but today, I feel sure, we will discover if our suspicions are true.

Suspecting that one way or another the weeks of uncertainty will soon be over, the tension we have all been trying to ignore grips at my throat as I turn to inform the Queen that the gentlemen are here. As soon as my words are out, the blood floods from her cheeks as a murmur of dismay ripples about the ladies at the hearth.

When a loud banging falls upon the outer door, we draw close about the Queen. The Countess of Rutland and Lady Lisle shush at the younger women to make us cease our grizzling, and we do our best to stifle our fear. Anna stands tall, allowing them to approach. Those who do not know her would think her calm, for she allows no fear to show in her eyes, but I can see how she clenches her fists to keep her composure.

We ladies fall back a little, giving her privacy, and I cling to Bella's elbow, my breast pressed against her upper arm, my heart beating like a scared rabbit's. *What is going to happen? What is going to happen?*

Stephen Gardiner, a tall man in black, is speaking. His voice is courteous and clipped as he bows low, keeping his eyes averted although it is impossible to tell if this is from respect or embarrassment. The murmur of his voice reaches to where we shiver in our corner and I know straight away that he is speaking too fast for Anna to follow.

Jane Rochford silently urges the interpreter forward, and the girl hurries to the Queen's side and begins to rapidly repeat the official language of government that none of us can comprehend. I am impatient to know what is to befall us all. *Why does he not just speak his message plainly?*

Queen Anna is blinking, a slight frown on her forehead as the interpreter wrestles to make sense of the meaning and then Anna tries to understand it too. Suddenly, one word stands out from the rest.

"Divorce."

The image of Caterina of Aragon and her miserable end flashes before me and when I turn to my companions, I see they are as horrified as I. My body is rigid. Poor Anna will be sent home, just as we had feared. She will become the laughing stock of the world. Divorce and disgrace may be better than death or imprisonment, yet I am furious. She deserves more than this; the King is just a spoiled child!

Beside me, Bella presses a cool hand over mine, urging me to remain quiet. We both keep our gaze on Anna as she locks her eyes on the Bishop and repeats the word, turning it into a question. Her voice is guttural and foreign in this room of Englishmen.

He bows stiffly from the waist and abandons the petition to adopt simpler language. "Your Majesty, the King is concerned that your pre-contract to the Duke of Lorraine forbids him to consummate your marriage.

66

He feels it would be better, for all parties, were the marriage submitted to the judgement of the Convocation."

Time is suspended as his words slowly infiltrate our understanding. I wonder what that means. Then the Queen puts a hand to her chest and releases a long held breath, and immediately the tension in the room lessens. I give a confused half laugh, glance at the other ladies whose faces are flushed pink with indignation, but I still don't fully understand.

Anna seems to feel no indignity, no shame. She inclines her head graciously and I strain my ears, for she is speaking and her words display a composure she surely doesn't feel. It is times like this that her royal dignity is most evident.

"I live only to please my King and happily concur with all of his wishes. Please, present my most humble and loving commendations to his most gracious majesty."

When Gardiner bends over her hand, I notice that his hair is thinning into a natural tonsure. Suffolk also takes a stiff bow before they back from the room, their men shuffling out behind. The door closes softly. It is over; the King has moved into the open and his intention is delivered. I expect there to be relief but there isn't, not immediately.

But then, quite suddenly, the combined whispers of the ladies rush like a flurry of butterflies about the room as the Queen drops to her knees, her prayers as loud as Fritz' yapping as he leaps up to lick her face. His claws snag the pearls on her gown and they cascade to the floor, rolling and bouncing about the chamber while we all cluster about her, to console her fears.

In the three days that follow, our anxiety is drawn so tight that scarce a word is uttered within the

Queen's chamber. Both day and night the constant monotone of the Queen pleading with God is our only entertainment.

We try to tempt her with card games and dainties but she waves us away, her plain face made ugly by fear. Anna is not a fool. She knows what became of Henry's former cast-off wives. Caterina, his first wife, left to moulder to death in a damp and chilly manor house; Anne, the celebrated beauty and Henry's great passion, destroyed to make way for another fancy. And Jane, sacrificed for the want of an heir, left untended, so the gossips say, on her childbed while the country celebrated the birth of its new prince.

What will become of Anna, friendless and powerless in a foreign land? Sharing her fears, I creep to her side and, with great daring, clasp her hand. To my surprise she does not snatch it from me or order me away, but instead she grips it so tight that I fear the blood in my fingers will cease to flow.

It is three days until they come again, and while my belly rolls and rumbles as it gives voice to my inner turmoil, I take my place with the other ladies. Beside me, Mother Leow, the German overseer of the ladies, prays audibly beneath her breath, her fleshy jowls trembling. We are all suspended in dread, as if the axe that has hovered just a little way above our heads for so long is slowly descending.

I see Blanche and dizzy little Catherine Basset's linked hands hidden within their skirts, and Bella with her hand tucked beneath Lady Lisle's elbow. Alone by the window, I clutch Fritz to my ribs to stop him from running off to bark at the solemn gentlemen who face us across my lady's chamber. He squirms and wriggles like an eel but, ignoring his farty excitement, I squeeze his scruff and force him to acquiescence.

Gardiner is speaking, his voice not as steady as it should be. As he clears a frog from his throat and begins again, I fear the worst. "Your Majesty." He bows his knee to the soon-to-be-disgraced Queen but, to my surprise, instead of acknowledging him, Anna turns sharply and all but marches from the room, bidding the gentlemen to follow her into the privy chamber.

Left alone, we all gape at each other until I drop Fritz to the floor and dash across the room to press my ear to the door.

"What are you doing, Mistress Bourne? Come away at once."

Usually I would not dare to disobey Lady Lisle, but when the other girls follow to do the same, I know she cannot punish all of us and we cluster, ears pressed against the thick oaken door and try to decipher the muffled words from within.

I hear faint male voices, patient tones, gruffly apologetic, and then the higher, almost pleading notes of my mistress, but I cannot make out the words although I linger so long my ear becomes sore from the pressure. Then we hear the sound of approaching footsteps and we fly back across the chamber. I seize Fritz again, his doggy breath an insult to my nose, and turn to watch them re-enter the chamber, pretending that my interest had been caught by something taking place in the gardens below.

I cannot tell the gravity of the news from the Queen's face. As ever, she keeps her emotions well concealed beneath her all-enveloping calm. The party of men bow, not as deeply as before, and leave us, closing the door softly, their feet tramping along the corridor. When the sound of their departure has faded away, we turn as one to face our Queen and are amazed to see tears glistening upon her cheeks. I am

69

the first to step forward, although it is not my place. "Madam?"

She stares blindly in my direction, her throat working, and I know the news is the worst it can be. I want to run to her and clasp her in my arms but something stops me. She deserves some dignity but it is difficult to watch her attempt to smile through her tears. She opens her mouth, her guttural voice rasping on the words that she forces from her throat.

"I am not to die." She blinks through her tears and holds out her hands, lifts her face to Heaven. "And I am not to be divorced and sent home, after all. There is to be no shame, for the King, in his graciousness, seeks an annulment and wishes me to live on in England as his beloved sister."

We stare at her in astonishment as we absorb the fact that, amazingly, our Queen will escape both the axe and disgrace. Anna is not to die, instead she is to become the *King's Good Sister* and live in all comfort here at Richmond Palace, or Hever. Moreover, the King has promised her such presents that she will be rich, rich beyond words, yet spared the revulsion of his affections.

She is a lucky Queen indeed.

"Oh," she cries, as her tension lessens and we see for the first time her full potential for prettiness. She spreads out her arms to us. "My dear, dear friends, I thought I might have to die, but instead I am to live here in England and be free. I am free of my brother and I am free of Henry! Now I can hold parties, lots of parties and feasts, and you will all be my guests. And I will buy gowns, many, many gowns, all in the French style. Oh, I am not to die! *Mein Gott*, I am not to die!"

Joan Toogood

The King is presiding over the bear baiting. I weave and push myself through the crowd, exchanging greetings and ignoring sneaky squeezes from unknown hands. I see the pennants of the royal party fluttering, glimpse a fair laughing face at the King's side, but I pay his new Queen little heed. My mind is not really on the festivities and I care nothing for the presence of the King. I am, as ever, hoping for a sight of Francis, for I have not seen him in ever so long.

Sometimes, I fear he has forgotten me and every day I pray he keeps himself free of all the trouble that we hear is happening at court. The goings on in the palace don't take long to reach this side of the river and I listen, more for news of Francis than for tidings of old Henry.

Recently the King has put Queen Anna aside, and we must all learn to think of her as the King's Good Sister now. It seems a funny thing to me, to be sister to a man you've wedded and bedded, but there's naught as queer as the carry-ons at the royal palace and it's not my place to question.

I will not trouble myself to attend yet another royal wedding. Most people expect to see just one royal pageant in their lives, but having witnessed three, I am bored to death with the King and all his wives. I pray God this fifth one is his last. He is growing old and, pray God, he can now be content to settle for what he has.

It pleases me that he let German Anna go free, and mayhap this new one will delight him enough and happiness will come to England again. She is bonny enough to please any man. Barely sixteen they say, poor mite, and as sweet as a nut too. The pamphlets tell us that the King has dubbed her his 'rose without a thorn'.

Well, time will tell, won't it? It always does.

London is teeming with visitors and most of them find their way across the bridge to the stews at sometime or other, and boost business nicely indeed. I buy myself some thick bed curtains and a sturdy dresser to hold a jug and bowl. It isn't new of course, and bears the mark of many an owner, but it's new to me and I'm proud to own such a thing. I have a meagre store of firewood put by too, in readiness for the winter cold. These days, I am so wore out that I fall into bed at dawn and sleep the sleep of the wicked, but before I close my eyes, I make the time to pray that Francis is safe and that the French disease will pass my sisters and me by.

The sickness, that seems to come in waves, is rife in Southwark again and the King is threatening to close the brothels down. They've tried that before, of course, but we just lie low for a bit and offer our services beneath another name. As long as the gentlemen come, there will always be whores, there's nothing even the King can do to change that.

Sometimes I fear I am growing old, for these days my work hangs heavy on my shoulders. Maybe it's the lack of hunger, but I can no longer revel in the bright pennies that are pressed into my hand or find satisfaction in the ale that my customers tip down my throat.

Even when I am stone drunk I lie beneath the sweating, wine-sloshed bellies of my leman, sick at heart, wishing there was another way. But there never has been, not for women like me. When the working night is over I often lie awake and wonder what became of Francis. It goes hard with me, never knowing if he will ever come to me again, or if he has forgot his Joanie for good this time. It's the not knowing that is worse, but only in the cover of night do I face up to my fears and admit that the joy in my life has gone with him and that life is harder now that I am no longer a merry whore.

"Joanie!" A young man grabs my waist, spins me round and for a moment I think it is Francis, but it isn't. It's the son of a Costermonger from Gropecunte Lane that I have known since he was an infant. "You coming to see the fun?"

He grins hopefully but I shake my head. I've seen enough beheadings to last me a lifetime.

"It should be good," he continues. "They say this one isn't likely to depart well. They expect him to die craven, begging for mercy." I rouse a smile at his gory enthusiasm. Some say it's thoughtful of the King to provide such merry japes to entertain us, but there is something about watching a fellow die that I cannot stomach.

The weeds will never grow rank along the scaffold way while Henry is King, for when he is unhappy heads will roll and these days, King Henry is not happy very often. They are saying on Bankside that Master Cromwell is in the Tower too, and like to lose his head. The gossips also say that he who rode so high and carried out such evil deeds in the King's name is gutless in his defeat. Now that it is his turn to be punished, he cannot summon the bravery to do it well, but they say that the King turns a deaf ear upon his pleas.

Old Cromwell smoothed the road for Henry, and regardless of who he had to bring down to do it, he put things within his reach that he'd no business to. Because of him, even the way we worship God seesaws back and forth to suit the comfort of the King.

73

There is not one among the common folk who can keep track of it, each of us unsure which road leads to Heaven, and which one to Hell. Sometimes it seems to me there is little difference.

One day we must love the Pope, the next we mustn't; one day we worship the Virgin, the next her image is taken down and burned in the market square and we, the common folk, must all be pleased to have it so. We just keep our heads down and go with the flow, back and forth like refuse caught in the tide, our only way that of the King.

We've all heard tales of what happened to the people from up north when they took offence at Henry tearing down the abbeys. I can't vouch for the truth of it, but they say that the man who is to die today, Walter someone or other, Hungerford I think, was caught up in the pilgrimage and none of us want to die in the manner he will.

Even Cromwell, who served his master better than any man, will receive no royal pity when his time comes. Some say Cromwell's enemies brought him down, but either way, it is his own laws that he has fallen foul of – sanctioned by the King or not. Master Cromwell's friend dies today and he will follow soon after, and who knows whose turn will be next.

The men who are to die are accused of heresy and treason, but it seems to me, although I am but a simple soul, that in these changeable days such a claim could be laid against any man. For of course, every man, woman and child in England knows that he really dies for no other reason than displeasing the King and offering Anna of Cleves as Henry's bride. Such is the value of the King's friendship. I swear to God I'd sooner be me, living in the gutter, than be a bosom-friend of the King.

On the face of it, Cromwell has done little wrong. As far as I can see he obeyed his master in all things, doing his master's dirty work so that Henry's hands stayed clean. And if he praised the charms of Anna of Cleves too much, where is the crime in that? The old saying about one man's fancy being another's poison has never rung more true. If Cromwell saw her plain sobriety as queenly potential, it is hardly his fault that fat, lusty Henry didn't agree.

But I, and others like me, care not one way or the other. My main worry is for Francis, who I fear is too mixed up in court intrigue for his own good. I've not the time to pity any of the others. At least this Queen escaped, and I hope the next one will too, for when you come to think about it, it's like my head being lopped off because a punter finds another whore up the road that he likes better!

Well, we are all whores when it comes down to it, fancy clothes or no, all subject to a man's lust and greed. Queens are no different.

"Come, come with us.'Twill be a lark." Peter's laughter pulls me back from me thoughts and I reluctantly let him lead me from the bear pit, knowing that he will want to use me later. Oh well, he has an ample purse and it may save me the chore of turning out for punters after dark.

As we near the river's edge a great cry goes up from the crowd and we turn, craning our necks to see what all the fuss is. To our amazement, those gathered at the pit are scattering, men, women and childer fleeing, wide eyed, half laughing, half afraid, their great shrieks tearing the air while the tormented bear, who has broke free of his chains, comes lumbering after.

The dogs are still following, baying and yelping as they snatch at his bloodied fur with their lathered jaws. Women snatch their bairns into their arms and hide in doorways as in a great, snarling, madcap parade, they pass close to us. Peter the Costermonger gallantly pushes me behind him and I cling to his goose-turd green jerkin to peer over his shoulder, watching in astonishment as the bear lumbers past and casts itself, with a great splash, into the stinking river, the yelping dogs not hesitating to follow after.

With wild hoots of laughter the crowd rush to the bank where the sudden appearance of the bear and his savage train are causing a deal of trouble on the water.

Several passing barges are thrown into disarray, rocking wildly in the murky waves. I see a man standing in the prow of an abandoned wherry, the other occupants having leapt into the water. With flailing arms they struggle for the shore. I nudge Peter in the ribs as the dripping bear clambers onto the side of the barge, over-tipping it, dragging it down so that it begins to fill with water, throwing the hapless cleric into the drink. The air around us is filled with screeching laughter.

Peter's arm is tight about my waist and, with the sharp edge of the balustrade digging into my ribs and the sun warm upon my back, I open my mouth to bellow insults at the struggling man who, with his books and parchments floating rapidly downstream, cannot decide which is the greater danger, the bear or the water.

He is a sorry sight, his robes streaming water, his hat lost, his face turning blue with cold. The onlookers roar with merriment as he wades up the bank, sits on the mud and begins to empty his shoes of water. Then, on seeing the bearward preparing to lure his charge home, he gestures to his treasures that are threatening to sink beneath the waves. The fellow runs obligingly along the water's edge to fish them out with his stave and dump them some way up the river bank.

The spectacle has raised my spirits and, in a better mood now, I follow Peter across the bridge. The hand on my waist may not be the one I long for, but Peter is a merry lad and will warm me for a while and help to keep a roof over my head.

I can be content with that for now.

Francis Wareham

I am a married man. I wake up and lay back, head on hands, and look down on my sleeping wife, fighting the urge to wake her. She did well last night for her first time and deserves her sleep. I look forward to all I have yet to teach her.

Fair hair tumbles over her pillow, her oblivious face is pink and serene, one leg thrown free of the blankets, showing a slim calf and knee. I think of the fleshy thighs and the cleft of Heaven that lies between.

With care, I slowly slide the sheet from her and gaze upon the bite marks still visible on her snowy white arse. It stirs again. The desire to possess her, bend her to my will whether she welcomes it or not. She is mine to have, whenever I want her and right now, I need to hear her cry out again in mingled pain and passion. I reach out. Touch her.

Breath rushes from between her lips and she rouses, opening one eye to look at me through her matted hair. Her lips stretch in welcome. "Francis?" she questions, half rising, but I push her face down again and, straddling her, begin to knead her fleshy rump, pinching and squeezing, making her squeal and wriggle before I anoint it with soothing kisses.

Afterwards, as I am tying up my cod-piece, Eve slides up the pillows, wincing as her well-used quaint comes in contact with the mattress. Her taut breasts peep at me through the ends of her hair and I am filled with the sudden regret that her body isn't as round and motherly as my Joanie's. I've always favoured large, pendulous dugs, the sort that suggest nourishment and comfort, and as the memory of Joan stirs my mind drifts to the south side of London Bridge.

Joanie will think I have forgotten her but I have just been intent on other pleasures … and work, of course. I never neglect my duty to Nicolas Brennan, although now that Master Cromwell has been taken, the exact nature of my task is unclear.

My latest instructions were to lie low, watch those about the King, and particularly Cromwell's direst foes, Norfolk and Gardiner. It is no hardship to do so. I am happy to lurk at the King's court, noting who comes and who doesn't. There is no real work in scratching a few cryptic reports on parchment and, ensuring I am not followed, delivering them to Nicholas' rooms. It means I spend less time with Joan but, now I am married, a night time spent at home with the wife has a certain novelty.

Eve is bending over a bowl of water, one knee on a stool as she rinses her nether regions with a linen cloth, the water trickling down her legs onto the floor. Her bottom is slapped pink, the softness of her inner thigh bruised from my attentions. She glances up at me through her hair, her nipples still red from my mouth, her face flushed, her eyes gleaming. I feel the urge to go again, but as I move toward her a sharp double knock falls upon the outer chamber door. When I open it, I find her narrow-eyed sister, Isabella. As she breezes in, I make my bow and hastily take my leave.

I saunter among the throng. I have no cares in the world and call a happy 'good morning' to a bevy of girls as I pass beneath the town gates and onto the bridge for a casual encounter with Nicholas. His chambers are close to Becket's church, as we must now, since the reforms, remember to call Our Lady Chapel. Before I approach Master Brennan's door, I ensure that I have not been followed. But my stealth is unrewarded for the door remains closed, and I surmise that Nicholas is from home. I stroll on, my feet taking me, against my better judgement, toward the south side of the river.

Then I spy a great hubbub on the water and see, of all things, that a bear has escaped the baiting. He plunges into the drink, a train of hounds on his tail, onlookers streaming after. For the first time since I left my wife this morning, I relax a little and smile, leaning over the better to see as those on a nearby barge leap into the waters when the bear scrambles on board. A great spectacle ensues, and not wishing to miss the fun I hurry over the bridge, pushing and elbowing through the jostling crowd.

I arrive at the riverbank in time to see a clerkly fellow flounder onto dry land, water streaming from his clothes. The crowd shows him little mercy, pointing and laughing at his predicament, and I notice he is anxious for his possessions that are in danger of floating downstream. Someone dumps them on the bank further upstream and, my curiosity piqued, I sidle forward. Unobserved by the onlookers, who are more concerned with the antics of the bear, I snaffle the dripping documents from sight, secrete them about my person and melt away into the commotion.

It is as I am mingling with the throng passing back over the bridge to London Town that I see Joanie. She is with some low fellow, his hand possessively on her waist, her head laid lovingly on his shoulder. The twist of jealousy just beneath my heart is so sharp that I look down to ensure someone has not wounded me. I know too well the privileges her ragamuffin lover will soon enjoy, and barely able to breathe for envy, I stand stock-still and watch them until they are lost in the crowd.

I am astonished that my affection for Eve has in no way cured me of love for Joanie. I'm at a loss as to know what to do. They are ahead of me and she doesn't see me, doesn't know my pain. Yet as I watch her walk happily away from me, I realise that the bonds that tie me to Joanie are unbreakable. I will have to see her again ... and soon.

I am in my chambers squinting at the cipher scrawled like a spider's journey upon the stolen parchment when Eve comes up behind and peers over my shoulder. Instinctively, I cover the paper with my hand.

"What is it?" she asks, and sidles round me to perch on my knee, lifting my fist from the document.

"Nothing to concern you." I push back her hair and begin to kiss her neck, inhaling her lemony scent, enjoying the silkiness of her skin beneath my tongue. She leans forward, her corsets creaking a little, and I slide my arms further about her waist.

"Is it a code, Francis? A cipher? Oh, do let me see properly."

"No." I have no way of knowing what the secret message contains, the information therein could be a matter of life or death. "I was supposed to deliver it but the recipient was from home."

It is easy to lie to her. I slide my hands up her bodice, the stiff brocade of her frock is rough beneath my fingers, denying me the pleasure of her soft contours. But at the top I find warm flesh that seems to pulse a little beneath my touch. My fingers wander, pushing awkwardly beneath the stiff garment to the softness beneath. She gasps as I pinch her nipple but still her attention is on the document. I no longer care what it contains and wish I'd left it on the river bank.

She lifts the paper closer to her face as I impatiently cut away the lacing on the back of her gown. I have them at last; small, round, hillocks of perfection, one in each hand. I groan with rising ardour.

"This word here …" she says, straining to see the paper as I twist her toward me so that I can rub my face between her breasts, "it is the same as this one … and this one … look."

She struggles to pull away and I lose my grip, the parchment waving beneath my chin, the smell of the wax seal in my nostrils. "Let us see if we can work it out, just some of it, come on."

She slips from my knee, shrugging her bodice impatiently back up her arms, and brings the candle closer to the table. "You see this word? What can it be?"

She bites her lip, her eyes alight with intrigue, at that moment more a spy than I am. I watch her lean over the table, her bottom an unintentional invitation I cannot refuse. I get up slowly and while I pretend to look over her shoulder, I press myself against her rump. Ignoring my attempt at seduction, she taps the signs and symbols with one long finger, biting her lower lip with small white teeth.

Her reading skills are limited but that doesn't seem to hinder her capacity for unravelling a coded message, for suddenly, I see quite plainly that she is right. The same word is repeated several times; if we could just discover the meaning of that one coded word we could use it to decipher the rest.

A quiver of excitement runs through me that, for once, is quite unrelated to my cock. Pulling out a chair, I sit down and draw her back onto my knee. With our heads together, we begin to closely study the parchment.

The chamber is almost dark when I straighten up and look at my wife properly for the first time in several hours. She has long since removed her cap and her hair is dishevelled, her fingers inky, a streak of indigo marring her parchment brow. For several minutes we stare at each other unsmiling, both of us aware that the document we have almost unravelled is important indeed. The hand is Cranmer's I suspect, or his secretary's, and the contents detrimental to the Queen.

"I must hand this to Cromwell, he will ensure it gets back to Cranmer."

"Cromwell is in the Tower!"

"I'd forgotten ...."

The silence stretches, a cock crowing far off, a bell chiming, a dog barking ....

"So Katherine Howard was a decoy, dangled before the King by her uncle to lure him back to the old religion. Are you for Reform, Francis?"

Her question astounds me. I've never given it much thought, never looked past my next meal or my next woman. I have little care for the church. I shrug and bluster, and begin to roll the parchment up and tie it with ribbon. I wish to God I could reseal the wax and pretend I'd never looked on it. If it falls into the wrong hands ... My wife interrupts the train of my thought.

"You must have an opinion. Katherine, it seems, is essential to her uncle's plan to keep the King on the side of conservatism. This – this letter and the information that it holds, is vital to the future of reform. Our duty is clear, but just think Francis, what will it mean to the Queen? She is just a girl."

"And a pretty one, at that." An image of the Queen's laughing face flashes before me, her kindling eye, her bouncing breasts. I had never thought of her as 'just a girl', and neither it seems had others before me. "This paper says she is no maid nor has been for some time. The King, it seems, was not the first to plough her furrow. Norfolk must be a fool to think he can get away with this. It could bring them all down, and the reformers will be glad to see them fall. The manner in which the pious choose to say their prayers

83

makes little difference to me. I have no preference and worship as the King demands. I just keep my head down and try to stay out of trouble."

Eve snorts inelegantly. "The day you picked up this parcel of papers hasn't exactly kept you from trouble, has it?" She stares through the black window for a while. "Katherine's downfall could help Cromwell. If you hand this to the right person, you may even keep him from the scaffold and aid the reformation at the same time. You have to decide, Francis, whether to pass these papers on and endanger the life of the Queen, or burn them and let your allies burn also."

Something stirs in my belly; I smell riches. Cranmer will pay a tidy sum to lay his hands on this, but on the other hand, so would Gardiner. Opposite sides, vying for information that is in my own keeping. A fleeting image of a fat purse, perhaps enough to buy some property and a new suit of clothes, passes through my mind's eye but I do not speak the thought out loud. I know Eve wants me to destroy the evidence and forget what I have read, but a rosy future beckons. I forage for another lie to appease her.

"I will take it to Nicholas on the morrow." I watch her yawn and stretch and hope she never discovers my deceit.

It seems there may be more to my wife than I'd thought. Before today I'd never imagined there was anything in her head beyond the latest dance steps. I find this newly discovered side to her not just intriguing but attractive too.

Her bodice is still loose, her breasts peeking through the stuff of her chemise. I realise I have spent the last six hours in her company and not once thought of humping her. That thought is as surprising as her newly discovered intelligence. "Ring for supper, wife," I say, "I will deliver the papers in the morning. Nicholas must be the one to decide what should be done."

She scowls at me but does as she is bid. Clutching her gown to her body she summons a servant and orders food to be brought up. I watch as the maidservant scurries about the room, closing the shutters against the night, drawing the curtains and bending over the hearth, stoking the fires. I decide I have just about time to take Eve to our bed before the food arrives.

The next morning Eve wakes up in a tetchy mood so, after enduring our first marital discord, I take myself off to contact Nicholas again. Ever alert for Gardiner's spies, I take a circular route to his home but when I go to bang upon the door, it creaks open a little way at my touch. I step over the threshold. "Hello?" I call, but there is no reply.

It is unlike Master Brennan to be so careless as to leave his door ajar, so I tread cautiously along the corridor and pause outside his chamber before lifting my hand to make my presence known. There is no reply even when I knock quite ferociously, and I draw out the papers, pondering what I should do. Deciding it might not be wise to shove them beneath his door, I tuck them into my doublet again. I turn to go but something stops me, and I reach out and lift the latch.

The high-up window provides insufficient light to leaven the gloom within, and it takes some while for my eyes to become accustomed to the dark. As I look about the familiar room it doesn't take me long to realise that the chaos that meets my eye is unusual even by Nicholas' standards.

The table is overturned, a stool is upended on the flag-stoned floor, a pot leaks ink as dark as blood onto a scattering of parchments and rolls. The beat of my heart increases, making me nauseous. Nicholas is in trouble and I know that if I am not to follow him, I must make myself scarce, as quickly and as completely as possible.

I slide along the passageway and pause momentarily at the door. Everything appears normal. I scan the usual crowds of traders and shoppers. There are urchins rolling in the dirt and a fellow across the street is eyeing up a doxy. I furl my cloak about me and melt, as inconspicuously as possible, into the crowd. For a while, my heart performs a clog dance in my chest, and I hurry along the bridge, unsure of which direction I should take. Then I dart between a gap in the tenements and pause for a moment at the edge of the bridge. Above me, the heads of traitors stare bleakly across the sullen river, but I have no care to dwell on their fate today. Instead, my eyes are drawn to the dark brown waters that ferment into a cauldron before rushing furiously between the starlings. I watch a boat caught in the current, struggling to pull free, the passengers on board white-faced with fear that they may have to shoot the bridge after all. Such pass-times are only for the brave or the foolhardy, and their relief is evident when the boatman steers them successfully to the safely of the southern wharf. While I determine my best course of action, I watch them clamber from the boat and hope that anyone watching me will be fooled by the casual manner I assume.

Master Brennan is nowhere to be found and our master in the Tower, in as deep a trouble as a man can find himself. I curse beneath my breath, hoping Nicholas has not been taken too. There is no way of telling what danger I may be in, but if anyone knows of my connection with either Nicholas or Cromwell, I may soon find myself following in their wake. I can brazen it out, return to court and pretend that nothing is amiss, or I can run, scurry to Joanie until such time as I can get myself away from London Town.

But then I remember that I have a wife to think of now. I look at the sky, pondering what to do. I tell myself that the best way to protect her is to first save myself. But then an unbidden memory stirs, and the thought of her tight little body and the tentative touch of her fingers changes my mind and draws me home.

Evelyn Wareham - 1540

It is late, the sun already high when I finally wake and slide up the pillow, my limbs aching from the night before, to blink about the empty chamber. Francis' pillow is cold, his side of the coverlet thrown back, his clothes gone. While I wait for my maid to help me dress, I rise from the bed to wander to the window and look out across the gardens.

The household is already up and about. If my father were here he'd call me a slattern and a lazy bones, but my husband kept me from a good night's rest and I needed the extra hour. I yawn and stretch, sighing impatiently as I wonder why Maud is so tardy in replying to my summons. Fed up with waiting, I cross the chamber in my nightrail and open the door to the outer chamber.

For a moment my mind does not acknowledge what is before me and I blink, trying to clear my vision, trying to convince myself that what I am seeing is false, a mistake ... a mirage.

Francis is beside the fire, his head turned from me, his face burrowed in Maud's bosom. Her head is thrown back, her fingers tangled in his hair, their bodies squirming.

Sickness overwhelms me and knowing I am about to disgrace myself, I gasp and turn, floundering blindly back into my chamber to heave into the chamber pot. My body is consumed with shivering, my mind a horrible whirl as my stomach twists and churns. I gag and cough, bringing up nothing but bile.

"Eve." Francis is at the door, too afraid to come hither. I ignore him, I cannot bear to look on him and know I will never be able to bear him near me again. Sweat soaks my shift as I heave once more, retching, my eyes streaming, the tears mingling with the moisture on my face. I hear him step closer. "Eve? Are you all right?"

When I stagger upright and turn toward him it is as if someone has removed a blindfold and I am seeing him clearly for the first time. He is no more my gallant Francis, he is like a child, a frightened little boy, as ignoble and as spineless as a man can be.

"Of course I'm not all right!" I screech, brushing away furious tears. "How the hell can I *ever* be all right?"

Another step forward and he is close to me. Too close. He needs a shave, his eye is shifty, avoiding mine. Shame sits sadly upon him. He cannot look me in the face but he shrugs as if to turn this gargantuan thing into nothing.

"It doesn't mean anything, Sweeting. All men dally with the maids."

I am astounded at his words. We have not yet been married a month and already he is 'dallying with my maid'. After a heady, glorious night with me, he has found it necessary to 'dally with my maid'.

"Really?" I snarl, scaring myself as fury unfurls like a demon in my heart. "I don't believe my father would dream of dallying with servants, nor would any man of refinement."

"It's good enough for the King," he mutters as I turn sharply away from him. I wish that I were dressed. It is not easy to be dignified in a night gown. I feel like a little girl; a stupid, gullible child. Like a burning brand, the memory of the last few nights flickers in my mind. I have given him every piece of me, let him do things to me that I'm sure no decent wife is ever asked to do. It strikes me that it all meant nothing to him, that I have been used. He has treated me like his ... like his ... like a whore!

He reaches out and touches my arm but I wrench myself away.

"Don't you dare touch me!"

He gives a half laugh, the dimple that I once found so intriguing appearing momentarily on his cheek. Had I a knife I would use it, my body is trembling with hatred. Hatred and bitter, bitter sorrow that he could use me so shabbily.

I could have wed anyone I wanted but I chose him, a nobody, because I loved him and had thought he returned that love in full measure. Oh, there is no truth in men, none at all!

Love is nothing but a word a man uses to get beneath a virgin's petticoats. As I stand there looking upon the wreck of my marriage, the wreck of my life, I remember a thousand small things that I have pretended not to see.

His eye sliding about the hall, fixated upon the trim of Katherine Howard's bodice, upon Mary Norris' swelling bosom. Francis, laughing in a corner with Jane Guilford until he sees me coming and moves away. All the time I have known him I have intercepted secret smiles, sly winks, unexplained absences, and I have loved him too well to question them. "How many women, Francis?"

The words are out before I've thought them and he gapes like a fish, flaps his arms like a pinioned bird and turns an unattractive shade of red. There is no need of an answer. I can see it in his face and know already that there have been too many, there are too many still.

He disgusts me. I turn my back, looking blindly from the window.

"Evie," he pleads, using his bedtime name for me, but I do not turn around.

"Don't ever use that name again. Go away, Francis, just go about your day and leave me alone. I care not if you never return."

There follows a short silence, then I hear his feet shuffling.

"I'll come back later, when you are calmer." *When I am calmer,* I scoff silently, humourlessly, my mind screaming. *I will never be calm again.*

He is at the door, his voice quavering like a miscreant boy. I want to claw out his eyes but I turn my face away and try to quell my temper. I say nothing.

"Bye then ..." He is still waiting for me to turn and bid him good day as if everything were well between us, as if there is a chance I will ever forgive him.

My heart is pounding with a rage I can no longer contain. I want to hurt him, draw my nails across his face, make him bleed as I am bleeding inside, spoil his pretty looks for ever, make him so ugly he is disgusting to *all* women. Instead, I reach out for a green baluster jug that stands before me on the table and, spinning suddenly upon my heel, I hurl it at him. As it flies through the air, he sees it coming and makes good his escape. The jug collides with the heavy oak door, shattering into pieces, along with my heart.

I am back in my bed, a bed that still reeks of our lovemaking. I claw at my pillow, tear at the sheets, trying to staunch the pain. Since I was a small child I have been loved and nurtured, always safe, always knowing what tomorrow will bring. But now, I know nothing. I *am* nothing but a commonplace wife with no future but to be further ill-used by her husband.

I hear a soft footfall, followed by a voice. "Eve? Whatever is the matter? Your servant said you are ill?"

It is Bella, come to gloat no doubt. I sit up and wipe my nose on my night gown, preparing for her lecture, waiting for her to say, "I told you so."

"What is it, my dear?" Her face, so full of concern, undoes me and I fall into her arms, blubbing like an infant all over again. Her jewelled bodice scratches my cheek as, little by little, between sobs and further attacks of despair, the story comes out. I see how Bella's lips tighten, how her eyes darken. "He was kissing Maud?" Bella's chin knobbles in righteous anger. "You've sent her off, I take it?"

I shrug. I have no idea where Maud is but I imagine she has fled. Maybe she has even gone off with Francis. At the thought my mouth begins to square again but Bella forestalls the tears.

"No. No more of that. Come along, sit up and drink this."

She offers me a cup of something strong, something that makes me cough and splutter as she begins to fasten back the bed curtains. "You must get up, wash and dress. When he comes back you must be contained and calm, dignified. You are better than this; you are a Bourne. Come along. Think how Mother would behave."

"Our Father would never treat her like this!"

She ignores me, rings the bell to summon a servant and ask for warm water. Then as we wait, she busies herself at my clothes press until a kitchen boy knocks and enters with a slopping bowl. He begs my pardon for bringing me the water and says that Maud is nowhere to be found. I wonder again if she is with Francis. The servants must all know what has happened, I will never be able to hold my head high again. Bella dips a finger into the bowl, testing the temperature.

"Things aren't as bad as they seem. It would have happened sooner or later, you know that."

Tight lipped, Bella is sorting my linen, holding out a shift. I step from my nightgown and allow her to help me dress. She pretends not to notice the marks Francis' passion has left on my body.

"We've been married for such a little while and … I thought … I really believed he loved me. How could he do it?"

Bella snorts. "Don't ask me the workings of a man's mind."

There is a short silence while we both let our minds travel different paths. Then she pulls me back to the painful present. "I did come this morning with some news of my own but … you may not receive it so gladly … now."

She looks almost guilty and I find my curiosity piqued. "What is it?" I ask. "What news?"

With her hands clasped in her lap as if she is seeking to contain her feelings, Bella looks at me, her white face unreadable.

"Oh, I am to be wed at last, that's all. I wager you thought it would never happen."

I had never imagined Bella marrying. She is so composed, so tightly laced I cannot imagine a man unleashing her passions. For a long moment I am silent, contemplating all the emotions that she has in store. The courtship; the heady torment of a desire that cannot be sated; the blissful relinquishment of virtue on her wedding night. I am filled with both a tearing envy and a wrenching fear that her marriage will be as miserable as mine. But I must try to be glad, for her sake. I must not taint her experience with my own knowledge.

I try to smile. "Married, Bella? How lovely. To whom?"

Her face is pink and for once she looks pretty. She bites her lip, waggles her head on her shoulders and will not look at me.

93

"Sir Anthony." Her voice is but a whisper.

"Sir Anthony Greywater?" I am dumbfounded. Bella is marrying my cast-off suitor. The gentleman I found too old and dull beside the exciting temptations of Francis. She will be mistress of a fine house, wife of a good, honest man while I am tied to a louse: a lecher and a rogue involved in the shady dealings of the King's chief minister. While she gets a gentleman, I get a monster that consorts with whores and slatterns.

At once the future appears even bleaker than before. It will be hard to watch Bella take the place that could have been mine, breed a bevy of fine little boys. While she can act the lady, giving alms to the poor and succour to the needy, I will be lucky if I ever rise higher than her knee.

"I am glad, Bella," I say at last but I am not glad, I am green with envy.

She stays for the afternoon, dragging me from my chambers to take the air in the gardens, forcing me to go about my business as if nothing has happened. "Perhaps you should get yourself a little dog, like Fritz," she says, as if a dog will solve all my problems. "You liked him, didn't you? And we should pay the Lady Anna a visit, she often enquires after you." I stare at her blankly. What good will it do? How can I enjoy the friendship of the ex-Queen or the lick of a puppy dog when it is common knowledge that my husband has shared the bed of half the court?

I can feel them all looking at me, their pity as sharp as loathing. When night comes I lock my chamber door, climb onto the mattress and curl into a ball. Yet although the fresh sheets are a balm to my aching soul, sleep does not come. There cannot be another wife in all the world as miserable as I.

All night I am kept awake wondering where Francis is, why he does not come. And although I tell myself that should he come home I would drive him from my presence, I long for him with every beat of my heart.

It is early when I rise and struggle into my clothes, lacing my sleeves awkwardly and struggling with my stockings. I have done nothing about replacing Maud. In truth I am afraid to, I had thought she was a good girl and I had believed she liked me. Evidently I am a poor judge of character. I fear I will never trust another female servant, not so long as Francis remains with me. That is, if he ever comes back.

My footsteps seem to ring loudly as I make my way along the palace corridors. Only servants are abroad and the place is deserted as I hurry toward the water gate to summon a boat to take me down river to London Town. Here, the common folk are already well into their day and I am surprised to discover such a throng.

All night I have been thinking of Francis, wondering where he is, who he is with, and then I recall the package that he was to deliver to Master Brennan in the morning. I think I recall him saying that his chambers are on London Bridge, and my intention is to seek him out and ask if he knows Francis' whereabouts. It will be humiliating to admit that I have lost my husband, but I cannot bear to pass another night like the last.

As I push my way onto the bridge people look at me curiously, for gentlewomen do not usually venture abroad unescorted. But I want no one to witness what I might discover this day. He might be drunk or tucked up in bed with Maud. He might have been thrown into The Clink for all I know.

The way is rough; ragged children peer from corners, a pie-man shouts his wares, a woman chases a dog from her step with a broom. I keep to the middle of the bridge, for the muck is much thicker close to the houses and there are too many dark corners that might conceal a cutpurse. Across the crowd I can see the towering walls of Our Lady's Chapel and I make toward it, casting about for someone who looks honest enough to ask the direction of Master Brennan.

I shoulder and elbow a way through the throng until I find a breathing space. A woman is sweeping straw from a doorway, tossing it out into the street with the other refuse. I step over a dead cat and wend my way toward her. She has an honest, gap-toothed way with her and when she sees me, she stops and puts up her broom.

"Are you lost, Lady?" she asks, one hand on her hip, noting my finery although I am dressed in my simplest cloak and cap.

"I am looking for the chambers of a Master Brennan. Can you direct me to him?" To my bitter disappointment she gives a sorry smile and shakes her head.

"Sorry, Lady, what's he look like?"

"I – I have no idea but thank you, I will enquire of someone else."

I move away and she watches me go with curiosity and a sort of pity on her face. I raise my chin and battle on, past a group of boys who are tormenting a flea-bitten cat. A man hollers at them to stop and they scatter, one of them running into me, forcing the breath from my lungs. He falls back onto the ground but I somehow manage to keep my footing.

"You all right, missus?" one of his companions asks. It seems that my predicament is obvious even to the likes of them. I nod and offer my best smile.

"I wonder, do you know of someone by the name of Master Brennan?" The grubbiest of them, his face daubed with the dried wipings of his nose, surveys me from one eye.

"Maybe," he says, holding out a filthy fist for a coin. But I am not that gullible. I am daughter of a Bourne. I jerk up my chin.

"You must take me to him first," I say, "and only then shall you have your coin."

He scrambles reluctantly to his feet and begins to lead me through the throng. He makes a rapid progress and I struggle to keep up, my shoes that are made for court slipping and skidding in the muck. After a while I realise he is taking me to the far side of the bridge, toward Southwark and the stews where I have no wish to go. I call to him to stop.

"Are you sure Master Brennan lives this far over?" My voice rings loud across the gap between us and I see a woman lift her head sharply.

"Master Brennan?" she says, stalking slyly toward us, an ominous eye on my child guide. "I know him and he lives back the way you come, up by the chapel. What are you up to, you young villain?"

She fetches the child a clout about the ear and he ducks out of sight to be lost among the crowd. The woman looks me up and down, taking note of my quality clothes, my lost expression. She folds her arms across her generous bosom and cocks her head to one side.

"I know trouble when I see it," she grins, "you're lucky I happened along. You'd better tell Joan all about it, me dear."

And so I find myself explaining my errand, although of course, I don't go into detail. But she is wiser than she looks and nods knowingly, half closing one eye.

"I'd lay good money on you being the lady wife of Francis Wareham. I know your good 'usband well. Would you like for me to take you to 'im?"

97

If she offered to take me to dinner with the Pope I'd not be more surprised.

"You – you know my husband? How so? And where is he?" All sorts of unsavoury pictures are flooding into my mind as to her precise relationship with Francis, but she seems a goodly type, a sort of honest rogue if there be such a thing. "Is he safe?" I add as an afterthought and she opens her mouth in a wide smile, her grubby prettiness suddenly shining through. She is younger than I had first thought.

"Oh yes, Francis is perfectly safe. You come along with me, I will take you to him."

Joan Toogood

My rule has always been 'no money, no cunny', so I hope Peter has a long purse for he is on his third humping. The rule doesn't apply to Francis of course, but Francis is different, always turning up with some dainty to tempt me.

I am peering over Peter's shoulder at the cobwebbed ceiling, my legs about his waist, my heels drumming on his arse, when the door flies open and Betsy bursts in. Peter leaps away from me, clutching his fallen hose and dragging them up to hide his nethers.

"What on God's earth is going on?" I cry, scrambling from the mattress. My sister's in a sorry state, her hair scat asunder and her eyes wild. Her chest is heaving.

"It's Sybil, she's been cut. A punter didn't like 'er price and took his blade to 'er."

She continues to grizzle as I scrabble into my gown and make for the door with Peter at my heels. As I reach the balcony I see a crowd bearing my sister home. She is holding a bundle of rags to her cheek and even in the dim light I can see the blood seeping from beneath it.

"Oh, Joanie," she wails as they hoist her over the threshold, "whatever shall I do? I am spoiled, spoiled."

Her mouth gapes wide, her limbs flailing as they dump her on the mattress and begin to fuss about her. The chamber is not built for a crowd and I can barely reach the bed. Pushing a way through to where Sybil lies prostrate, bleeding on my fancy counterpane, I force her hand away and gingerly lift the makeshift bandage.

I close my eyes, swallow vomit. Her cheek is open to the bone. She needs a surgeon but I can't afford one. Not even if I worked on my back day and night for a sennight.

"Is it bad, Joanie? Is it bad? I can't really feel nothin'..."

I swallow and look up at Peter who stands, white-faced, on the other side of the bed, his ardour vanished.

"Not so bad, Sybil," I lie, "'tis just a lot of blood but it's sure to heal up fine."

Betsy sits by the hearth with her skirts to her face, rocking back and forth, weeping and wailing like Sybil is about to die. I turn back to Peter. He is young but able.

"Peter, can you get them out of 'ere so I can see to 'er?" After a moment he comes back to his senses and tears his eyes from poor Sybil.

"I will, Joanie, leave it to me," he says and while I begin to warm water on the hearth and tear my best petticoat into strips to bind her broken cheek, he chases our neighbours from the chamber.

At the first touch of the warm cloth Sybil's body stiffens, her hands clawed, her legs taut. I try to wash away the blood but more comes, as fast as I try to staunch it. The cloth is reddened and the water in the bowl turns scarlet. Peter looks over my shoulder, his young face furrowed with concern.

"Why would someone do this?" he asks, bewildered. "Sybil is a fine gel, gives a fellow a good time. Why would anyone hurt her?"

I sigh, continuing to bathe my sister's ravaged face that was once so 'andsome.

"Some men like to hurt us. It soothes something within them, some secret sense of guilt. Maybe it

100

makes it easier for them to go home and bed their wives … who knows?"

It was true, girls like us did get hurt, and often died at the hands of their customers too. It wasn't always a punter, sometimes it was a jealous wife or sweetheart, sometimes it was a bawd. My mother told us a tale once about her childhood friend who'd been marked by the bawd who ran her. The girl had wanted to marry but the woman she worked for, unhappy at the loss of earnings, had other ideas and opened up her face for her. That girl had died of her wound, her cheek festering until she expired in agony. A glance at Betsy, still howling at the fireside, tells me that she is remembering that tale too.

"My ma's a midwife. I could get her to come."

Peter's anxious face is paler still and I know he hopes I will decline the offer. "She'd come here and sew up a whore?" That doesn't sound very likely to me. Peter shuffles his feet.

"She would if I asked her, she is a Christian soul."

Sybil is shivering and moaning, half asleep, half reliving the horror. "Go on then, me little darlin'."

I give Peter my best smile and he takes himself off. I watch him go and make a silent vow that I'll never ask payment from him again but will lay back for him for free until the end of my days.

As Sybil drifts in and out of sleep, I stoke up the fire higher than we can afford in July and tempt Betsy to get to bed. She curls up next to Sybil, her pretty unmarred face contrasting with the livid marks on Sybil's. *Oh God, let her heal well,* I pray, but in reality I have long since given up believing in the power of prayer.

I am more grateful to Peter than I can say and since his mother helped our Sybil, he is a constant visitor in our lodging. She is no pretty picture but at least she lives, even if she no longer laughs. The mark has healed crooked, one side of her mouth taut as if she is always about to break into smiles, but her smiles don't reach her eyes which remain dark and wary. One cheek is unblemished, as pretty as it ever was, but the other is as red and as angry and as knotted as her wounded heart.

She is afraid to go abroad now and refuses to leave the chamber. When my 'gentlemen' call she shuffles off to sit on a stool just outside the door. Rain or shine, she will not set foot further, although I tell her she should. She ain't that bad lookin' and could still work if she would, most men aren't fussy about the state of the mantle when they are poking the fire. I understand her fear but she won't even work in a twosome with Betsy or me. All she wants to do is sit at home, eating and using up all the kindling on unseasonal fires.

"Good day, Joanie." Peter puts his face in at the door and I smile up at him before putting down the shawl I am mending.

"Come in, me little darlin'," I say and he whips off his cap and steps over the threshold. I haven't gone back on the promise I made and accommodate his needs most days. He is a needy boy but I've learned what he likes and manage to keep things efficient. He is welcome to call but I don't let him linger long for I've a living to earn, after all.

Sybil shuffles outside, the door closes and when we hear the stool creak beneath her weight, I begin to undo my bodice, watching the eager blood surge into his cheeks. Once my dugs are bared he fumbles with his lacings and we leap into bed.

Poor Peter, his visits are always interrupted lately and not two minutes later, there is a squeal from

102

Sybil and the rumble of a masculine voice outside the door. Peter's face is red and contorted and he lets out a loud groan of frustration when the door is thrown open and there is Francis, large as life and twice as handsome.

"Get out of here," he yells and Peter, with one terrified look at his rival, whips himself out and scuttles from the chamber, tying his lacings as he goes. Feigning nonchalance, I pull down my skirts and swing my legs from the bed as Peter's hasty footsteps clatter down the stairs.

"Joanie." Francis holds out his arms but I shun them. Although inside my heart is alive with joy, I have to show how angry I am at him for disappearing for so many months. And what gives him the right to treat my customers as if they are trespassing?

I regard him unsmilingly for several moments. "I was working, paying a debt," I say pointedly as he swoops toward me, takes me in his arms. I close my eyes, inhale the man-smell of him, the velvet of his doublet as smooth as swansdown on my cheek after the roughness of the costermonger's tunic.

"Did you miss me, Sweetheart?"

I look at the strong bones of his face. He hasn't shaved this morning and his doublet is open at the neck, giving me a glimpse of ruddy chest hair. I want to kiss it. "No," I say, deliberately trying to hurt him.

"Oh, I've missed you." Like a bear he nuzzles into my neck, squeezing me tight and flattening my dugs against his torso. "I'm starving, is there anything to eat?"

"No," I say again, but his wide smile and sunny, open face is thawing my ice. Before I can stop myself I add, "But we could send out for some, if you've a coin about you."

And so, without an apology or an explanation, he is back in my life, and as I lay beneath him,

103

enjoying the familiar surge of gratification that I only get with him, I am glad.

He is my Francis and I love him.

Afterwards he lays his head on my bosom and while I twiddle his hair where it curls into the nape of his neck, he tells me he has wed another. At his words, something dies inside me.

It is as if he has forgotten he ever promised he would wed no other but me. I push my jealous fear away and pretend it doesn't matter. At least he is here. He prattles on about her, even going so far as to tell me how she mislikes him humping the maids. *Oh, Francis*, I think to myself, *for all your adventures with women, you know us not at all*.

"What is she like?" I ask, although I don't really want to know. I should have known better than to ask, for envy and dislike writhe like snakes in my belly as he describes her.

"She is a gentle lady," he says, "to look at her you'd not imagine she'd ever enjoy the rough coupling she gets from me. She is petite, like a daisy … no, no, finer than that, more like a primrose, yellow haired and delicate with small, pink tipped breasts like a child's."

I hate her even more now and hope she is barren and that she will soon grow ugly and all her teeth fall out. Francis shifts in the bed. "Pour some more wine, Joanie. We can share the cup."

He watches me go naked across the room to do as I am bid. When I climb back into bed with him, his arm slides about my neck, his hand wandering down to play with my dugs.

I try to console myself. At least he is back, and now the stew pot will be full again and the firewood store replete, the coming winter may not seem so harsh. There is nothing pleases me more than the clink of money in my purse, for coin means food and warmth and there has been little of that while he has been gone.

Francis burbles on about his bloody wife until I can't stand the mention of her, but his dribbling praise means that when I bump into her on the bridge early one morning, I have such a clear picture of her that I recognise her almost straight away.

She is lost and some small boys are tormenting her when I come upon her and, although it is plain to see she is in sorry straights, to my shame, jealousy prompts me to torment her further. Pretending to help her, I lead her into trouble, and as a result of my meddling, Francis' wife and I will suffer together until the end of days.

Isabella Bourne – June 1541

We have searched everywhere, high and low, near and far, but neither Eve nor Francis can be found. Their chambers are left empty, their bed unmade, the morning meal uneaten. It is as if they have been spirited from the world and I am distraught with worry.

From the very first I knew it was a mistake for Eve to wed a man like Francis Wareham, but she would not listen, not even to Father. There was nothing he could do but give in to her and now he regrets it. We all do. Each one of us wishes we could travel back and live that day again. I'm sure that if he had that time again, Father would shoot Francis dead on the first encounter.

I had to tell my parents about Francis' indiscretion and we all fear that their disappearance is connected with that shameful act. We are afraid that Eve did something stupid and reckless, but we cannot imagine what. It is the not knowing that is worst. I cannot rest and although I am to be wed in a few days, I can think of nothing else when my mind should properly be on other things.

Poor Anthony doesn't know what to do with me. He hovers about me like one of those striped beasties that linger about the marigolds in the garden. Although, God knows, I am no flower.

The face that peers back from my looking glass is pale and shadowed around the eyes. I miss my sister, my naughty, disobedient, defiant, infuriating little sister, as I would miss my right hand.

At court there is so much happening that no one has time to spare for the loss of a young woman. They treat us, not as if we are the victims of some misfortune, but more as if we have been rather careless. Not one of our acquaintances, high or low, has bothered to help us in our search for her. Francis and Eve have disappeared as thoroughly as an early morning mist on a summer's day.

I am dressed in my wedding gown and the pearls that are closely sewn onto the bodice and hood hang like shining, unshed tears. Father kisses my cold cheek and says I am beautiful but it is just the dress that is fine, not me. My looking glass tells me that I am made plainer than ever by grief.

Eve should be here, teasing me, bearing my train, sprinkling me with petals as I adorned her on her wedding day. I miss her each moment of every day and when my husband meets me at the church door, it is not of him that I think, or the night that will follow. In my mind's eye all I can think of is Eve's lifeless body washed up on some unnamed shore.

The stone chapel floor where I kneel is as cold as my heart.

I do not tremble when my husband looks upon my unclothed body for the first time. Indeed, I barely shudder when he takes me. I have long ceased to fear, or to anticipate, the heady, blood surging passion that Eve promised I should feel. Anthony's attentions have no more effect on me than a troublesome fly. I am dead. My body feels nothing and my mind acknowledges only pain.

As I lay beneath my husband's labours I think of Eve, seeking ways to discover her whereabouts, wrack my brains trying to remember each word of our last conversation, some tiny detail that might lead me to her. When Anthony emits a great sigh and his body goes rigid, I feel a surge of warmth between my legs.

Then he rolls off to lie panting on his back while I stare at the ceiling and try to remember exactly what Eve was wearing the last time I saw her.

"Did I hurt you?" My husband's voice drags me from my thoughts.

"What? No, no. I am quite comfortable. Thank you."

"Good," he says and leans over to leave a kiss on my brow. "Goodnight." He falls straight into a heavy slumber while I lie awake, wondering and plotting in the darkness.

In the morning when he takes me again I am surprised, I hadn't realised it would be a regular occurrence. I had imagined it to be something I should have to indulge him in once a month or so. It occurs to me that such attentions might soon prove tedious. He slavers at my breasts, gropes between my thighs, moving me not at all, and I am greatly relieved when he is done so I can wash and dress. Perhaps, since I have pleased him so well, Anthony will humour me and take me into the city to enquire if anyone has seen Eve there.

I sit up on my pillow as he dresses and watch his man laboriously tying his laces, brushing his shoulders. As soon as he is dressed and the servant departed I can keep silent no longer. "He drinks, you know, far too much."

Anthony's calm grey eyes turn upon me. "Who does, my dear?"

"Francis Wareham, of course and, and …" I hesitate, wondering if it is indelicate to continue. But I am a married woman now and surely can discuss intimate matters with my husband. I drop my voice to a whisper. "Eve told me that he dallies with the servants."

Anthony's eyebrows shoot up into his cap.

"Indeed? I can't say I am unduly surprised."

"Why?" I pierce him with my eye, wondering if all men dally likewise.

"He looks the type. I warned your father at the time."

"Did you?" I watch him gather his belongings from the washstand. "Do you wish Eve had married you instead?"

The words are out of my mouth before I have thought what I am saying, and my husband's hands hover above his belt before he turns and comes to sit upon the bed.

"My dear, I did not know your sister well enough when I asked for her hand. I was merely blinded by her youth, her lively wit and I thought, fleetingly, that she would adorn my table. Now I realise that she would have made me miserable and led me a merry dance. I am very happy with the wife I have."

He leans forward and leaves a kiss upon my hair. "And I hope that she is likewise happy."

I swallow and blink away tears. I have scarcely given it any thought but I nod and try to smile.

"I – I wondered if perhaps we could go into the town, look about and make some enquiry and discover if anyone has seen her?"

He turns again, takes my hand. "Isabella, you must let this go. She has been gone almost a month. There is little chance of discovering her whereabouts now. If she comes back, she comes back. Think on it no more, it is time now for you to think of our marriage and the sons you will bear me. Besides, the Queen has requested your presence today, has she not?"

I make a rude noise. "Oh, Katherine," I say contemptuously. "If only Anna were still Queen."

If she were Queen she would make certain Eve was found, living or dead, but Katherine thinks only of gowns and jewels and dancing ... as everyone had known she would ... except for the King. But the Lady Anna is ensconced in her new house at Richmond and can offer me no help at all.

As I had feared, Katherine invites me to join her household and I am constrained to accept her request. She is as unqueenly as it is possible to be. Like a child she grabs my hand and shows me her new gowns, and I feel quite impatient with her although I daren't show it. Instead, I put on an act and gush over her fine silks and brocades, and when she lets me hold her newest string of pearls, I let them trickle through my fingers as if I really adore them. Her world, for all its glamour, is really very small.

"It will be such fun, Bella, like old times when we served Lady Anna, only more so now that I am Queen. We can have pageants and dancing and private parties. There will be no end of fun."

I watch her preen herself before the glass. She holds her new gown before her, turning this way and that, watching the way her hair trickles down her back.

"Yes, Your Majesty," I murmur, wishing that Eve were here. She was the one to relish serving a woman like Katherine, both of them as vain as peacocks, each as pretty and as gay as the other. I know I will hate serving her. I shall not help but measure her every movement against Anna's, judge her harshly and suffer her ill.

The Queen's childish giggles dwindle away as she turns back to the mirror and, almost at once, my mind wanders back to Eve. How am I going to bear the superficiality of the Queen's household when, for all I know, my sister is in dire need of me? If only there were some way I could escape the duty.

The sing-song voice of the Queen draws me back to the present ... to a reality that is more like a child's play-time. "We travel north in a few days, Bella, so make yourself ready for a journey. There are still rumblings of discontent in the far counties and the King desires to show himself to his people. And to show off his new Queen, of course …" As usual her conversation dissolves into giggles. She reduces everything to laughter and I wonder how on earth anyone can imagine that a girl as superficial as she could hope to keep the interest of a man like Henry – a man, for all his faults, of intellect and acumen.

But, for all her ill-manners, Katherine is a Howard, niece to the Duke of Norfolk and therefore influential. She raises her hand to her mouth and whispers something to Jane Rochford, and the latter spins on her heel and leaves the room to attend the Queen's bidding, whatever it may be.

After a further twenty minutes or so of Katherine's prattle I find I am desperate to escape her presence. The windows are closed to avoid the stench of the river, and the air inside is stale with a cloying perfume that sickens me. I feel as if I am ailing. I cannot concentrate on anything for the whereabouts of Eve is like a fever in my mind, blotting out all else. I let my eyes travel about the chamber, taking in the new tapestries, the heavy drapes, the heap of new gowns upon the bed. Searching for an escape, I seize upon the notion of gowns, groping pitifully for a way out or even just a reprieve. I cannot concentrate on the Queen and royal duty just now.

"I will need a few days, Your Grace, to organise my wardrobe, but I can come Tuesday next should that please you?"

She turns from the mirror in which she has been admiring another necklace and beams upon me.

"Of course, Bella. I shall look forward to it. It will be deliciously amusing." Thankfully, I bow myself from her presence and once in the corridor, turn on my heel and march too briskly for gentility back to our married quarters.

I had hoped, now I am wed, that I would be spared my duties at court. Anthony has promised me a visit to his manor in Wales but that trip must now be postponed. "Damn her," I mumble, but as I turn the corner into our chamber, I am unsure as to whether I am damning Katherine or Eve.

Joan Toogood

She must feel strange, walking here beside me, lifting her skirts above the foulness of the alleyway. Her feet slip in the mire and the hem of her gown is besmirched with mud but still she follows, although I can tell she wishes she wasn't here. She is pale, glancing anxiously from side to side, her lips colourless as she shivers and her hands are trembling as if she has the plague.

"I cannot be responsible for the things you see here, my dear," I say. My neighbour, Bertha, is scolding her sozzled husband as we pass by and I raise a careless hand in greeting. Beside me, my lady averts her eye, raises her nose and flinches away from the stench of my world. We might as well live on separate spheres. I shrug. It isn't my fault if she doesn't like what she finds here. I stop suddenly and point a finger along the route she is to take.

"See there, past the midden where the pigs are rooting? It's up that stairway you must go, just behind the inn, but be careful on those rickety steps; my room is right at the end."

I wonder what she will make of my musty chamber with its damp spots and draughty shutters. A fine, pretty lady like her will have never seen anywhere like it before, of that I am certain.

"Go on up, my dear, that's where you'll find him." I bite my lip, gesture her forward, knowing he will have thrown off his cloak and be growing impatient. To my surprise, as she goes, I feel a twinge of conscience and wonder what she will say when she finds her husband sprawled on a whore's bed. If she mislikes him dallying with her servants she will not like to find him here. Maybe I should call her back …

113

But she is gone, sidling past the pigs, tiptoeing through the mire and climbing gingerly up the unsteady stairs. Her gloved hand reaches out to throw open the chamber door and I hold my breath, listening for the rumpus that promises to be as good as any bawdy play.

Instead, a few moments later I hear a scream so grisly that my hair prickles on my scalp. For a few moments I stand amazed and then, wrenching up my skirts, I fly across the yard and scramble up the steps behind her.

Just as I reach the top My Lady stumbles backwards across the threshold, a hand to her mouth. Her gown is spattered with spots of blood and her eyes are wide open, her mouth squared and ugly as she gropes blindly at my arms, scrabbles at my hands, babbling nonsense.

I am afraid of such madness and cannot bear to let her touch me. Crossing myself, I wrench away from her clutching hands so violently that she loses her footing. I mean her no harm but her ankle turns on the top step and I see her face open like a flower as she realises she is going to fall.

Before I can stop her, she tumbles backwards and I watch helplessly as her body bounces loosely from step to step.

After a moment, I peer down to the bundle of fine linen and velvet in the mud. Her face is white, her eyes closed, but I can just determine the rise and fall of her chest. I am torn between running to help her and venturing inside to discover what horror waits inside.

No sound comes from within and with my heart hammering like a drum, I glance back at Francis' wife and then at the door before, holding my breath, I push it open.

Francis! Oh, my God. Oh, my life! He stares back at me, his eyes wide open, seeing nothing, his best slashed doublet daubed in gore. Rooted to the spot, I put a hand to my mouth, feeling my gorge rising. I want to grab the jewelled dagger that is sticking from his heart and thrust it into my own.

For a long time that might be only moments, I look upon my poor dead lover, my mind empty of everything but the loss of him. I make no plans, concoct no cure for our predicament, and do not move a muscle until a small sound behind me makes me leap in fear. With a hand to my chest, I turn to find that Sybil has left her stool to creep indoors behind me. She moves toward the bed, a hand clamped across her lips, her hair tangled, a drool of spittle on her chin. She turns her ravaged face toward me. "Christ and his saints, Joanie, what 'as 'appened 'ere?"

As usual she is looking to me for answers. *Why do they all look to me*? I am just Joan the whore. I don't know what happened or what to do about it.

I shake my head dully, my eyes still fastened on his motionless body. Since the day he walked into my life he has ne'er kept still. He has always been full of life and movement, even in sleep he twitches and wriggles like a bag o' eels.

"We 'ave to do something before someone comes."

Slowly, very slowly, I pull my gaze from Francis and know that Sybil is right. If we are not to bear the blame for this, we must act and act now. I shake myself, fumble in my leaden brain as to what to do. There is no one who can help us. I have no man to turn to now. Francis will never come again.

A whimper erupts from my breast but I push it away. It's no time for panic now. I have a corpse in my bed and another at the foot of my stairs. Southwark is no stranger to trouble but this is the worst crime I have ever witnessed. I need a man to help me and of all the full grown, strong-bodied men I consort with, there is only one I trust, and he hardly more than a boy.

Grabbing Sybil by the shoulders, I shake her roughly. "Run and fetch Peter, quickly."

She shakes her head, gaping at me, still afraid to go abroad, even now. I want to slap her.

"It's but two streets away," I cry. "You have to go or, if you don't, then when the justices come I will tell them it was you as done it and you can rot in The Clink for the rest o' your days."

Her chin trembles but I do not heed it. I push her cruelly toward the door, over the threshold, and as she clatters down the stairs and leaps nimbly over the prone body of Francis' wife, I remember that I have yet to move her.

At the end of the alley Bertha is still berating her old man. I lift my petticoats and run toward her. "Bertha," I whisper hoarsely and she lifts her head, noting the urgency of my tone. "There's a drunken toff at the foot of my stairs, come help me get 'em to bed."

Before hurrying to my summons she lets fly a few more insults and spits on the floor at her husband's feet. Glad to see her go, he settles back on the step and prepares to sleep it off.

"Bloody men," she sneers, displaying her lack-tooth gums. "What are they good for, Joanie? You tell me that."

I have no need to give her an answer, even if I had one, for we have arrived at the place where M'lady Wareham is still lying like a broken flower. Bertha makes a noise through her teeth. "She's a lady, by all that's holy."

"Yes," I say, "grab her feet." And between us we haul Francis' wife up the stairs and shove her onto Sybil's seat by the chamber door.

"Thanks, Bertha," I say. "I will see you all right later, if you keep your gob shut."

She lays a finger alongside her nose and closes one eye while I lean on the door jamb so she doesn't seek a way inside. Casually, we chat for a while and all the time, although my insides are churning, I pretend to be calm. While she lingers, cursing the day she ever set eyes on her old man, I know that on my bed Francis' body is stiffening, his blood cooling, and he will never warm me again.

Peter and Sybil appear in the alley, their faces red from running. I nod in their direction. "Business is on its way, Bertha. You must excuse me."

"This one looks eager for it too, I'd say," she cackles as she hauls her bulk down the stairs, winking at Peter as he rushes toward me.

He climbs the stair two at a time and frowns, running an eye over Mrs Wareham who, for all intents and purposes, is snoring, her fine, bright clothes like a flag against the drabness of my world. I jerk my head, bidding him follow, and turn into my chamber to reveal the tragedy upon my bed.

The sight turns his face white. "What have you done?" he groans, pulling off his cap. "Joanie, what in God's Heaven have you done?"

"I've done nothing, Peter. I loved him with my whole being and he were alive and kicking when I left him. I think it was her."

I jerk my head in the direction of the fine lady who stirs and snorts, her mouth open, head lolling.

"Who is she? Is she drunk?"

I shake my head. "Nay, she fell down the stair, she is knocked silly and will be right when she comes to. She's his wife, I do believe."

117

"You must call the constable …"

"Don't be daft, Peter. Who will they believe? Me, or her ladyship here?"

He shifts from foot to foot, twisting his cap in his hands, biting his bottom lip. I feel a twinge of guilt. Maybe I shouldn't have got him involved; he is little more'n a lad really. It isn't fair on him.

"What then, Joanie? What are you going to do?"

I try not to remember happier days as I turn again to look at Francis, the blood soaked counterpane, the pool of gore on the boards. With a blood stained fist, I rub my nose and fix Peter with a serious stare. "Get rid of the body."

"What? Are you run mad? What about her?"

"You get rid of him, and I will take care of her."

"Me? Get rid of the body and …what do you mean you will take care of her? You don't mean to harm her?"

"'Course not. Once he has gone," I nod toward Francis' still form, "I'll put her to bed and hope that when she wakes she will 'ave no memory of it. She is in a bad way, she may not even last the night. If she does I will take her after dark and put her where her own kind will find her."

Peter sighs and rubs his forehead, chews the inside of his mouth. I can see he can't decide what's best and I am suddenly full of remorse. I put a hand on his arm. "I'm sorry, Peter, it's the shock of it all. I can't expect you to be part of this; I see that now. Go home and forget it. I will sort it out. Visit me next week when it's all over …"

He grabs my hand, kisses it, and looks me in the eyes, his beardless chin set firm. "No, Joanie, no. I will help; you have no one else. When dark falls I – I will drop him in the river. I will need to use your counterpane as a shroud."

118

At his words I have a sudden unwanted picture of Francis, eyes wide open beneath the surface of the shite-filled Thames, turning and drifting with the current, battered against the starlings, buffeted by boats, chewed by fishes until he is just bones; bones that were once living, laughing, loving flesh.

A sudden sob escapes me and I clamp a hand across my mouth, try to stop the tears, but they find a way out and course down my cheeks. Peter ignores them, his mind on practicalities.

"I need something to weigh him down, to take him to the bottom and keep him there." In this nightmare Peter speaks as if he does this sort of thing everyday, as if every broad-shouldered costermonger on every corner of Southwark is party to murder. I hand him the cooking pot.

"Fill this with stones and wrap it up with him."

Many tortured hours later, Peter bears my love away and the last I see of Francis is a tuft of ruddy hair poking from the blanket. Red-faced, for Francis is a well-built man, Peter hoists him onto his shoulder and carries him furtively down the stairs. I watch them fade into the darkness, my heart heavier than it has ever been, and turn back indoors.

I cuff Sybil to stop her snivelling and she wipes her nose on her sleeve before helping me strip the bed and turn the mattress. She takes a scrubbing brush to the wooden floor and it is only then that I go outside. Taking M'lady beneath the arms, my hands clasped just above the pretty, pink-tipped breasts that Francis spoke of so fondly, I drag her toward the bed where her husband died. Then I sit down and wait for her to wake up and tell me why she did it.

Isabella, Lady Greywater – August 1541

After a wet and dismal start to the journey the sun has finally come out, and the royal cavalcade is on its way again. The Queen has been under the weather but seems better now, although her indisposition was so acute it set the court ablaze with gossip that she is already carrying the King's child. In the end it proved to be no more than a piece of bad fish, and now her cheeks have colour again and her silly giggles are once more grating on my nerves.

I didn't want to come. My heart is in London with Eve, wherever she may be, but Anthony insisted that the honour was too great to pass by. Although it is early days, I had hoped that with all Anthony's attentions I could plead the indisposition of early pregnancy, but I have failed to get with child. Now, I watch the cycle of my courses as eagerly as the Queen watches her own, for of course, the King's incessant quest for male heirs never stops, and he will not be content until such time as Katherine produces a Duke of York, a back-up plan should any ill-fate befall Prince Edward. God forbid.

Poor Katherine. If the King's constant caresses are anything to go by he is an ardent husband indeed. Now that I am party to all that passes between a man and his wife, I find it quite repellent to watch the way the King mauls her even in company. I turn my face away from them. She is so very young and he a ravaged old fool who cannot keep his hands off her. I notice the way she turns her face from him so his lips are upon her neck rather than her mouth, and I wonder she can bear even that. I hope the jewels she loves so much are some recompense for so distasteful a bed-mate, and I pray she bears him a son soon and is spared of his company, at least for a few months.

To my relief, we break the journey for five days at Collyweston, an impressive palace in the midst of the most beautiful countryside. Although the house is far grander than home, the sight of the gently sloping meadows and wide green river makes me long for Bourne Manor. I close my eyes and let my mind rush back to my childhood and a time when Eve and I were always happy.

But I cannot keep my eyes closed forever and I know that when next I open them, I will still be here in a strange palace, surrounded by people I do not love and married to a man who does not move me.

I am uncertain if he has noticed my lack of ardour when we couple. It is not a requirement that I receive enjoyment, but I am careful to embrace him and accept whatever he cares to do to me. But while he gyrates in the throes of ecstasy, I stare into the darkness, bite my lip and pray for him to make a child on me quickly so that I can have some respite, both from him and from court.

We are making ready for the ride into Lincoln. Katherine, bedecked in a gown of cloth of silver, holds out her hand for her rings to be placed on her fingers. While Jane Rochford has that honour, I scurry about, my gown rustling as I pick up her fan and offer it to her with a deep curtsey. Then she holds out her arms and raises her pointed chin for our approval and I must confess, she looks more a Queen today than she ever has before. Her youthful charms are quite overshadowed by the grandeur of her glittering costume and even though we are all in our very best for the entry into the city, beside Katherine's splendour we are like sparrows beside a peacock.

With Katherine all in silver and the King in cloth of gold, she boasts that she is the moon to Henry's sun; a royal sun and moon with the ladies in waiting playing the part of attendant stars, shining in reflected glory and ready to do their every bidding.

It is the first time I have seen pageantry such as this and for a while my mind is drawn from my own troubles. I drink in the tabarded heralds, the sword of state held aloft as the King and his child-Queen follow the carpet through the great west door of Lincoln Cathedral.

There, before the Bishop, the King and Queen kneel before God while they are censed and a *Te Deum* is sung in their honour. Eve would have revelled in this. The pure voices of the choir bring a lump to my throat and I surreptitiously wipe away a tear. Perhaps Katherine will prove to have the stuff that Queens are made of after all. A good Queen is what Henry needs; it's what the country needs; it's what we all need. I pray that it be so.

The other ladies whisper that the King secretly plans to crown Katherine when we reach York, but I cannot imagine the ceremony will be any grander than this. Henry's eyes shine with joy at the crowd's reception of his enchanting new wife. He smiles fondly upon her as she graciously inclines her head, her gaze dancing on the cheering people before she lays a hand on Henry's forearm and allows him to lead her away. Her ladies and I follow, skimming along behind her, basking in her glory. It is a good day for the King and Queen, a good day for England, but unable to rise above my personal sorrows, it is a heavy day for me.

Long before the ceremonies end, Katherine's eyes are red. Like a child who has been allowed to stay up too late, she constantly yawns behind her hand. In any other woman such behaviour would be frowned on, but Henry's child-bride can do no wrong. She wilts prettily, like a Lenten lily in want of water, but on our return to Lincoln castle, when the King

122

retires straight to his apartments, Katherine's yawns immediately cease.

She claps her hands and demands music and refreshments and while the lady of the bedchamber helps her change, we scurry about making her room as cosy as we can. We are all prepared for an evening of supper and cards, when Katherine suddenly pleads a headache and asks to be left alone. Only Jane Rochford is allowed to stay behind, and a smug smile plays on her lips as she closes the door firmly upon us.

The other ladies pout and whisper together in corners but without sparing it another thought, I skip off to the apartments I share with Anthony and to my relief find them empty.

Oh, the luxury of an evening alone. I slip early into bed and try not to let my thoughts return to Eve. I have to make myself believe that she is well and will come back when she is ready, but before I sleep, I pray earnestly for her safety and ask that it please God to send her home to us.

The next morning, for the first time, I vomit before breakfast and the face that looks out of my glass is as white as death itself. I clutch my stomach in a relief that is short lived, for I realise that pregnancy has come too late to spare me from attending the Queen. Soon, we must journey inland across Yorkshire, calling at Pontefract, Hull and York; a journey that entails a fortnight spent in tents and swaying litters. Just the thought of it sends me running for the chamber pot again, where I retch like one damned.

After I share with Anthony the suspicion that I bear his child I tell him that I wish to return home. He hesitates. "Give it a few weeks, my dear. The sickness may yet pass."

He is gently unmovable. My place, as he sees it, is with the Queen although to me, my duty is to

123

nurture our child, not be buffeted about the countryside like a pig on its way to market.

The Queen, when she learns my news, is tight-lipped and envious. I stand, hands clasped, fighting the ever-present nausea, while she offers her insincere congratulations. I do feel for her. The whole court is eager for the news that she is with child and I have heard her uncle of Norfolk's constant haranguing that she should conceive, as if the matter is as easily arranged as a day in the tilt yard.

There were rumours while we were still at Grafton Regis that she had fallen, but it proved not to be so. And it is not just the royal couple who wish things were different, for as soon as the Queen presents Henry with a son everyone will breathe a little easier. When the King is happy it is as if his court bathes in sunshine, but his displeasure is like a dousing of frozen rain.

It is the Queen's duty to provide an heir and I, and many like me, do not envy her. Few of us would wish to be in Katherine's shoes. Just the thought of sharing the bed of the sick old King makes my bile rise. A woman, when she is little more than sixteen years old, dreams of youthful knights, tall, handsome figures with a well-turned leg. The King is certainly tall when he stands, but that is where the similarity ends. Poor Katherine is to be pitied. I would not swap all her jewels to be forced to yield to the corrupted, stinking body of the King. I don't believe there is a woman alive who would envy her that. There are those who whisper that Henry cannot mount a woman anymore, and that Katherine has about as much hope of bearing a prince as Master Cromwell. I begin to wonder if they are right.

The Queen's gown rustles and I remember she is waiting for my answer, so I tear myself from my thoughts. But as I open my mouth to make reply, a knock at the door reprieves me and I step back as a young man enters. Thomas Culpepper, a gentleman of the King's privy chamber, bows before his Queen and she tosses her head, a twinkle in her eye, her demeanour changing as it ever does in the presence of a goodly looking man.

"Master Culpepper," she says, "is the King's leg still troubling him or is he better today?"

He rises, keeping his eye respectfully on her hem, and offers her a small parcel. "His Majesty is well. He sends his love and apologies for failing to join you for supper last night."

I watch her accept the gift and notice their fingers touch as, for a brief moment, his eyes rise boldly to hers. I catch my breath, for the look I intercept is one I have seen before; a hot, sly dart of yearning, like the exchange of unspoken secrets. Once I saw Francis Wareham share such looks with Eve.

My eyes flit from Culpepper to the Queen, but the moment has passed and he is backing away, taking another bow before he departs. As soon as we are alone, the Queen bends her head to the offering and tears open the box, her giggle trickling about the chamber. It is yet another pretty trinket from the King, yet another token of his undying affection, although some would see it more as payment.

The next day, due to my condition I am spared the jolting of the hunt, but the King and Queen and most of the court set out early, for the day promises to be fine. Glad to be free of ceremony for a few hours, I wander about the gardens among the flowers, looking for a likely spot to take my ease.

I settle in an arbour and lean my head against sun-warmed stone. It is as quiet and peaceful as the grave, with only birdsong to break the silence. I close my eyes and lose myself, just for a short while, freeing myself from care.

After a time my ears, accustomed to the joyousness of the birds and the droning of lazy, fat bees, become aware of a less soothing sound. Voices intrude into my quiet world, male voices, and the tone is so subdued that I am alerted to their intrigue and prick up ears.

I cannot see them, as they cannot see me, and I find myself holding my breath, my heart beginning to dance unsteadily within my breast as I realise I am hearing secrets that I would rather not be party to.

"Of course, if the King really knew her he'd not be spouting of love the way he is. He had no cause to marry her. She drops quite willingly to her knees at the slightest bidding …as I, for one, can vouch."

I hear muffled laughter but when he makes his reply, the other fellow keeps his voice low and I cannot make out his words. But his companion's response is loud and clear, and even to my mind indescribably foolish. "She is a trollop of the first degree, I tell you, and our monarch is made to look a fool by the association. Why, between you and me, when she was little more than a child in her grandmother's household, I was the first man to bounce upon her belly but I wasn't the only one to tickle her velvet, I can tell you."

I have heard that Katherine's grandmother, the dowager Duchess of Norfolk, keeps a lax household and it is no great surprise that the Queen has turned out as she has. The men are moving away, their voices dwindling. Determined to know their identity, I stand up and peer above the rose bushes at their retreating backs. I raise my brows; surprised to discover that one man is Master Dereham, lately engaged as the Queen's private secretary. The man who accompanies him I do not know, although I have seen him many times about court. Infuriatingly, I have no idea which man has just unwittingly made such a dangerous confession.

I should, of course, be shocked at such a frank discussion of the Queen. Loose talk is dangerous and I should be hot in her defence, indignant at such disregard for the truth. To my dismay, I discover that I believe every word.

From the moment I met Katherine I noted her lax morals, her silly, vain, greedy, single-minded regard for the opposite sex. For the first time I am ashamed that I ever compared her to Eve, who I am quite sure would never give herself lightly to any man.

I linger for a while until I am quite satisfied that they are gone. The garden is no longer as restful as it was, and lifting my skirts, I hurry back across the daisy-strewn lawn toward the palace, passing through the kitchens in search of something to eat.

I am constantly hungry these days but once my stomach is filled, I find I cannot contain it and hurry to my chamber to vomit all into a pot. If this carries on I shall grow weak, and if I am to produce a healthy child, I must be strong. My breasts are larger now, my nipples hot and tingling. I slide a hand across them, feeling a dart of pleasure before I stroke my still-flat belly, cupping an imaginary bump, cradling the child within although he cannot be any larger than my thumb.

The sun is beginning to slide toward the west, and when I move to the window I see in the distance a puff of dust on the road that denotes the returning court. My peaceful afternoon, which lasted only as long as I was alone in the garden, is over and I must prepare to greet the Queen again.

With the knowledge of her past writ large in my mind, I hope that should Master Culpepper be in the company, they make no action or speak a word to confirm my suspicion that they are indeed lovers. I,

127

for one, have no wish to be party to the Queen's most dangerous secrets.

The weeks pass slowly and although I try to keep my eyes closed to the goings on of the Queen, I cannot help but be aware of the night-time whispers, the furtive locking and unlocking of chamber doors. Jane Rochford has a look of wary devilment in her eye and I tell myself that perhaps it is she who has taken a lover with the Queen's endorsement, and not the other way round. Katherine is young enough to enjoy romantic intrigue and would surely not be so foolish as to risk the same fate as her cousin. It *must* be she who shields Lady Rochford, not the other way around.

One morning, as I am passing along the corridor toward the chapel, someone comes whirling down the stairs. There is no time for me to retreat and we collide. She is moving so fast that I am almost knocked flat. As I grab at her gown to steady myself, I am engulfed in fragrance, and when I gather my wits I realise that I am grasping the richly jewelled sleeve of the Queen herself. Her cheeks are flushed with laughter but she straightens her face and snatches her arm indignantly away when she recognises me.

"Mistress Greywater," she says, as haughty as ever. I wonder at her formality for she usually addresses me as Bella, or sometimes Belle, which I can't abide. She swallows, licks her lips, her eyes darting up the twisting stair as if she expects someone to be following. "I was looking for you. I have mislaid the emerald ring the King gave me. I would have you go to my apartments and search until it is found."

She speaks loudly, her clear voice filling the corridor. I know she lies for the benefit of some companion hidden up the stairway, but I sink into a curtsey and turn on my heel to do her bidding. It is not my place to question the directives of the Queen.

In her apartment the maids are turning her mattress, the chamber windows stand open wide and soiled linen is heaped in one corner, fresh ones in a neat pile on a nearby stool. The maids' chatter ceases when I enter and they turn to bob a curtsey but I wave my hand, indicating that they can relax.

It is as I am casting my eye about the room, stooping to peer under stools, lifting and shaking cushions, that Jane Rochford enters the chamber. She stops dead in her tracks when she sees me. "What are you doing here? You should be taking the air with the others."

Her face is icy cold, making me feel I have violated her domain. I bob a curtsey. "The Queen bid me search for her emerald ring."

With an impatient huff Jane crosses the room to the Queen's jewel casket, fumbles for her key, unlocks it and opens the lid. She waves the great square ring beneath my nose. "Is this what you seek, you foolish girl? Do you expect me to believe the Queen wishes you to fetch this, a priceless jewel?"

"N-not fetch it, just discover its whereabouts. I will inform her majesty that it is safe."

Jane locks it into the casket again and I make my escape, hurry back to where I last saw the Queen, my feet soundless on the stone floor. As I reach the far end of the corridor, close by the chapel, a man approaches and I stand by to let him pass, keeping my eyes lowered.

It is Stephen Gardiner, the Bishop of Winchester, closely followed by his servant. He makes to pass right by but, to my surprise, he stops suddenly and speaks my name. "Mistress Bourne?"

I bob a curtsey, keeping my chin lowered, not daring to meet his eye. "I am Mistress Greywater now." I am greatly daring to correct so great a personage as Stephen Gardiner but I keep my sight on the hem of his gown as is fitting.

"Of course, of course. I was forgetting. Tell me, how is your sister? Evelyn, is her name?"

Totally astonished that he has knowledge of either one of us I raise my eyes to his, my mouth suddenly void of moisture. "I – we, I do not know, Your Grace. She is missing."

"And that fellow she married, a merry rogue. Francis Wareham. Do you know his whereabouts?"

"I do not, Sir." For all his friendly manner his eyes are penetrating and the answer he makes is vague.

"No matter," he says, preparing to move away. "Pray, when you see them, give them my regards."

I curtsey again and as I rise, I notice the bulbous eyes of his servant on me, his eyebrow raised quizzically as he seems to burrow into my soul. For a moment I wonder where I have seen him before, and in no small puzzlement I watch him and his master walk along the corridor. The Bishop's gait is curiously soft and stealthy for so great a man. He looks to be a great keeper, and seeker, of secrets. *What on earth can he want with Eve or Francis*? I wonder as I hurry off in search of the Queen.

It is not until much later, when I am preparing for bed, that I realise that Stephen Gardiner's man is the very same I saw whispering in the gardens with the Queen's secretary at Collyweston.

By the time we return to Hampton Court, the summer is sliding into decay and my morning megrim is beginning to subside. The leaves along the wayside are yellowing now and the grass in the meadows is tall and lank. We ride past men and women labouring to get the harvest in before the seasons turn. They turn to watch us as the lively wind snatches at our cloaks and sends the curtains on the ladies' litter bellying in the breeze. At each hamlet the peasants appear at the roadside, and for all their hardship, they call out with good wishes to the King and his pretty bride.

His rose without a thorn.

Joan Toogood

She is slow to wake up. When I try to rouse her, her head lolls and her moth opens, but she does not speak. She sprawls on my mattress, her hair streaming across the pillow, her face bone white, her eyes staring at nothing.

Sybil leans over, puts her nose an inch from the girl's mouth. "She's breathing, Joanie."

"I know that." I push her away so I can get a better look. Against the coarseness of the sheets she is like an angel or a nun fallen among whores. *What in God's Heaven am I going to do with her?* I wonder. I can't just let her wander off alone for it is clear she will fall straight into danger.

Francis' stricken body floats before my eyes and I sink sharp teeth into my lower lip to leaven the pain in my heart as I ponder what to do with his wife. I know a wherryman who, for a favour or two, would take her upriver and put her back among her own kind, but I fear that as soon as she regains her wits she will start blabbing and have the justices down upon me. And there ain't a hope that anyone will believe my word against the word of a woman like her. No. It will be better if I keep her comfortable until such time as she can tell me why she did it. Once I know her reasons I can decide what's best to do.

Betsy curls her hair, pinches her cheeks and takes herself off to work, but I lack both the heart and the courage to go. Sybil curls up in the corner with a blanket and I sleep, half on and half off the bed with M'lady curled like a cat beside me. She snores like a sailor and does not wake for all my prodding, so I lie

132

wide-awake and watch the pitch-dark ceiling lighten with the rising of the sun.

It is around dawn when I become aware of her sliding off the bed and fumbling at the walls. I rub the sleep from my eyes and go to her, take her by her narrow shoulders and guide her back to the bed. She is unresisting, her mouth open, her lips moist, and as I tuck the covers beneath her chin again, I see there are tears glistening on her cheeks.

"There, there, my dear," I murmur as I wipe a calloused finger across her smooth skin. "Go back t' sleep now. Things will look better in the mornin'."

But in the harsh light of day, nothing looks better. Everything is as bad as it was before. Betsy has returned with a torn frock and a pocket full of coins, and I do my best to persuade Sybil to run down to the cook-shop. She can't spend the rest of her days cooped up in here, hiding from the world. She has to learn that we must each play a part.

I prod her cruelly over the threshold and watch her progress tardily down the stairs and across the yard. Then I turn back inside where M'lady still snores, drool trickling from her open mouth onto the mattress.

It is the smell of hot pie that rouses her. She stirs on the bed and I go to her, smile my best smile as if she is a visitor as I haul her into a sitting position. To my surprise she smiles crookedly back at me, but the faraway look is still in her eye.

She is sort of vague and daft and puts me in mind of a girl I once knew that was hit by a runaway horse. I am sure she was not like that before. When I hold out half a meat pie she all but snatches it and begins to stuff it into her mouth, although it's hot enough to raise blisters. I offer her a cup of ale to take the heat away.

Betsy yawns and stretches, tired from her night, and I know she will want the bed for an hour or two. Sybil will have to give up her stool for a bit and shift herself to tidy this place up. It's not fit for scullions let alone our present company.

Francis' wife watches my every move, her blank eyes rarely blinking. I am reluctant to leave her in the care of my sisters but I have things to do, places to go. I need to wander the streets and discover if Francis has been missed or even discovered on his lonely, night time journey down river.

"Come, Betsy needs her beauty sleep," I say and, taking her by the hand, I begin to tug her off the bed to settle her on the stool close by. As she shifts I notice she has wet herself, her petticoats are soaked, the mattress too.

"Oh, charmin'." Betsy stands, hands on hips, and surveys the ruined bed. "Dead man's gore on one side o' the mattress and piss on the other."

I shove her with a rough hand. "It ain't the first time you've slept in a pissed bed," I say. Then, after untying M'lady's petticoats and hanging them over the balcony to dry in the sun, I take a piece of wet cloth and begin to wash her nether regions. She jumps at the sensation of the cold water.

She is made from a different mould to me. Her legs are long and slim and her quaint is small and neat, while my body is fleshy and full and makes hers look like that of a child. When I am done, I retie her skirt and lace up her bodice. She can do without a kirtle for the morning. Then I sit her down, cup her cheek and give her a cheery smile in farewell.

The more time I spend with her, the more confused I am as to how she came to do the terrible thing she did. Her attack on Francis was fierce and fatal yet the child before me is fragile, in both mind and body, and I can only surmise that it must have

134

been jealousy of me that drove her to such frenzied passion. I feel a twinge of guilt at that, knowing I am as much to blame as she.

Since I trust neither sister to watch her as well as I do, I resort to tying her to the bedstead with one of Betsy's ribbons. "You wait there, Sweet'eart, 'til Joanie gets back," I say and she gapes at me. All the time I am gathering my shawl and slippin' a couple of coins into my pocket, I feel her eyes upon me.

The sun is brave this morning. I wave to Bertha as I pass her door, hoping she will not stop me to ask about my curious visitor. Her husband is, as ever, snoozing on the doorstep, his chin on his chest, oblivious to the sober world buzzing around him. Bertha ceases her sweeping to draw her hand across her forehead and sends me a cheery wave in reply. I hurry by, thankful that she hasn't the time to stop.

The market place is heaving. Blind Tim is in his usual place, making his scrawny dog dance on its back legs for a few pennies. I watch for a few minutes. It's a mystery to me how he can tell if the mutt is dancing or has run off with the butcher's bitch. As I move on, I call out 'good day' to him and he gapes in the direction of my voice and raises a hand.

Nearby, a fellow calls his wares and, suddenly ravenous, I buy another pie and sink my teeth into mutton and gravy as I continue on my way. No sooner have I wiped m' lips clean than I bump into Thomas Bluer, who has need of me. For the exchange of a few pennies he takes his pleasure in an alleyway.

I look over his shoulder to where Winchester Palace glistens in the sunshine, like a star that has had the misfortune to fall into a pile of turds. When Thomas is done and paid his due, I move on, cheered to have a couple more coins clinking in my purse. Happily, it is a busy morning and I add to them further when I come upon a printer's boy in want of company.

135

This one wants me on me knees and I grovel before him in the shadow of the palace wall and loosen his piece. I come away from him, wiping my chin and mentally counting my wealth.

With the money Francis left on the dresser and the little Betsy and I have earned since, perhaps the winter will not be so hard after all. I decide I can go home early and venture out again at nightfall when the more affluent fellows begin to trickle over the bridge.

On my way home I stop off and buy half a cooked goose and some fresh baked bread, confident that I can make more coin later. Feeling more positive than I have since the moment my eyes fell upon poor, dead Francis, I walk toward home. But as I turn into the alley alongside The Cock's Inn, I hear a screaming and hollering the like you've never heard. I wrench up my skirts and sprint up the stairs, flinging the goose on the table and slamming the door behind me. "What in God's holy acre is goin' on?"

Betsy is leaning over the bed, hollering at M'lady, who in turn is wailing fit to burst, her mouth squared, her eyes spoutin' like a gargoyle in a rainstorm. As I slam the door, she turns her head, her face a drama of fear. To my great surprise she opens her arms to me.

I plump onto the mattress and she falls sobbing against my chest, her pretty cheeks sinking against my motherliness as my arms slide instinctively about her. "There, there, my dear," I croon. "Joanie's back now, there, there … cease yer blubberin'."

That evening, instead of venturing out to turn tricks with Betsy, I sit at M'lady's bedside and feed her strips of goose from my fingers. She has taken a shine to me and every time I leave her side, her eyes follow me about the room as if I hold the answers to all her unasked questions.

Her hair is snarled and tangled, damp with tears, and there are still splashes of dear Francis' blood on her bodice. I take up Betsy's comb and begin to loosen her hair. It is thick and long, the colour of honey, and it feels like satin compared with my own coarse curls. The comb has few teeth but I go slowly, taking a tress at a time and working my way from bottom to top so it pulls less.

She sits cross-legged on the mattress where Francis died and sways gently, crooning a tune I have never heard before. I wind a strand of hair about my finger, making the perfect curl before laying it gently across her shoulder.

"You've gone soft, you 'ave." Across the room, by the hearth, Sybil is watching us, her own hair in haloed disarray, a sneer of disapproval on her lips. "She ain't a doll, Joanie. She ain't yours t' keep. You will 'ave to send her back."

"Back to what? The gallows?"

Sybil stands up, slams the bowl of peas she has been shelling onto the table. " 'ave you ever heard her speak? She ain't said a word so far, Joanie. I don't think she can talk. I reckon that bang on the 'ead done somethin' to 'er. So she won't be confessin' nothin'."

"She could lead them back here to us or, if they do suspect her and you are right and she can't talk, how will she defend herself? Would you just let her hang? Does she look like a villain to you? Does she?"

"'Tis not our problem."

I look at Sybil for a long time, remembering how I have kept her from harm, worked twice as hard just to keep her from having to go back to whoring until she is ready. I know the dangers out there. I understand her fears and am happy to tide her over for a bit. The shame of it is, she is as ungenerous as a tithe-taker and don't see that charity should work both ways.

Although it is August, I am suddenly chilled. I rise slowly from the bed and regard her sadly for a few moments before I move toward the hearth, hold my hand out to the meagre flame.

"I think, Sybil, that my problems should be yours an' all. I can't find it in my heart to send Francis' wife back to face God knows what. He was the closest thing any of us have had to a husband and I will respect him as such 'til the day I die."

She fidgets on her stool, not meeting me eye, but I fix her with mine and make my words as strong as I can. "Francis would expect me to have a care for her and have a care I will. You, Sybil, owe it to me to do likewise … unless you'd care to make your own way in the world, of course."

I turn me back again as she begins to snivel. Her grizzling has always got my back up but now, with things the way they are, I am forced to trust her. Yet of all the women I know, Sybil is the one I trust the least. She's no Judas but she ain't too sharp neither and her loose lips have led us all into trouble more'n once.

But it is growing late and I've had enough of the day. Betsy will be out for hours yet and the fire is slumping in the grate but instead of feeding it, I leave it to die out and crawl into bed. Sybil makes do with the pile of bedding in the corner, grumbling like an empty belly as she tries to get comfortable.

I have no choice but to settle down with M'lady for a second endless night. I undo my bodice, step out of my skirt and slide in beneath the blanket beside her. She snuggles against me for warmth and falls asleep right off, while I lay wide-eyed, listening to her breathing, soft and regular. My right arm is across her shoulder, my fingers playing with a silken curl as I wrack my brains to remember her name.

138

Isabella Greywater - November 1541

"Come and dance, Belle." Katherine holds out her hand, a half pout on her face, her cheeks still flushed from the last dance. I cannot refuse a request from the Queen so I put down my sewing and take her hand.

Katherine and all her ladies are bored, there have been no visitors all day and outside the weather is relentless. Grey November clouds hang over the palace and, every so often, they let loose a deluge of rain to rattle against the windows.

The King is unwell. No one has seen him for several days and since the men of his household attend him, we are starved of male company. Forced to entertain ourselves, we sew and gossip and now, it seems, we must dance together also.

The older women gather close to the hearth, keeping a watchful eye on the younger girls clustered around the Queen at the window seat. Elizabeth Fitzgerald picks up her lute again and Mary Norris joins her in a song while Anne partners Dorothy. My heart is heavy as I attempt to turn and hop as gracefully as my royal partner and I can barely keep time with the music.

Eve should be here, not me. She is the one who loves to dance; her step is light, her carriage graceful. Dancing always makes me feel like a bear, lumbering and clumsy, and now that nausea is making my head swim, I am more ungainly than ever.

Katherine, on the other hand, is as light and graceful as a nymph, her fair hair bouncing on her shoulders, her face pink with exertion. Her perspiring palm warms mine although the tips of my fingers remain chilled. I try to smile, force myself to pay attention to the steps, but her breathless giggles grate on my nerves. It is not long before I take a wrong turn and stumble to a stop. "I am so sorry, Your Majesty, I cannot keep up with your light step."

Katherine's laugh is like a burst of sunshine on a dull day, blinding in its intensity. "Don't worry, Belle, perhaps Bessie will have the next turn." I gratefully bob a curtsey and scurry back to my seat, but as I take up my needlework again we hear the sound of heavy boots outside. The door is thrown unceremoniously open.

The music slithers into discord.

As silence drops like a stone upon us, the King's guards march in and surround the Queen, their pikes levelled at her chin. Katherine freezes while Dorothy and Mary run squealing to Lady Edgecombe's side. The Queen glances rapidly about the room, her eyes wide, her lips as white as her face. A tear trickles down her cheek. "What is it? What is the matter?"

Her eyes dart from face to face, seeking a friend, and her voice trembles like that of a reprimanded child. Behind her, Lady Rochford lets out a moan and drops suddenly to her knees, groping for her crucifix, her lips moving in silent prayer.

She has been in a like situation before.

The sergeant steps forward, not meeting the Queen's eye. "You are under arrest by order of the King and are to remain here within your apartments."

Katherine makes a sound that is half-laugh, half-sob and, for the first time, I realise that she is not so much a wanton as a little girl. A silly, heedless child playing a deadly game, and she doesn't understand the rules. "There is some mistake," she says, fear stark in her voice, "I will speak with my husband, the King."

As she makes a move toward the door their ugly weapons are immediately raised against her again. She shrinks back in alarm, her mouth downturned, shoulders hunched in supplication. Beneath my bodice my heart begins to bang, loud and sickeningly slow, as I taste the doom that is to come. Katherine Howard in her tarnished jewels stands alone in a sea of faces, a babe among wolves.

"You are to remain within this chamber." The sergeant's voice is loud, harsh. It is no way to speak to his queen. Her chin wobbles as she looks this way and that about her chamber, seeking someone to tell her what she should do. But her ladies turn their eyes away. Only Jane Rochford remains with her in the circle of firelight. Still on her knees, she prays too loudly, her voice discordant, her face wet with tears, fingers fumbling at her beads.

When nobody else moves or speaks I force myself forward and, with shaking knees, move quietly to Katherine's side. I take her frozen fingers in mine and raise my chin. Together, we look upon the guards. "Very well," I hear myself say, "we will stay within the chambers until the morning when, God willing, the King will be recovered enough to receive Her Majesty."

The guards' tramping feet diminish, giving way to the sound of weeping. Katherine stands silent, staring at the closed door, her fingernails digging into the back of my hand. I can feel the fear travelling through her into me, and I know she is remembering her cousin, Anne Boleyn, the ruined Queen of whom we are forbidden to speak.

But I remember another Queen. Queen Anna, who chose compliance to escape the King's displeasure, and I realise that Katherine must give Henry whatever it is he wants.

141

"Your Majesty," I say, wishing I had Eve's winning way with people. "Come away to the fire, you are shivering." I tug gently at her hand and to my relief she follows meekly and allows me to ease her into a chair. I signal to a maid to bring wine.

"Your Majesty ... Katherine," I speak in urgent whispers as I thrust a cup into her hand. "Do not despair. There are ways to overcome the King's discontent. Remember the last Queen, the Lady Anna?" I glance about the chamber, making sure there are none close enough to hear my silent pledge of allegiance. "Anna of Cleves escaped by agreeing to everything the King requested. That is what you must do."

She suddenly becomes aware that she is holding the cup and lifts it to her lips, slurping the wine like a woman dying of thirst.

"Norfolk," she croaks, ignoring my counsel and drawing the back of her hand across her wet lips. "I must see my uncle of Norfolk. He will instruct me."

She is right. Her powerful connections *should* provide protection such as the Lady Anna never had. Of course, Norfolk was the Boleyn's uncle too, but I do not remind her of it; it is best she doesn't think on that now.

I squeeze her hand and, clutching at the arm of her chair, rise from my knees. After bobbing a curtsey that she is too distraught to notice, I whirl around and call a page to summon the Duke of Norfolk.

As I had feared he does not come, and with each passing hour the tension in the chamber becomes more stifling. Katherine paces to and fro before the window, watching the water gate, longing for someone to come to her aid. She wears a trail across the floor, from the hearth to the window seat and back again, and all I can do is watch helplessly.

142

She can be no more than seventeen now. I cannot imagine what 'bad things' a child can have done to get herself into such a scrape as this. I forget that I am addressing my Queen and grasp her by the elbow, give it a gentle shake.

"What things? Tell me."

"I was just a little girl but they were all doing it. Well, most of them were anyway. I thought it was just what girls did. It was sort of expected of me. I didn't know it was wrong. Not then."

"What was, Your Majesty? What things?"

She sniffs and wipes her nose on the back of her hand, looks at the royal snot gleaming in the half-light. "It was Henry Manox to begin with. He taught me music. He said my voice was like a bird's and that my dance steps were as light as a fairy's." Briefly, her eyes gleam at the remembered compliments and then she blinks as she searches for the lost chain of her narrative. "One day he kissed me. I was very young, eleven maybe, or twelve, and flattered that such a grown-up person should want to woo me. After that I sat upon his knee often and gave him lots more kisses and sometimes ... other things."

"Other things?" Cold grips my stomach as I anticipate her answer. My own innocent girlhood flashes through my mind, games of catch-as-catch-can in the garden with Eve and our little brother, Tom.

"He said that he loved me and that if I'd let him feel the secrets of my person then he should know I loved him too."

"Y-you didn't though, did you?"

After a moment, she bites her lips with pretty white teeth and nods. "I did. It was nice. Nice that someone noticed me and thought me pretty, liked me enough to bring me presents and want to kiss me."

"And did none of the women notice what was happening? Did nobody stop him?"

147

"Oh, yes. A girl called Mary told my grandmother and she was right cross with me and gave me a spanking and forbade me to be alone with him ever again."

"Is that all? She should have had him horsewhipped!"

Katherine grips my hands tight. "No Belle, I wouldn't have wanted that. Manox was nice to me and I liked him, although it didn't last. It wasn't true love, not after Dereham joined the household."

Bells begin to ring inside my head, warning of danger, and I feel a little giddy. I should listen to no more of this; it isn't safe to do so but my lips form the questions nonetheless. "Not your private secretary, Dereham? For God's sake, Katherine, tell me that isn't so."

"That's why I took him on when he sought me out at court, so he wouldn't tell anyone about us. My uncle would be so cross if he knew."

Not so cross as your husband, should he discover an ex-lover installed in your privy chamber. I don't want to know the answer but I can't seem to stop myself from asking.

"So, Master Dereham. He just kissed you and gave you presents, did he?"

She flushes to the roots of her hair, lowers her chin, as pretty and as delicate as a bird. Then she shakes her head. "He used to come creeping into the dormitory to share my bed at night time. We lay together often, but it wasn't wrong for we were trothplight. He called me 'wife' and I called him 'husband'. We were going to marry as soon as he had made his fortune."

Oh God have mercy, it was worse and worse. If they were trothplight it meant she was not a true wife to the King. No wonder Henry was furious.

"Did he take your maidenhead?"

148

"He did. I lay with him in my bed for more nights than I can remember. He took me in many ways and taught me little tricks; tricks that have served the King well. Then he told me he had to go overseas, but he said he would be back. But he was gone so long and by the time he returned, my uncle had married me to the King."

"But you confessed all this before you wed him, did you not?"

She shakes her head, her eyes fearful. "Should I have, Belle?"

Lord God on high. I cannot believe my ears. My head is teeming with images I would far rather not see. Katherine the child, pawed by her music master and used shamelessly by an adventuring braggart, a man whom everyone at court whispered was little more than a pirate. It would be bad enough were she just a gently born girl, but she is a *Howard* and married to the *King.* Things could not be very much worse. I can barely bring myself to utter my next words.

"You've not lain with Dereham since you married the King, have you?"

She shakes her head violently and my anxiety lifts a little. If all took place before Henry married her she might yet escape. Fornication is a sin but it is not a crime. If Henry can bear the humiliation she may yet survive. He can put her aside and marry again. But, try as I might, I cannot imagine he will lightly bear the cuckold's crown.

Eve always said that for all his lusty nature, the King is the biggest prude in the world. He has a great abhorrence for immorality and, more than once, has tried to shut down the brothels over the river. And give him his due, for all the illegitimate children he's bred, he is not indiscriminate like some men. When Henry fancies a woman, long before he takes her he seeks to preserve her reputation and ensures she is safely wed to one of his favourites. Of course, we all know it to be a screen for his nefarious doings but there are plenty of men who care not at all for the fate of a woman once they are done with her.

It is hard for a girl to refuse a King, as Katherine's own story proves, but this King treats his concubines fairly, showering them with property and wealth and looking after their offspring. This should make me feel better but of course, so far, Henry's courtesy does not extend to his queens. Katherine might have been far wiser to have just bedded rather than wedded him.

"Do you think Henry might have discovered my secret, Belle?"

Her face is a ghost in the darkness, her hair a streak of gold against the shadows of the bed hanging. I have to be truthful, there is no point in lying.

"I fear he may have, Your Majesty," I whisper, and her head droops as she begins to weep again. "Hush," I croon as I rock her back and forth, "hush. If you confess all, Henry will be angry but it is not a crime, Katherine. He can set you aside, you can then wed another and so can he. It will be better so."

"Do you truly believe that?" she asks with a little hope shining from her eyes.

"I do. As long as you tell the truth, all should be well." Purple thumbprints mar her eyes that now seem larger than ever in her wan little face. She smiles uncertainly and pushes her straggled hair from her face.

"Belle, should I tell them about Culpepper as well, or is it better if I don't?"

I turn to look at her, all hope withering in my chest.

We have just broken our fast when the waiting ends. Cranmer, the King's most trusted statesman, sends the women curtly away but Katherine grabs my wrist and asks that I may stay. He reluctantly allows me to wait, as unobtrusively as possible, by the wall, out of earshot.

A frigid draught blows from beneath the rich tapestry, freezing my feet, but I do not move. I try to pretend I am not really there and think of the garden at Bourne Manor, with the roses nodding in a summer breeze and Eve's laughter mingling with the scent of honeysuckle. I long so much to be back in my girlhood where I was safe and happy, but I cannot dream for long. Soon reality pulls me back to the Queen's chamber where she sits before the hearth, knee to knee with Cranmer.

As if he is teasing a whelk from its shell, he leans forward and begins to gently prise the sorry tale from her. She is tragic and I know it is no act. Sometimes she weeps with her head in her hands, rocking back and forth while Cranmer waits, his eye on the leaden skies outside the window, his fingers slowly drumming on the table top.

Once, she leaps to her feet, pacing back and forth, beating her chest, waving her arms in the air. Her voice is raised and although I try to block my ears, I cannot help but hear the agony of her shame as the confession is torn from her throat. Cranmer closes his eyes, shakes his head sadly and asks her to sit down again. She lowers herself stiffly into a chair and begins to tremble violently when he offers her the pen.

Poor Katherine can barely form her letters and I wonder what the King will make of such a confession. What will the punishment be? As I watch her slowly scratch her name at the bottom of the parchment, for the first time my child leaps inside me and I place my hand upon my womb, wondering what his future holds. What my own future holds. There are many better than I who have been brought low by their association with a doomed Queen.

I start in surprise when the legs of Cranmer's stool scrape across the floor. He places a hand on her shoulder, more fatherly than statesmanlike, and clears his throat. "The King desires that you and three of your ladies retire to Syon until the trial, Madam."

After that, Katherine does not speak for many hours.

We are no longer to address her as 'Queen' or 'Majesty.' Instead, we must remember to call her 'Lady Katherine.' She watches like a punished infant as stern-faced guards enter her apartments and bear away casket after casket of her jewels, precious gifts from a besotted King. Her gowns are heaped in resplendent piles ready to be carried away in their arms. She is allowed to keep only six of her plainest dresses and six of her most unbecoming hoods. It is a far cry from the luxury she has lately enjoyed but she doesn't seem to care. She remains unnervingly silent.

There is not long to wait now, for we are to leave for Syon shortly after noon. I am folding her plainest petticoats and placing them in a pile when the bells ring out loud for morning mass. Katherine is suddenly on her feet.

I jerk up my head at the abrupt movement but before I can stop her, she runs swiftly across the chamber and wrenches the door wide. Taking the guards outside by surprise, she darts like a small silver fish between them and is half way along the corridor before they have even begun pursuit.

"Henry!" she shrieks, lifting her skirts and running. I dash after her, glimpse her cascading hair as she turns a corner. She is heading for the chapel where she knows the King will be at prayer. "Henreeeeee!"

Her voice cracks. The guards are closing in on her, their broad backs shutting her momentarily from my view. When I next see her, she is at the chapel door, hammering on the thick oaken panel with her little-girl fists, her body writhing in the pain of defeat. "Henry!"

As I draw near, the bones of my bodice digging deep into my ribs, I see them lay hands upon her. She struggles, writhing and kicking hopelessly in the face of their strength. "Henreee, please hear me, my lord! Henreeeeeeee!"

Her voice grows shriller and more frantic as they haul her backwards, her feet dragging across the stone floor. She twists and turns in their grip as, with bland faces, they lug her back toward me. There is no sound from the chapel but the King must surely hear her. Such cries will echo down these corridors for centuries.

I hurry along behind as they march her relentlessly back to her chamber, throw her to the floor before the hearth. She falls to her knees, weeping helplessly, her pretty face contorted into red, misshapen ugliness, her fragile arms encircling her own shoulders.

Never in my life have I seen anyone so alone. All the grief I have felt at the loss of Eve merges with the pity I now feel for Katherine. When I fall to my knees beside her it is as if I am gathering them both into my arms.

Joan Toogood

It will be a meagre Christmas this year and that's for sure. It's hard for me to work now, what with Sybil afraid of her own shadow and M'lady tied to the foot of my bed. I turn a few tricks about town but earn barely enough to fill our bellies. And to top it all, my little sister Betsy is set on wedding a farmer's boy from way up river, some far flung place I've never been to. Good luck to her, I say, but since Betsy is our best earner, it means we are deeper in the mire than anyone'd wish to be. It don't seem to worry her none, she flounces about as gaily as you please, as if I haven't had the care of her since she learned to walk.

Since early November the rain has fallen without easement, the wind blowing it in beneath the shingle, the damp chill filling the air and settling in my bones. Now that December is here, the cold increases, casting a layer of hoar frost upon the heads of the Queen's lovers that the King has pinned to the bridge by way of warning. We've heard no word of the faithless little Queen herself, but I imagine her fate will not be one to envy. I'd sooner be me, hungry as I am.

But I've no time to worry for her overmuch for I've mouths to feed and a gently born lady to keep warm. I've pinned my Ma's thick shawl across her narrow shoulders, it's a plain home spun thing against the tattered silk of her gown but it warms her a little. I still don't know what to do with her and she shows no sign of improving or remembering who she is or ought that happened.

Sometimes now, she shouts. Loud sometimes, crude words that I'd never have thought to hear from the likes of her. Other times she hollers words that we can't understand and when these times are upon her she fidgets and strains at her bonds and nothing will soothe her but a cuddle from me. But most of the time she is quiet, as if placidly waiting for something to change.

But nothing does.

Every day I wash her face and hands, make sure her petticoats are clean before I set out to make a penny or two along the Bankside. I do not tarry if I can help it for my absence makes her fractious.

The smell of roasting meat from the cook-houses sets my mouth alive; I can all but feel how the juice would run down my chin if I could only bite into it. At home, all that awaits me is a week-old pot of pease-pudding, but at least I've earned enough this morning to buy some bread to sop it up with.

When my customer has had enough I drop my skirts, and he lets a couple of pennies fall into my hand. "I'm grateful, Ned," I say and leave him to go his own ways. I see a baker's boy with a tray of wares and relieve him of a couple of loaves, reluctantly hand over the pennies before scurrying off homeward.

The steps to my chamber are slick with ice so I climb them with care before throwing open the door and unravelling my shawl. "I'm back," I call, although in the one room we share they won't have missed the blast of colder air that heralds my arrival.

M'lady is straining at her leash, wanting to give me welcome, so I dump the loaves on the table and go and take her hand. The strange, animal sounds she makes when she's happy scare Sybil silly, but I just smooth back her hair and stroke her cheek and she calms down, retreating into silence.

155

Before I fill my belly I clean myself, using the bowl of rainwater that has filtered through the shingles. It is cold enough to shrivel my nethers and a curious shade of yellow, but it cleans me well enough. Meanwhile Sybil doles out pease-pudding into three bowls and rips the bread into chunks, saving one loaf for supper. Then, tucking a cloth beneath her chin, I begin to spoon the food into M'lady's mouth. When it has near all gone, I soak the bread in the remaining gravy and put it into her hand.

"Stoke up the fire a bit, Sybil," I say, putting my feet up and folding my hands across my belly. Outside the wind still howls and night is falling early, making me wish for thick curtains to draw against the cold. Such is the delight of December, short days and long nights. I think of the frigid days still to come, the relentless cruelty of January and February. I long for the springtime, when the very air makes it good to be alive.

"Tell us a story, Joanie," says Sybil, settling herself close to the hearth and poking at the glowing embers. M'lady, hearing her words, sits up on the bed, crosses her legs and appears to listen too. As I launch into a tale of brave King Arthur and his lusty knights, her eyes do not leave my face but seem to drink the story up. It is just as I am reaching the part where the boy hauls the great sword of England from its stone that we hear heavy footsteps on the stair and the door is thrown wide. We all turn in surprise.

"Peter! By all that's holy. Where have you been, boy?"

He blushes, pleased that I've missed him, and holds a jug of ale aloft. "I had to go to Kennington. My uncle was ailing and I helped out for a while. I am back now and hope to stay."

The glance he casts in my direction leaves me in no doubt as to which way his mind is wandering.

156

But I can hardly throw Sybil out in the cold and M'lady is taking up the only bed. He passes the jug to me and I tip it to my lips to let the rich, cool liquid flow down my throat. Then I pass it to Sybil and after she has had her fill, she hands it back to Peter. When my turn comes round again, I see M'lady watching and I go to her and hold the jug to her lips. A trickle of ale runs down her chin and along her throat, disappearing beneath her bodice, making her laugh.

The jug is soon empty and when Peter gets up to fetch another from the Cock's Inn on the corner, I follow him outside and wait on the balcony for his return. When he reaches the top stair, he puts down the jug and I slide my arms about his neck, wanting to feel the touch of a friend. I turn my face from his kisses but welcome his fondling hands, and before we go back in we couple quickly and efficiently, my bottom slapping against the roughness of the wall. The moon looks down unabashed while Peter smiles sheepishly, as red as a cock's comb to the roots of his hair as he refastens his piece. I pull down my skirts and open the door to stumble inside.

It is not long before we are all as drunk as lords. While Sybil sings a bawdy song about a priest and a gander, Peter begins to dance an unsteady jig and I scramble up to join him. I lift my skirts to my knees and circle the room, my boots making a din on the wooden floorboards, my dugs doing a separate jig all of their own.

When Peter and I fall laughing and panting to the floor, M'lady kneels up on the bed, clapping her hands, her mouth gaping in delight.

"She wants to dance too," cries Sybil, with the spirit of Christmas upon her. I go merrily toward M'lady to untie the ribbon that holds her fast. She is still giggling when she grabs my hands and begins to dance, forcing my feet to move in steps I do not know.

After a while, I pull away and she dances alone, her movements more graceful than anything any of us have ever seen before. We watch her in silence, the coarseness of the celebration suddenly seeming out of place.

Her arms are arched like a pair of swans' necks and she tilts her head, a dainty foot appearin' and disappearin' beneath her skirts in time to music only she can hear. She is a ragged Queen in the company of whores. A winsome smile plays upon her face and there are tears upon her cheeks, as if she is remembering another dance in some other place.

Isabella Greywater – February 1542

I am at my wit's end, for as we wait here at Syon for her fate to be decided Katherine will not speak, even to me. Her entire household has been questioned; some members who were summoned for questioning have not returned. We fear they are languishing in the confines of the Tower, and I dread to think what they have been constrained to confess. We all know the methods used to satisfy the King's quest for 'truth.'

Jane Rochford was the first of our household not to return and word filters through to us that she has lost her mind and raves like a lunatic in her cell. The only comfort I can take from this is that such madness will ensure she can endanger the Queen no further. Even the King's men take no heed of the insane.

While I worry for the future and try to guess which of the remaining household members we can trust, Katherine sits silently at the hearth, agitatedly plucking threads from her skirt. Poor Katherine, she never dreamed she would ever fall so low. Her status has diminished so far that she is allowed just four gentlewomen to attend her.

She has been allotted only three paltry chambers and this room is chilly, the walls covered with shabby hangings, the floors strewn with rushes that are in need of changing. Even the cushions are worn and full of moth. There is no majesty here and few comforts although, I must confess, she doesn't appear to notice.

For hours now she has sat with her chin on her chest and she refuses both food and drink. I hope her mind takes her to happier times, the days of dancing, flirting and courtly games. Does she still believe she is Henry's little darling and that he will forgive her in the end? Or does she despair? Does the shadow of her cousin flicker upon the walls of her imagination, as she does in mine? I cannot know what she is thinking and sometimes I think her mind has closed down and that nothing can touch her now – unless it's the edge of Henry's blade.

The knowledge of what befell Anne Boleyn haunts me night and day. The King loved her, too. For seven long years he pursued her, he fell foul of the Pope and took on the power of the mighty Roman church, sent his wife and daughter into exile just to make her his. He killed his oldest, dearest friends to secure her hand but, when she failed to give him a son, the quick-silver agility of her mind soon ceased to enchant him.

They say that on the day of her execution, the King rode off to dally with his new love, the soon-to-be-Queen Jane. If the quick-witted Boleyn could fall so swiftly from grace, what chance did a giddy child like Katherine stand?

I have tried to keep her in ignorance of events that are happening in the outside world. She does not yet know that the King has denied her the right of an open court and has tried her in her absence. Even the lowest in the land are offered a fair trial, but it is not to be for Katherine. In this world, where a woman's rights are few, she is not even to be allowed the chance to defend her actions.

Such is the power of Queens.

Without recourse to her own testimony, her alleged lovers were tortured and her friends interrogated. Culpepper and Dereham were indicted for treason, as she has been. In November they found her guilty of living the vicious life of a harlot, and since that day we have been here awaiting her fate.

160

None of us are dead yet but the existence we suffer can certainly not be described as 'living.'

She is quieter than ever today and I am not sure if she realises that we are now waiting to be taken by river barge to be housed in the Tower. That place must have such sharp memories for her. Even I, who was a child at the time, will never forget the horror of her cousin, Anne Boleyn. It was unthinkable then and it is unthinkable now that a Queen should suffer execution. My mind cannot encompass it, but it is to the Tower we must go. It is there we must wait a while longer, balanced upon the edge of sanity until such time ... *I can barely voice it*. It is there we must wait at the King's pleasure, until the time of execution.

None of us is brave enough to tell the Queen – or Lady Katherine as she is now. The few of us that are left have come to love her too well to be able to face the further crumbling of her wits. And so, she remains in ignorance that Culpepper is dead, and Dereham too, and that the Tower dungeons are replete with members of her friends and family, even her feckless grandmother, the Dowager Duchess.

Norfolk has fled court and, after denouncing his niece, has taken himself off, pleading sickness until such time as the crisis has passed. *May the plague take him.*

Although I had no love for them when they were living, my prayers are for poor Culpepper and Dereham. For all their sins, they were too young to die and so is Katherine, silly laughing little Katherine whose only real crime was to be born into the wrong family. If only there were something I could do!

I can barely stand to think on it. Sometimes I fear I will run as mad as Jane Rochford. Perhaps when the time comes, they will have to drag me away from Katherine's mutilated body, a foaming, muttering wreck. There is only so much I can stand.

I gasp as a hefty kick beneath my ribs reminds me that the luxury of madness cannot be mine. I have responsibilities. As my child's heel travels across the globe of my womb, I let my hand drop to my stomach. God knows where life will take my little one, if I can bring him healthy into this world.

There has been no word from Anthony. He knows my whereabouts but has taken no action to bring me home. No doubt he is humiliated by my proximity to the Queen, and wishes not to draw attention to himself. He will not wish to displease his King and, in the present circumstances, who can blame him? So much has happened since I saw him last that I can scarcely recall my husband's face or remember his voice. Indeed, if it were not for my swollen belly I would not believe I'd ever been married at all.

My head snaps up in surprise when the door suddenly opens. Katherine, dragged back from wherever her mind was wandering, leaps to her feet. Sir John Gage fills the doorway, his gaze not quite meeting ours. He begins to bow and then remembers himself, straightens his shoulders and clears his throat. "The barge is waiting, Lady Katherine," he says. "You must come with us now."

"Where are we going?" Katherine asks, her voice sounding small and bewildered but, lacking the heart to explain, I take her elbow and, while her other women gather up the few possessions left to her, lead her traitorously from the room.

We pause at the exterior door, blinking at the brightness. It is one of those bright, crisp winter days when the sky stretches in an endless arc above our heads. It is reflected in the smooth surface of the water and as the boat glides downstream, tranquil sounds float toward us from the riverbank. Birds call, a coot scurries into the rushes and a pair of ducks emerge and accompany the barge for a while, their small brown bodies effortlessly matching our speed.

When the barge passes beneath a line of trees, the temperature drops and the curtains flap a little in a sudden breeze. I draw a blanket about Katherine's shoulders, as if it still matters whether she catches a chill or not. I scoff at my instinctive nurturing of a girl whose corpse will soon lie disgraced beneath the English soil.

Slowly, as we near the capital, other vessels begin to fill the waterway, and soon we navigate a bend in the river to see the Tower of London looming before us.

It stands sentinel on the river bank, the walls stark white against a fair, blue sky. But first we must navigate London Bridge, where the water rushes apace between the starlings. I settle myself more firmly in the seat beside the Queen and while fear writhes in my belly, I hold on tight to her elbow and prepare for the wild ride.

As we draw closer the water takes us, lifting the vessel, pulling us on whether we want to continue or not. There is no turning back now. It is all the boatman can do to guide his vessel, keeping us away from the edge and trying to prevent the rough current from tipping us all into a watery grave. Behind us the other women cling together, as we are doing, whimpering as the white water churns beneath us. Katherine, shaken from her reverie, grips my sleeve, her white face close to mine. I hear her breath jerking sharply from her lungs. I glance at her to see her mouth is slightly open, revealing pretty white teeth that a lifetime of sweetmeats has not yet had time to mar. I am still looking at her when I see her fear turn to terror and her eyes darken. Her faces stretches as she opens her mouth and begins to scream.

"Katherine," I screech above the crashing water. "It will be all right. You must stay calm. Please." But she does not listen, her mouth is quivering in terror, her breath rasping from her throat so violently I am sure she will faint. Her eye is fixed on something high above the boat and, following her line of vision, I realise too late that it is not for herself that she screams.

Her own end means nothing to her now for grimacing from the gatehouse at the Southwark end of the bridge are the severed heads of her erstwhile lovers, Dereham and Culpepper. Their wet hair is plastered to tattered scalps, their expressions frozen in the terror of death, and looking upon them is like a physical blow.

I cannot tear my eyes away, and neither can Katherine. The crows have been busy, stripping the skin from their cheeks, yet they are recognisable still. There is nothing I can say or do now but restrain her writhing panic until we are safely under the bridge.

The people of London, passing to and fro beneath such grisly spectacles every day, have grown used to such sights. It is different for Katherine, it is different for me. I have seen these men in happier days, when they were animated and alive. I have passed the time of day with them.

I remember Culpepper, the first time I saw him in Katherine's presence. I recall how he bowed over her hand, his misguided, lusty eyes sending out a deadly message … although he did not know it then. And now they have come to this; death and dishonour, and the ruin of us all. If the short duration of my acquaintance with them accentuates the horror of their passing, then how must it feel for Katherine, who once lay naked in their arms.

I try to calm her but she fights me and the boat is lurching, the women screaming, the guards shouting. All is chaos and I am sure the vessel will founder, but thankfully, the boatmen know their business and at length we are brought safe to shore. She ceases to fight me and slumps suddenly into my arms, still weeping helplessly. I look up and watch the black hole of the Water Gate loom above our heads. The shadows increase, the chill intensifies as it swallows us and sucks us into the confines of the Tower; a place from which few return.

The time seems so long in coming that I am almost glad to leave the confines of our chamber. The royal apartments offer more comfort than a cell but it remains a prison; any place from which you are forbidden to leave can be a prison and confinement is driving me mad. But the time is almost upon us. From the high-up window I can see the King's council arriving in twos and threes, stepping from the barge onto the slick, black stone steps. They are come to do their duty and witness the execution of Henry's faithless Queen.

I see Walsingham and Denny pause just above the Watergate to pass the time of day, as if they attend a pageant. Denny shakes his head, scratches his beard as the Duke of Suffolk arrives, and they all move off together. There is no sign of Norfolk and I imagine that, like Anthony, he is still keeping his head low, trying to keep it on his shoulders.

What will the future say of Katherine? I turn to watch her women tucking her hair beneath a white linen hood. *What will it say of any of us?*

"Is it time?"

It is so many hours since she has spoken that the sound of her voice makes me jump and I have to clear my throat before I can answer. "I think so, almost."

This is ridiculous. It is as if we are waiting to go down to dinner. "Katherine!" My voice is anguished as I push past her women to cling to her hand but she quickly covers it with hers, patting to offer me comfort.

"Please, Belle, be strong for me. I – I must be brave and I don't think I can be if you don't help me."

The tears gather painfully in my throat again but I nod, my voice cracking. "I'll try, Your Majesty."

"I need to pray again."

She hurries back to her prie dieu and falls onto her knees, knees that must be red raw from prayer. I can do nothing more than pray with her and while she begs for strength, I silently scream at God to intervene, to send some heavenly angel to save us.

But he doesn't hear me.

When she rises from her knees she seems a little calmer, her white face bleak with sorrow, her eyes red with weeping. I thank God the screaming has stopped. I try to offer up a brave smile but fail miserably. "Are you ready now?" I ask, as if we are setting off to chapel. She nods and attempts a smile in return; a smile that wobbles and falters.

"Be brave, Your Majesty," I mouth, for my voice betrays me and I can make no proper sound. She accepts the illicit title gratefully but doesn't refer to it.

"Oh, Belle, promise me, I beg you, that when this is all over, you will follow your heart. If only I had been brave enough to stand up to them and married where I pleased …"

There is an unbearable pain in my throat and I know it is also in hers, for when her voice breaks, her throat works to stifle the tears. It is the closest she has ever come to confessing to me that she loved Culpepper, and the painful honesty in her voice makes me think of Eve and Francis, who likewise loved … and perhaps died.

A loud rattle of keys tells us that they have come for us. I try to smile, urging her to have courage and she raises her chin, takes a deep breath and turns away to greet her gaoler.

The walk from the Royal apartment to Tower Green is very short, although it doesn't seem so. I follow in Katherine's wake, keeping my head low and fixing my eye upon her heels as they flick from beneath her skirt. Along the way we are joined by Jane Rochford who, although her face is ravaged with fear and looks twenty years older than the last time I saw it, appears to be as sane as I. In solemn procession we cross the Tower Green, the ravens rising noisily from the naked treetops to spiral in the winter sky.

A traitorous sun dazzles our eyes as Katherine places a foot on the lowest step to the scaffold. The wood creaks beneath our feet, the aroma of sawn wood and warm, wet straw rising strongly. There is little time left and I am suddenly reminded of all that has not been said between us. I am blind with tears when Katherine turns and offers me her beads and prayer book. "Be strong, Belle," she says kindly, as if I am the one about to die.

I nod wordlessly and watch her address each of her women in turn before facing the crowd with her little-girl chin held firmly in the air. She has nothing of which to be ashamed. Desperately I try to catch her words, aware that it is the last time I will hear her voice, but no matter how I strain my ears, the noises inside my head block out the sound. My panic increases as blackness encroaches. I fight for stability and faintly, as if it is coming from a great distance, I hear her speak of the King's majesty and goodness. For a moment I am furious and inwardly scream for her to tell them all the truth; he can hurt her no more than he has already. Why doesn't she tell them all of her uncle's duplicity in pushing her toward the King;

167

of Henry's unspeakable cruelties, the offences he committed upon her girlish body, the thousand indignities he heaped upon her and thought to recompense with trinkets and jewels? Why doesn't she use her last few breaths to curse them all?

But then I realise she is playing a game.

It is *all* a game, known only to Kings and princes. Whereas I, a commoner, would spout recrimination and, in protesting my innocence, defame the King, she will do no such thing. Katherine is a *Howard* and a *Queen*, and she is determined to die like one. With sudden understanding, I fall to my knees and join her in praising God and blessing our King. It is all that is left for me to do and I have never felt so proud of anyone in my life.

With a demeanour like nothing I have known her adopt before, she blesses the executioner, offering her forgiveness and a few coins. "Katherine…" I whisper her name like a prayer.

I can barely watch. As if in a nightmare she kneels and, with great care and precision, positions her head upon the block as she practiced last night in the privacy of her prison.

With her beads and prayer book clutched to my chest and tears burning my eyes, I utter my last ever prayer. *Let it be quick. God, please have mercy and let it be quick.*

The moment is here and as the long silence begins, I close my eyes, feeling the cold wind rushing in my ears, ravens calling high up in the sky. The birds and the wind are all I hear until, close by, I sense a rush of air and hear a sickening thump, followed by the communal sigh of the crowd.

I keep my eyes screwed tight. I dare not look up and I do not discover until much later that it is not spring rain that splatters on my face … but Katherine's blood.

168

Joanie Toogood

When the King struck off the head of Anne Boleyn, nobody really blamed him once we heard what she'd been up to. Of course it came as a shock, I mean, Queens just don't get executed, do they? Or they didn't then.

His first wife, another Catherine, had been loved by everyone since the day she first set her Spanish foot on English soil to marry our King's brother, Arthur. Caterina, they called her, and she was a fine woman; loved and well-received wherever she went. It was Anne Boleyn and her self-seeking ways who pushed Queen Caterina from her rightful seat and as a consequence, Anne was never liked. The King was so besotted that there were those who spoke of witchcraft and enchantments, and many spat abuse at her when she dared appear in public. Although we were all aghast at the Royal goings-on, few of us mourned her passing.

Henry's next Queen, Jane, kept herself quietly at court and we saw very little of her. She set her mind on other important things, such as birthing a boy for the King's peace of mind. Henry has always been big on the succession, as was his father before him. I even went as far as to feel glad for him when he finally got his little lusty prince, and sorrier still when he paid the price by losing himself yet another Queen.

Then, of course, we had the fiasco with the German princess, another Anne this time, or Anna, as they call her. Eeh, Henry has had so many Queens and all with similar names, it's a wonder he can keep track of 'em. This one, Anna, didn't suit our fastidious King though, and he rid himself of her quick enough.

Before I had time to turn myself around there was another one stepping into the shoes of the German.

This last one though, the baby-faced Katherine, has not been such a stranger to us. We'd all seen her, before she wed the King, when she was little more than a babe in arms. Night after night they ferried her back and forth across the Thames to dine at Winchester Palace, close by my yard. And I recall one summer's day when I saw her at a bearbaiting, as bright as sunshine she was, laughing at the antics of the bear. She was such a dainty young piece next to the bulk of our King, it didn't really seem right.

Come to think on it, she might already have been Queen then, or as much Queen as made no difference. Anyway, as I was saying, the common people knew Katherine and we are sorry and angry at her passing. As for King Henry, well, his true colours are nailed to the mast now and no mistake. I doubt any right-minded lass will ever wed him now. I warrant he will die a widower and it'll serve him right too. The gossips say that his heart is broke over Katherine but, to my mind, he had no right loving a little dolly like her in the first place.

We are sick of it all; the burnings; the hangings; the quarterings. All of it. If you had told my old mum that bluff King Harry would ever come to this, she'd have called you a liar to your face. London is no more a merry place, that's for sure, and nobility and commoners walk in fear alike, each and every one of us keepin' our heads down, none of us knowin' what changes will be forced upon us next. And as for me, well, I have problems of my own, and more than I can rightly cope with.

Food, that had become so plentiful when Francis was around, is now my main concern. The winter has been cruel and all three of us are thin and ailing. Only M'lady who, as well as her own, gets what share of my own ration I can spare, has any flesh on her bones. My paps hang like empty sacks, my belly loose an' groaning for want of a decent meal. Now, when a gentleman buys himself a whore, he craves a comfortable one, not a bag of bones, and it's getting harder every day to make a living.

More than once I have had to protect M'lady from going the way of me and my sisters. She looks like one of us now, you see, and her fine clothes didn't last a year, and so she is dressed in an old fustian gown of Betsy's. Her hair that used to curl so well is no longer so shiny looking, and her once rounded and pink face is becoming sharp. Of course, she is still a pretty piece and as different from me as a star is from a chunk of coal.

"You should make 'er work." Sybil is envious and bitter, knowing her own looks are marred forever, and her own chances of getting out of here worse than my own.

"Don't be ridiculous," I say, placing an arm about M'lady's shoulders. "That's a terrible thing to say."

"She wants to eat, don't she? So, she should work, or go back where she come from."

It's true that I could earn a pretty penny if I became her bawd and set M'lady to work, but the thought of her sweet body defiled by lechers is too much for me, as hungry as I am. My belly growls suddenly and the girl giggles, puts out a hand to my cheek.

"If I didn't know different, I'd think you were sweet on 'er yerself."

"Shut up, Sybil, before I thump you."

She subsides onto her stool, scowling at me and curling her lip at M'lady. It is true, I am fond of her but not in the wrong way. She is more like the child I never bore; my only link with Francis, and besides, she depends on me and is miserable when I am away.

I can never send her back to her own.

But we are only just hanging on. Once the few pieces of kindlin' in the bucket are gone and supper eaten up, there will be nothing left.

Nothing at all.

No wood for the fire or bread for our bellies. Things have never been so bad.

As February gives way to March, and the frost is replaced by a bitter wind that no matter how much I stuff the cracks and crevices with straw and sacking creeps in beneath the door. I know I have to do something. We can't go on like this or we'll all be dead come spring. As soon as I've plucked up sufficient courage, I pin on the remnants of M'lady's French cap, pinch some wanton roses into my cheeks, hoist up my paps and make my way toward London Bridge in search of a fat purse or two.

Of late there have been gangs of youths, young sons of the nobility, making trouble for us girls. One night a bevy of them sailed down the river, shooting arrows at us as we worked on the bank. Since then I keep myself as far from them as possible and ply my trade with men I know and trust ... as far as I trust any man.

Even in daylight hours they make a nuisance of themselves, drinking and rampaging through the streets, accosting innocent women as well as those on sale. It isn't easy for any girl to keep herself safe, but now times are so hard I must risk picking one of them up and mayhap get him so drunk he'll not notice when I steal his purse.

I hear them before I see them and I force myself to walk with a jaunty step until, sure enough, I come across a band of them sparring about outside The

White Horse. They are making such a din that at first they don't notice me, and I fear a quarrel is about to break out.

Sparse-bearded boys like these are ever ready for a fight and it will not take much for one of them to draw his sword. It's the sort of trouble I can well do without but, with my mind set on the depth of their purses, I push out my bosom and don my best smile.

"Good day, gentlemen," I call as I stroll toward them, letting my thin cloak fall back to reveal the mark of my trade. They turn as one and watch me draw near, their eyes burning through my clothes. Abandoning the argument, one of them pushes back his cap and gives me the benefit of his handsome smile.

"Good morrow, Madam," he says, mocking me with the title for 'tis plain to all of them what I am. "Can I serve you?"

I try not to let them see my nervousness when I laugh up at him and stare brazenly into his eye. "I'm sure you all can, Sir, given your purses are long enough."

They fall about laughing, slapping each other on the back as if I am some great wit. "Come join us, Sweeting," the boldest one cries, holding out his arm in welcome. Although they are young enough for me to have birthed them, I go forward and join their roistering.

An arm falls heavy across my shoulders and I am handed a flagon. Grateful to have a means of dulling what sensibilities I have left, I take a hefty swig. Nobody, not even a whore, really enjoys the company of drunks and villains, and these men are rogues indeed. I am well aware that there is every chance they will make use of my body and then cast me into the river like an empty wine vessel.

It's a risk I have to take.

We move off to a quieter yard, away from the eyes of the passing townsfolk, and I am glad of the flagon that is seldom out of my hand. My companions are far gone, stumbling and giggling, their words so slurred I can scarce understand. I cling to the hope that just one of them takes me off to some inn where I can service him well before lulling him off to sleep. Then, once he is snoring, I can make off with his money. Well, 'tis a plan of sorts, albeit a frightening one. It is only the thought of a full belly and the easement of Sybil's whining that gives me courage.

The youngling leans on the wall beside me, his narrow eyes seeking a way beneath my clothes. Experience tells me that he will want to be the first ... I pray he will be the last too. "What's your name?" he slurs, taking the wine from me and tipping it to his own mouth. A trail of liquid runs down his chin and I watch his Adam's apple bob for a bit before he hands the drink back to me.

For some reason, I shy away from using my own name and give the first that comes to mind. "Betsy," I say and try not to flinch from him when he draws me closer. The smell of his carousing engulfs me; stale wine and body odour mingled with a hint of vomit.

"Well, fair Betsy. Am I right in assuming you have been kissed before?"

I never kiss the punters, they can do as they like with me as long as there is no kissing. Kissing is for Francis, not the likes of this fellow. I try to turn my mouth away but he seizes my face with strong fingers and clamps my lips into a mockery of a kiss before forcing his mouth over mine. He swamps me, his furred tongue plunging down my throat as his cold hands pull apart my bodice and dive inward, searching and pinching.

He is strong and urgent and I whimper like a virgin in the face of this assault over which I have no control. Panic prickles at the edge of reason. *I have made a bad mistake in coming here.*

I must get away. But at the first feeble attempt I make to wriggle free, a fist hammers against my jaw. Bright lights flash in my head and I slump to the ground, the laughter of his companions loud in my ears as he throws himself down upon me. I can barely remember my own name.

It seems he pounds away at me for a lifetime and when he is done, I curl into a ball while he towers over me, fumbling to re-tie his piece as he reels away. "Who's next?" he calls to his companions and straight away, another steps forward to take his place. I scramble into a sitting position. "No, no, I never agreed to..."

But I am dragged upward, thrust against the wall and when I open up my mouth and begin to holler, rough hands are clamped across my mouth, restricting my breath and stifling my cries. He rips up my skirts and I know I am lost.

In all my days of whoring I have never felt so dirty, never been so ill-used. I am filled with hate for them and for myself. These young sons of lords and princes do not waste their noble courtesies on the likes of me. I am nothing to them. As they use me, one by one, tears slip from my eyes and the strength seeps from my body. My limbs are limp. I give myself up to their violence.

When it is finally over, I do not move. From my place in the gutter I see their feet milling around and know they are drawing lots as to who shall have me next. Boots come close to my head and loud voices clamour in my ears as they begin to scuffle. One of them treads on my hand and I draw it back, put my fingers in my mouth to deaden the pain as they thunder around me. Then, one of them drops his knife in the straw by my head.

Before I even think what I am doing, I grab the blade and scramble to my feet. Weaving amongst them, I dart from the yard and into the main thoroughfare. There, lifting my skirts to my knees, I dash back along the street, my dugs bouncing free as a cry goes up behind me.

I head straight for home.

There are just a few folk in the streets about my lodgings and they turn to watch as I fly by. "Are you all right, Joanie?" someone calls but I cannot risk stopping. They cannot help me now.

I hurtle round the corner and into the alleyway, where I almost collide with Sybil who is stalking a bedraggled hen, escaped from some back yard.

"Joanie?" Her face blanches as she becomes aware of the danger.

"Stay there, Sybil," I call over my shoulder. The breath is rasping from my throat. "Send them off, tell 'em I went some other way." I sprint onward, grab the railing and take the rickety stairs two at a time. As I burst through the door the warm fug of home engulfs me.

M'lady looks up startled from her bed as I fall to the floor on my hands and knees, my chest heaving. She begins to cry. "Hush." I crawl toward the bed and drop onto the mattress beside her. "It's all right, Sweetling, there, there…"

She is still blubbing when the door is thrown open and my attackers surge into the room, filling the space. In a flash of fury, realising how stupid I have been to lead them here, I spring to my feet, trying to shield her from their gaze, hating myself for putting her in danger.

Curiously, now that they have me cornered they seem uncertain, hesitant, and I am reminded of their youth. Their brightly coloured clothes stand out against the drabness of my home, but the candle light shows up their bloodshot eyes and ravaged faces. They are nothin' but drunken scoundrels, surely I can outwit them yet. I will dally with them, hold them off and pray that Sybil has had the sense to send for the watch.

While my eyes dart from one to the other, assessing the danger, deciding how to act, they mill about my room. M'lady clings to me, peering over my shoulder, her tiny body shivering against my back. One of them kicks over a stool and a jug smashes onto the floor. Her cries become more vocal, her panic increasing.

I do not move when the most brazen of them, the one that had me first, approaches the bed and leers down at me. All I can think of is the revulsion of our recent coupling but I stick out my chin and let him see my scorn. I force a smile and lead his eyes down to my open bodice. I am not sure I can stand to be taken again but if it will protect M'lady from harm then I welcome it, and hope that the constables will hurry. I try to smile as prettily as I can.

"Well, Betsy, we meet again and I see you have a sister ... and ... a delectable looking one too." He puts his foot on the edge of the bed and reaches past me toward her, placing a finger beneath her lowered chin.

"Get your hands off!" I snarl, prepared to defend her with my life. But before I need to take action against him, he draws back from her as if he has been stung. For a moment I am confounded by the horror on his face.

"Eve!" he cries, stumbling back to join his companions. They form a ring about him, every one of

177

them fixing startled eyes upon the pair of us. "By all that's holy," he spits, "the bawd has turned my sister into a harlot!"

Isabella Greywater – February 1542

By the time I regain my senses I am lost in a mob of people, far from home. I look about me, confused by the sudden hubbub. A woman with a basket bawls in my ear that she has some 'lovely fresh 'errings'. I spin around, not knowing where I am or how I got here. Someone barges into me, almost knocking me from my feet, and I am pushed this way and that, turning confused, frightening circles, searching for my senses.

"You all right, Lady?"

I blink stupidly at the rough looking fellow who is addressing me, certain that I do not know him. But that is all I am certain of.

"I am lost," I whimper like a child, "so very, very lost …"

I cannot even recall my own name. In my hands I am clutching a rosary and a bible, but have no idea how I came by them.

I feel I have to find somebody without delay, but I cannot remember who. And then a memory stirs in the bottom of my mind, shifting like a brown trout in a murky stream, unfurling slowly, unreeling like a serpent. I know that when I find it the memory will be painful, but I cling to it anyway, grab it by the tail and pull it to the surface of my consciousness.

"Eve," I whisper at last. "I have lost my sister, Eve. Have you seen her?"

My companion chuckles and rubs his beard. "That was careless. Sorry, Lady, I don't know anyone called Eve ..." He stops mid-sentence. "Listen, you are lost and I can't be leavin' you to wander about in this mob. Let me take you home. Where do you live? I'm sure your people are searchin' for you. It won't do for both you and Eve to be lost, will it now?"

Where do I live? My mind evokes a vague misty picture of a warm day and a rose-filled garden, a puppy barking, children laughing. I shake my head. I don't know if that is a vision of home or just a happy dream.

He takes my elbow and begins to clear a path through the throng and I realise we are passing over London Bridge, on foot, a thing I have never done before. Memory nudges again and I narrow my eyes, willing myself to remember something that will throw a little light on the reason why I am here. A gossamer word, a name floating in my mind, the name of someone I love, someone I must find, our future depends on it. Eve. But how did I lose her and why is it so important that she is found?

Then another name penetrates the fog, like a shout this time, or an insult, a slap in the face. Francis. Francis Wareham!

I stop short and my guide stops also. "Francis Wareham." I withdraw my hand and shout above the noise of the crowd, heedless of their buffeting. "I am looking for Francis Wareham."

His laugh is not so merry this time but tinged with something darker, something menacing. He throws back his head, showing his rotten back teeth and the tidemark of dirt about his neck. "Well, you've found him all right. He is up there, look."

My reluctant eyes follow the line of his finger, to the sky above the gatehouse where a cluster of pikes point heavenward, each adorned with the tattered remnants of a traitor's head.

"Francis?" I know that is not the man I seek but at the sight of Dereham's severed head my memory returns, slicing through my mind like a blade.

"Katherine!" I cry, and my knees buckle as I remember the blood. The vivid, scarlet gore and poor,

180

silly Katherine dying like a Queen, her blood coating my face at the moment her life was severed.

I lift a hand to my forehead. It has dried now and the blood flakes at my touch to float down upon her prayer book. They are all that I have left of her.

I clutch them tighter and raise my eyes again to the bleak and dreadful sight of Katherine's lovers. Tom Culpepper and Francis Dereham and their blind, staring eyes look back at me. We are worlds apart now, separated by the narrow divide that splits the dead from the living; a divide that is so easily crossed.

A few short months ago those men had been vigorously and misguidedly thinking to mock and cuckold their King. Now look what they are come to. How vain men are to run such risks for the sake of a pretty face, a high bosom and a girlish laugh. How trifling and sad the consequence. There will be no one to remember them, and their brash, short lives will be lost, like a drop of rain falling into the river.

"I don't 'ave all afternoon to tarry here ..." His voice cuts into my thoughts and I shake myself, take a deep breath.

"That isn't Francis *Wareham* up there; it is Dereham, the traitor," I say and, taking one last look, I turn to leave. His warm hand slides beneath my elbow again and he begins to fight a way through the crowd. I follow him as if I am in some sort of dream, a nightmare in which I don't know who or where to run to. But by the time we reach the town gate, I have remembered I am Isabella and that I was a servant of the late Queen. At my request he helps me reach the one place I know I will be safe. I return to Richmond and the care of my friend, the Lady Anna.

When Mother hears of my plight she sends for me right away and I take my leave of the Lady Anna and find myself bundled into a litter for the journey home to Bourne Manor. My head has ached for days and I rest my brow on the jolting cushions and close my eyes, trying to shut out the ugly images that haunt me. For just a little while I need to forget about Katherine, and about Eve.

It will be better now. At home, in the bosom of my family, I will be able to rest and recuperate and grow strong again. If only the horses could travel faster, I cannot wait to be back at my father's house that has always kept me safe.

The bitter late February winds blow in beneath the leather curtain, and the first scatterings of snow drift like petals at the edge of my consciousness as I settle down to dream of Bourne in the summertime.

But before we have gone five miles my bones are weary, the horses jolting and lurching over the hard rutted road. When at last we come to a halt at the door of my father's manor, I am stiff with cold and climb like an old woman from the litter and shuffle into the comfort of the familiar hall, calling for my mother.

Bess appears first, her smile as wide and plump as ever, her well-remembered voice cheering me as she helps me unfasten my cloak. "It's good to have you home, My Lady," she says. "Your mother is waiting in the solar."

I smooth the front of my hair, straighten my cap and go forward as quickly as my bulk allows. Father's hounds gallop to greet me, their bark of welcome loud in the quiet of the hall. I push them away and turn to where she is waiting before the hearth.

"Mother!" Warm in her embrace, I feel her shudder emotionally as she holds me, and I know that she is as glad to see me as I am to be with her again. Everything will be well now.

"Let me look at you," she says and while she notes my wan cheeks and bulging belly, I take note of her appearance.

She has grown older and there are new lines about her eyes, anxiety scrawled upon her brow. I imagine that, should she remove her cap, her hair will be streaked with grey. Like any bereft mother she has not been left unmarked by the loss of Eve. "You are well, daughter?" With a nurturing smile she reaches out to stroke my belly, and I cover her hand with my own.

"I am very well, Mother, or I will be now that I am home. And once the babe is born, I swear I will do all within my power to find Eve and bring her home."

My words are intended to paint her cheeks with a happier hue but instead her face clouds again and she shakes her head.

"She is gone, child. We cannot bring back the dead ... not any of them. The past is gone."

I open my mouth to argue but she shushes me and leads me closer to the fire to sit with her on the settle. I look about the hall at the rich hangings and the bright flames leaping in the hearth and feel sad. There is something missing, there will always be something missing now Eve has been taken from us. "Bella, my love," Mother says, drawing my attention back to her, "you must be very brave for there is something I have to tell you."

Mother's lips are moving and I can hear her voice, but it makes no sense. I shake my head, negating her words, but I am back in the nightmare, the one in which I am lost and the Earth is crumbling beneath my feet. The one where the people around me are slipping away, dissolving into a mist through which I cannot follow. I cannot grasp them, cannot hold them and keep them here ... with me.

"It was the sweating sickness." She is weeping as she speaks, her face contorting with grief. "He was struck down suddenly and violently …" Her voice breaks and she droops her head, muffling her words with her handkerchief. "The doctors did all they could, but he was gone before a week was out."

"Father…" It cannot be true. I saw him last summer just before I left for the northern progress with the Queen. He was so very alive, so very robust … it *cannot* be true.

It is more than I can bear. Leaping to my feet, I clench my fists, my senses reeling, my mind screaming. As the blood rushes from my head, I dig my fingers into my skull and fight against encroaching darkness. A chasm opens at my feet and I give myself up to it, prepare to fall, but Mother's voice arrests me and I am dragged back to the horror of reality.

Her soft words rush like poison into my ears. "And that is not all, my dear. I have to tell you that Anthony … your husband, was stricken with the fever too."

I try to focus on her face and find some comfort there but the skin on her grey cheeks hangs lose, her misery etched deep. She cannot ease me.

"I am a widow? You are telling me that my husband *died* and no one thought to even tell me he was sick?"

My child lurches in my womb and I sway, my head momentarily lolling. Mother is beside me, supporting me, forcing me back into the chair. My serene, dignified mother is kneeling on the cold stone floor at my feet. "No, no, Anthony lives, Bella. He is still very weak but he will live. He would have been there with you when you shared Katherine's punishment otherwise. You know he would."

"Anthony lives?" Relief that my child will not be left fatherless surges through me, briefly compensating for the loss of Father, but the feeling is quickly replaced with guilt. "I should have been here, Mother. Oh, why did he make me go on the progress with the King? I would have been content to stay at home with him."

Sorrow is heaped upon sorrow. I think of my staid husband lying alone in his sickbed and I grieve for the loss of my dear father. If only I'd had the time to say goodbye, to say the things I'd never thought to say. We never think to appreciate those who are close to us – we never take the time to tell them we love them – not until it is too late.

"You are distraught, Bella, you cannot be everywhere, for everyone. Take comfort that you were with your mistress when she needed you at the end."

Mother strokes my hair, murmurs soft words, and when Bess appears with a jug of wine she holds the cup to my lips and helps me drink.

"We must get you to bed. You are exhausted and need to rest. We must all think of the next generation, look to the future and the child you bear. We will be fine, you and I, just wait and see."

Isabella March 1542

The next day dawns grey, and the rain that lashes the casement keeps everyone with any sense indoors. Not that I have a wish to go anywhere. I am exhausted, the trials of the last few weeks crashing around inside my head, leaving me drained of energy. All morning I lay abed watching Bess, who has been taken from her usual duties to attend me, sort through my old linen closet. But lying abed has never suited me. No matter what it may bring, I've always liked to greet the day head-on. Now, however, I am listless and tired and my pillow is too soft.

I dream of the past. "It is funny, Bess, how it always seems to have been so sunny when we were little. These days the sun never shines so brightly."

"Well, it is March, My Lady, and the winter is loath to leave us this year." She pauses for a moment and adds quietly, "Besides, I think, we only tend to think on happy times, and happy times always seem sunny."

I let my mind meander back to childhood days when Eve and Tom and I used to play with Bess, running in and out of the flowerbeds, chasing across the lawns, and dangling our fingers and toes into the fountains. Bess is wrong. I am certain it was sunnier then, when our hearts were unburdened with shadows.

"I should get up. Father would call me a sluggard and a lazy bones." My voice catches a little at the mention of him but I force myself to sit up and smile at the grey windswept clouds that blanket my window. Swinging my swollen ankles from the bed, I slip my feet into slippers and wrap a gown about my shoulders. "Help me dress please, Bess, and then I will keep Mother company. We can offer each other comfort."

Sometime later I am in the hall, sipping frumenty with Mother before the fire. We have decided to organise the maids into a frenzy of spring cleaning, although Spring still seems to be so far away. "We shall start in the attics," Mother says briskly, tying on an apron, "and finish down here. Will you be all right if I leave Bess to see to your needs?"

It is good to see her with some purpose again and I am sorry I cannot be of more help. Bourne Manor is now in the hands of my brother, Tom, and Mother will want the place to be in good order. My brother was just on the cusp of manhood when last we met and full of the arrogance of youth, but although only two years or so have passed since then, he will now be fully grown. In my mind's eye I see a replica of Father, mild and thoughtful, a worthy successor to the Bourne title. Soon, he will marry and raise a fine set of sons, and we can form some semblance of happiness again. It is a happy dream and I linger there for some time, ignoring the activity in the hall.

Soon maids are scurrying up and down the stairs with buckets and brooms while I stay cosily settled before a roaring fire. I ask Bess, more for company than for need, to help me sort through some of Eve's things, and she fetches a big pile of her clothing so that we can work near the comfort of the fire.

It is a heart-breaking task. Not only are the colours and texture of her clothes evocative of her, but when I hold them to my cheek and close my eyes I can smell her perfume too. It is almost as if she is here in the room with us. "Have you thought of names for the little one, My Lady?"

I open my eyes and lower the garment I've been sniffing to my lap, blinking away tears. "If it is a girl I shall call her Evelyn, of course. If it is a boy, he shall be John after his grandfather. If my husband agrees …"

I concentrate, trying to recall Anthony's face, but it escapes me. Our time together was so short and I realise now that I was a poor wife to him. Pray God, he will live so I can make it up to him. I take a big breath to chase the maudlin thoughts away. "You will have to bring your little daughter to see me, Bess, one day I hope she will be a playmate for my child."

"Oh, I will, My Lady. Shall I fetch her tomorrow?"

"Yes, yes, that will be lovely." I pause and cock my ear to the window, listening. "Is that horses arriving outside?" Bess struggles to her feet and with her legs numb from kneeling, limps across the floor.

"Yes," she says, peering through the thick green glass. "Ooh, I think it is the master."

My heart lurches for an instant, thinking she means Father, and then I remember that Tom, whom I have not seen in so long, is the master of Bourne Manor now.

Moments later the door is thrown open and he strides over the threshold and
without greeting me, he demands, "Where is Mother?"

A little dazed by the fact that my baby brother is now a man with a deep voice and a sword on his hip, I wave my hand toward the upper floor. In a few strides he is at the bottom stair, hollering like a ruffian. "Mother, come down. I've found her! I've found Eve!"

I stand up as a small, skinny woman is led shuffling into the hall. For a moment I am puzzled but then she lifts her terrified eyes, just briefly, and something that I see there gives me pause. She looks like Eve and yet, she doesn't. There is almost no resemblance to the beautiful young woman I last saw. This woman is thin and ragged, her hair lank and lustreless, but it is her eyes that are changed the most.

There is no life in her expression. Eve is vivacious and naughty but in this woman, the wicked spark of intelligence is extinguished and all I see is bewilderment and fear. "Eve?" I whisper, and she gapes at me without recognition, a trickle of dribble running down her chin. I do not rush to take her in my arms.

I move forward but she pulls away, conceals her face in Tom's cloak. "What has happened to you? Who has done this?"

"That's what I should like to know." Impatiently, Tom all but rips his cloak from Eve's grasp. "I found her with a family of whores on the Bankside, romping on a bed with a slattern ... I'd the devil of a job to get her away from one of them."

"What?" This cannot be true. I look at her again, cannot take my eyes away, although the sight fills me with a curious mixture of fear, regret and revulsion. This cannot be my sister. In truth I am longing for it not to be her after all, but merely some freak of nature who resembles her.

While I watch, she crouches on the hearth and wraps her arms about her knees. Soon she is rocking back and forth like a chastised child. "Eve," I try again, and this time she looks up at the sound. "Come, sit on the settle." I move toward her and hold out my hand, but the eyes that look back at me are blank. She doesn't know me. I think this might be the final straw.

There is a movement at the doorway and Mother appears, her breast heaving from the haste in which she descended the stair. "Eve!" she cries, and the anguish in her voice is hard to bear. "Oh, blessed God, you are returned to me."

Ignoring the state of her filthy clothes and matted, probably lice-infested hair, Mother drags the terrified girl to her feet and into her arms. I look away, close my eyes.

Mother has noticed nothing beyond Eve's physical presence, she does not realise that she has lost her mind. "Tell me where you have been, Eve. Who took you away? Did they harm you? Are you all right?"

She stands back, holds her daughter at arm's length and, for the first time, looks into her eyes. Mother goes very still and her smile fades as at last she recognises the truth. There is nothing left of what made Eve, Eve; no joy, no wit, just a bleak emptiness.

189

Eve's hands drop to her sides when Mother releases them suddenly to cover her mouth. She closes her eyes.

"Oh no, not this, God, please not this."

Untouched by Mother's tears, Eve shuffles to the table where victuals are habitually laid out. She picks up the jug and begins to drink from it, rich red wine dripping onto her chest. Thomas emits a growl of displeasure. "Bess, take her to the kitchens and feed her. Keep her out of my sight until I decide what is to be done with her."

I stand up, outrage overshadowing my sorrow.

"The kitchens? Don't be ridiculous. You can't do that. She needs care and nurture, not shutting from your sight. Bess, take her to her old chamber while we decide what to do, and have the maids take up some food and hot water so she can be bathed."

Shaking herself from the shock, Bess moves forward and gingerly takes Eve's arm. "Come along, Miss," she says, "come with Bessie, she will look after you."

To my relief Eve follows her without protest. As the door closes behind them, Mother plumps into a chair, older and greyer than before, while Tom, from his position before the fire, looks down the length of his nose at me.

"You, Madam, will do well to remember that I give the orders around here now."

Joanie Toogood

"I'm scared, Joanie ..." Sybil's voice is stark in the gloom, making me jump. Usually, I'd scorn her fears but today I am as frightened as she is. The straw rustles beneath her feet as she crosses the cell to sit beside me, her body as near to mine as she can get. Sybil and I have never been close but, grateful for the extra warmth, I loop an arm about her shoulder and give her a little squeeze o' comfort. She tucks herself closer, her hand slipping about my waist, her head falling onto my shoulder. "Oh Joanie, what'll we do? I wish Betsy was 'ere."

"What good would it do having all three of us in Clink?"

Knowing that Betsy has escaped into marriage and been spared this punishment is the only small comfort I have.

We have been here for near on a month now and it is a dismal place; dark and damp and cheerless. It makes the squalor of my chambers seem like heaven. The only light that enters our darkness comes through a barred window high up on the wall, but when night falls, as it has now, it is blacker than a hangman's heart.

Night and day we can hear the restless creak of the gibbet that hangs on the outer wall just outside our chamber, so that when we do sleep, the soul that rots there creeps into our dreams.

Night time is the worst. During the day the turnkey unlocks our cell and we are allowed to wander about and mix with the other prisoners. I've even managed to turn a few tricks and earn an extra crust

191

and a chunk of cheese. But there are so many other girls trying to work the same patch that it ain't easy. Luckily, after a day or two, I learn that the turnkey is old enough to enjoy a little 'motherin', and I make a friend of him.

His name is Nick and of course, he is no man o' steel. There was a time when I'd 'ave scorned to lie with the likes of him but 'needs must,' as my mother used to say. He can soften our time here if anyone can and if anyone knows what is likely to happen to us, it's him.

Against my will I embark on a campaign to win him and, by my truth, he is easy won. I can barely stand it when he takes me, his great flabby belly banging on my arse as he bends me forward over a barrel. But that night Sybil and me enjoy a meal that has proper chunks of meat in it and the bread that we dip greedily into our pottage is the freshest we've eaten in weeks.

The next time I service him it doesn't seem so bad. I focus my thoughts on the herb flavoured stew and doughy dumplings that he's promised me and, once he is lodged inside, I wriggle my arse to make a quicker end to it.

Afterwards, barely able to see his piece beneath the bulge of his belly, he ties up his laces while I pull down my skirts and adjust my bodice. Then I smile winsomely at him and begin to pick his brains. "Nick, what will become of me and my sister, d'you know?"

He smiles through his broken teeth as he tugs his jerkin down and tightens his belt. "Well, Joanie, that all depends on which justice you come before. Some of 'em, the sort that like to dally with women, go lightly on whores, but there are others, the ones who want to clean up the streets, well … they goes heavy on 'em."

That doesn't sound very much like justice to me but at least he is honest. All I can do is wish for the right sort o' judge … or the wrong sort, whichever way you care to look on it.

Nick turns at the door. "Thanks, Joanie. I'll order up something special for yer dinner tonight. Oh, I forgot to tell you. You had a visitor yesterday but he come too late an' I sent him away, told him to come back today. If he comes back, d'yer want t' see 'im?"

My head jerks up. "Well, that depends on who it is, don't it?"

He scratches his scalp, examines his finger and squeezes a louse between his nails. "Said his name was Peter."

Peter! Peter is back! A tiny breath of freedom wafts beneath my nose. "Oh, yes," I say with too much delight. "I want to see Peter."

Nick's eyes narrow suspiciously. "He said he was your nephew."

"And so he is, Nick, so he is, and very fond of the boy I am, too."

I cannot rest. All morning I stride back and forth in the yard with my fists clenched, longing for Peter to come. The other whores, seeing my distraction, mock me, thinking I am waiting for a lover. I ignore them and they soon get tired of taunting me and begin to squabble over the few paltry inmates that have the coin to pay for their services. And when I finally see Peter, dressed head to toe in goose-turd green, creeping cautiously into the yard, I surprise myself and fly to greet him as if he is indeed the love of my life.

He drags off his cap, his face pink with embarrassment, and I step away, release my hands from around his neck, remembering he is now a

193

married man and no longer willing to continue our previous bargain.

"It's good to see you, Peter. You look well."

"It's good to see you too, Joanie … although … well, it's not so good to see you in here. I was shocked when I heard what had happened …" His eyes dart around the yard, where the other inmates are up to their nefarious business, and suddenly I realise how unkempt I must look to him. I know there are lice in my hair and on my body also. He must see the difference to the healthy, smiling Joanie of old.

"How did you know where I was?" I ask as an afterthought.

"Bertha. I went to see Bertha when I heard her husband had died and she told me … is there anything I can do to help, Joanie? I've been unable to sleep nights since I heard."

Knowing his involvement in my crime, he is brave to come here. The shadow of the boy is lurking visibly beneath the thin cloak of his manhood. He is as scared as I.

"What can anyone do, Peter? I think I am for it." I speak quietly, so as not to alarm Sybil who is sitting with her face turned toward the wall, as she often does.

"No, no. Don't think like that, Joanie."

"What else will they do with me? Thank me for taking care of her and give me a fat purse by way of reward? No. It's the rope for me and it's best I face the fact."

"Have they…? Do they …?"

"Know about Francis? Nay, I think not. You are quite safe. I am to be charged with abduction and abuse, no more."

"Abuse? But you treated her like she was your own child."

We exchange a long look before I whisper, "Aye, Peter, she was just that …the child I never 'ad. Who'd have thought I'd come to love her so?"

"Where is she now?"

I shrug. "I know not. Back with her own, I suppose, although her brute of a brother … well, it should be me bringing charges against him, not the other way about, but who'd listen to a rape charge from a woman like me?"

I try to stop the memory of the beating and the hurt that Thomas Bourne laid upon my body, but a tear drops onto my cheek.

"Aw, Joanie … don't."

His eyes are bright with unshed sorrow, making me smile ruefully and reach out a hand. "Don't pity me, Peter. Life hasn't been so bad and what other end would I choose? Dying of the pox in the gutter, old and withered and unwanted? I don't think so."

He stands up, screws his cap into a roll, and I realise he has put on his Sunday best to visit me. He has always been such a good, gentle boy. I was cruel to drag him into the violence of my world.

"I've given the turnkey some coin. Enough to ensure you don't have to … work … in here anymore. When I return, and I will return, you must tell me if the turnkey has scrimped in your comforts in any way, do you hear?"

I nod but cannot answer, for my throat is painfully choked with grateful tears. I know he cannot spare the coin but he is a good soul and will one day join the saints in Heaven. He takes my shoulders and plants a kiss on my cheek.

"I will seek some legal advice, Joanie, and see what, if anything, can be done."

It is hard to let him go. I want to cling to him. He is little more than a boy, but weak and powerless as he is, he is all I have. "Come on, Sybil," I say, "let's go in, it's starting to rain."

She shambles toward me, clutches my shawl and we walk slowly back to our comfortless cell.

Things are a little better now. The turnkey daren't deny us food since Peter has paid him well, but he resents the withdrawal of my favours. He turns up his lip and dumps the tray before me, and I know I have lost a friend. I just pray to God I never need to placate him again. Sybil pins all her hopes on Peter.

Terrified of hanging, she tells me, time and time again, that all will be well. "Peter is a good boy, I always said so. He will work some miracle and get us out of here, I know he will."

She is better company now she has hope so, for my own comfort, I do not disillusion her. Let her believe all will be well, it will make the days shorter … at least, for her. Day by day, my sister grows braver and even begins to speak to one or two of the inmates. There is no one more surprised than me when I spot her leaning against a wall flirting with a felon. I pause and watch, surmising if she is turning a trick or just passing the time of day.

He is not a bad looking man, his long hair would be black and glossy if it were washed, and the cut of his shabby doublet had once been good. Sybil has always leaned toward his type. As I watch, he reaches out and lifts her hair from her damaged cheek but she clamps her hand upon his and turns her face away.

His laughter floats across to where I am lingering beneath the arch. He puts a finger beneath her chin, lifts her face toward him. Sybil is blushing like a maid and I watch in astonishment as he kisses her, gentle-like, on the mouth. Then, with her chin

196

down and he with his head held high, he takes her arm and begins to squire her about the yard.

"By all that's holy!" I exclaim out loud, and Janet of the stews stops beside me.

"Whassup, Joanie love?"

"Who is that walking with Sybil? What's he in for?"

She squints her eyes, shades her brow with her hand. "That's Jack. I'm not sure what he is in for this time. I do believe he has a finger in most pies, smuggling, poaching, theft. In fact, it's a wonder he has a hand left to double deal with. He's an oily sort, always manages to slip out from beneath the noose."

"Not a good fellow, then?"

Her laugh is loud and raucous, and I feel my own lips stretching in response as she walks away bellowing over her shoulder. "Blow me, Joanie. What on God's acre is a 'good fellow' when he's at home?"

Jack and Sybil are soon behaving like man and wife, spending every hour together. The change in my sister is like the sun peeking from behind a dark cloud. At first she is wary and her smiles uncertain, but as she becomes more sure of him, she beams on everyone like an indulgent aunt.

"For God's sake, you two, can't you find anything else to do?" I bawl at them when I trip over them sprawled on the floor of our cell. Sybil pulls our only cover up to her chin and snuggles on Jack's bare chest.

"Are you jealous, Joanie? At least you don't 'ave to go outside and sit in the rain while we're at it."

Her words bring back the long afternoons I spent with Francis, the smell of his warm skin, the softness of his touch, the lash of his tongue on my breast. My heart sinks, the memory still as sharp as a knife. They were my good days and if only I'd known

197

it, I'd have relished them more'n I did. I never dreamed I'd end up here with the shadow of the noose swinging above my head. Maybe Francis was better off to go the way he did, taken sudden in the midst of living. It is this waiting that goes hard with me. Maybe Sybil has the better idea. I swivel on my heel and, as I leave the room, I turn to see Jack lift the cover and dive beneath it again, making Sybil squeal as he blows raspberries on her paps.

The corridor is dim, the courtyard slick with rain. The whores lurk in doorways, their shawls about their heads looking for likely customers. I hold out my hand and feel rain drip onto my palm. The weather is as grim as my prospects but unwilling to return to my cell, I lean against the stone wall and watch the falling rain.

"Joanie?" Nick the turnkey appears at my elbow. "Your 'nephew' is back to see you and he has someone with him. I've shown them into an upper room."

An upper room? Peter has someone with him? My mind is teeming with questions as I follow his unwieldy body along the corridors and up a twisting stair. It could be a trick but he shows no sign of tension as he puffs and pants his way to the upper floor.

At the top, he throws open a door to a well-lit room and I step inside. Peter is standing by the hearth, his cap in his hand, his face glinting between anguish and hope. He steps forward and takes my hands.

"Joanie. I've brought someone to see you. She wants to ask you some questions." His eyes are urging me to comply with whatever plan he has concocted and, with great curiosity, I turn toward my other caller.

As we face each other for the first time, she stands up and moves slowly toward me, as graceful and as grand as a Queen. My mouth gapes like a haddock's.

"Thank you for seeing me, Joanie," she says and offers me her stool.

Isabella Greywater – March 1542

It takes just a few days in his company for it to become clear to me that Thomas is not made from the same stuff as my father. There is no resemblance to the child I once played with. He shouts at the servants, is rude to Mother, and keeps ungodly hours. Mother blames the company he keeps, the younger sons of the gentry who, with too much time on their hands, have become wastrels and rogues. From the day of our reunion he leaves me in no doubt that he intends to rule Bourne Manor with an iron fist.

Despite the fact that we are a house of mourning, he invites his friends to stay and each night the great hall is filled with the sounds of roistering. I thrust my head beneath the pillow and try to block out the noise, comforting myself that once my child is born, I can travel to Wales to be reunited with my husband. My memories of marriage are vague, a few months of indifferent coupling and polite daytime conversation has done little to convince me my return will be a welcome one. But, since I no longer have a position at court, my duty is with my husband.

Tom, who cannot bear to look upon Eve, has denied her access to the lower floors and she is kept within her chambers. I spend much of my time with her and although she does not know me, I think she grows used to my presence. When she was missing and I feared her dead, I prayed only that she be returned to us. I did not dream it would be in this way. I never thought she could be here and yet … not be here. And so, I miss her still and it is hard for me to realise that she will never be the girl she once was.

Bess seems to be the only person my sister trusts completely, which is just as well since she relies upon her for everything. She has to be washed and dressed and her soiled linen changed several times a day, and it is only Bess who has the wherewithal to soothe her many tantrums.

My meals are taken with Mother in the dining hall, but afterwards I change into a loose gown and settle for the rest of the evening in Eve's chamber. Here, I am away from Thomas and can relax, put my feet up on a stool and try to make friends with the girl that Eve has become.

Although she can feed herself, the process is messy and disconcerting to watch, so Bess spoon-feeds her as if she were an infant. She sits quietly, opening her mouth like a baby bird, chewing slowly as she looks wide-eyed about the room while Bess dabs gravy from her chin and offers another spoonful. At least Eve is calm now, her bouts of rage are frightening and when the attacks come, I am at a loss as to what to do.

The first time the family were witness to such an attack, Thomas took one look at her and stormed angrily from the house while Mother and I stood back in hopeless horror. Thankfully, Bess instinctively knew what was required and launched herself at my sister, clamping her arms to her sides to stop her from harming herself. All the time she whispered soothing, sing-song words that seemed to penetrate Eve's fury and bring her to some semblance of normality. Since that day Bess has had full charge of her and I think – I pray – that she is making some progress.

But Mother, Bess and I all know that things cannot go on as they are. Some more permanent arrangement will have to be made.

"She has been a good girl today, My Lady. She has eaten her dinner all up." Bess places the spoon in the empty bowl and gathers up the tray.

"Eve isn't a child, Bess, please don't treat her like one."

"Oh, I am sorry, My Lady. I didn't mean to. It's not easy …"

"I know, Bess. I do understand. It's just that, even if she never comes back to herself, I want her to have some dignity …" My voice fails me and I battle back tears before speaking again. "I don't know what to do and it seems the doctors are at a loss also."

Bess puts down the tray. "Dr Malleon said that once she is used to us and has a routine, she will quieten, and she is quiet now. She seems happy."

"I heard her shouting earlier." I mop my eyes with the corner of my kerchief. "Was it very bad?"

"Oh, not really. She gets herself all agitated, that's all. I just wish I could make out what she is yelling about. It is as if she is trying to tell me something. She was shouting, 'bony' or 'pony', or something like that. It made no sense to me."

Eve's periodic bouts of noisiness border on madness and I know there are grumblings in the kitchens about lunacy and witchcraft. One or two of the lower staff have left, and Bess heard one of the cooks declare the 'young missus is touched by the moon.' They think she should have no place among God-fearing folk and there are those who would shut her away from the world.

I will never countenance that.

She is my sister.

She is Eve and always will be.

My child kicks and I place a hand over my womb, gently caressing. My ribs are sore from the drumming of his heels but I take comfort that the child I carry is lusty and strong.

"And how are you, My Lady?" Bess asks, bringing me a cup of watered wine. "Are you getting enough rest?"

It is Bess' way of enquiring if my nightmares have ceased, for bad dreams can have an undesired

202

effect on the character of an unborn child. I wonder at the truth of it; I must ask Mother if she suffered from such dreams when she was carrying Thomas, for something has turned him from a happy child into a bully.

Bess moves to the window to draw the curtains across and shut out the falling night. She pauses and looks down into the bailey. "The master has company again, I see," she says, managing in a noncommittal way, to convey very much.

My heart sinks. "Again?"

This means we will all be kept awake until the small hours, just as we have been every night for a week. I join her at the window and look down upon a bevy of painted women alighting from a carriage, their raucous laughter wafting up to the chamber. "Oh, Lord," I breathe in Bess' ear, "pray that my mother does not see the company he keeps."

A hand touches my shoulder and I notice Eve beside me, straining to see. "No, come along, sweetheart, you don't want to see them..." I try to draw her back to the hearth but she pushes me away, immediately fractious.

"Oanee, Oanee ..." Her voice is thick, as if her tongue is too large for her mouth and her words make no sense, although I am sure she is trying to tell me something.

"Help me with her, Bess," I gasp. Together we pull her back to her cushions and Bess distracts her with a loud song that I remember from our nursery days. When she relaxes into Bess' lap, I lay my head against the back of the settle. With the warmth of the flames on my face, I close my eyes.

It is much later when I am woken by a gentle touch on the arm. Bess nods toward Eve, who is now tucked up in bed and sleeping soundly. I look about the chamber and see to my astonishment that the fire has burned low. "Goodness, Bess, how long have I been asleep?"

"You must have needed it, My Lady. Come, let me help you to bed. There's another day tomorrow."

With a glance at my sister and a silent mew of thanks to Bess, we tiptoe from the room and along the corridor to my chamber. At the top of the stairs we pause and I raise my eyebrows at the sounds of music and the squeals of feminine revelry coming from the great hall. "How is anyone expected to sleep through that ruckus?" I complain as Bess opens the door.

I don't expect to but I fall sleep easily. It is not until I become conscious that there is somebody in my room that I open my eyes again, and find myself blinking into the yellow circle of Bess' candlelight.

"What is it?" I pull myself up on my pillow and try to force my bleary eyes open.

Bess' face is white, her hand trembling slightly. "Oh, My Lady. I am sorry to wake you but I didn't know what to do. Miss Eve is not in her bed. Something disturbed me and when I checked her, I found her blankets were thrown back and she isn't wearing her robe."

She is clutching Eve's robe beneath her arm and her hair is hanging in two long braids. I swing my legs over the edge of the bed and fumble for my slippers. "She can't have gone far, I shall help you look. It's best not to disturb Mother."

Together we tread quietly downstairs. It is quiet in the hall now and I hope they are all gone to their beds. If there is any justice, they will all have headaches come morning and live to regret their excesses.

"We should check the kitchens first, My Lady, Mistress Eve is always hungry."

We hurry toward the back of the house where the kitchens are situated, and as we enter the chilly stone passage, our candle illuminates a golden circle about us. Beyond the reach of our light the night is black, giving everything a false emphasis, the darkness seemingly alive with danger. A tiny sound brings us to a sudden stop and I give a sharp squeal as a mouse appears and scurries along the wainscot. We hold our breath until it has passed and I suppress a shudder – *dreadful little things* - and then we creep onward.

Night and day the old house creaks and settles, but tonight, with night wrapped like a blindfold about the windows, the sounds take on a new and eerie significance.

We stop abruptly again and listen. It could be footsteps crossing the upper floor above our head, they could be Eve's or they could be … something else. All the stories I've ever heard of ghouls and spirits come back to me. They are tales I would scorn in daylight but now I wish with all my heart that I were safe in my bed.

The house seems to close in upon us as we creep forward, suppressing our rationality until we are afraid of everything ... and nothing. Bess reaches for the latch, and as her hand touches it something clatters in the kitchen. It sounds as if every pot and pan has fallen to the flagstone floor. She snatches back her hand and emits a yelp of fear.

"Don't be silly, Bess," I say, with a conviction I don't feel, "it is only Eve." But I am now clinging to her hand too. We listen for a moment but there are no more sounds, and very slowly, so as not to startle Eve, Bess pushes open the door.

Our tiny flame throws a looming shadow about the stark room. The whitewashed walls are painted yellow by the flickering light and we see the long wooden table in the centre of the room holding half a loaf of bread, some discarded flagons and a covered pitcher. A scattering of copper pans litter the floor, but other than that it seems to be empty. We begin to turn away.

But just as we start to relax there is an enormous clashing and clanking of pans behind us and some devil streaks between our legs with an unearthly shriek. I scream and Bess drops the light, plunging us into darkness.

"Sorry, My Lady." Bess' voice is pale in the darkness as she scrambles for a tinderbox and drops it on the floor, the pieces scattering. I fight for my breath, a hand to my throat. "That damned cat!" I gasp, trying to still my thumping heart. My child stirs fretfully and stretches, his head pressing down hard on my bladder. I hold my breath until the pain has passed.

"There was a torch burning in the hall," I say when I have regained my breath and, groping for each other's hands, we fumble our way back along the corridor again. The night chill is creeping up my legs, and ignoring the pain in my lower back, I draw my shawl about me and feel my belly tighten uncomfortably. "Where can she be?" I whisper irritably. "The outer door is sealed so she must be in the house. We will have to check the great hall."

Our comfort increases a little when we locate the torch and can see a little way past the ends of our noses. The heavy oak doors open with a groan and we immediately recoil from the stench of wine and debauchery.

I put my hand across my nose.

"God's holy acre!" Bess looks around with wide eyes at the devastation of my father's once noble hall. It will take a fleet of servants a week to clear up such a mess. One corner of the great tapestry showing The Expulsion from Eden has become detached from the wall, and my father's carved chair is overturned; its legs pointing Heavenward.

A couple of hounds are finishing off the remains of the feast, upending platters and jugs as they wolf down meat and pastries. I inch forward, lifting the skirt of my shift to avoid a pool of vomit, and with Bess following, begin to tiptoe deeper into the room. Bess raises her torch higher and I let my eye trickle disgustedly over the prone bodies of men and women who, in various states of undress, are snoring by the hearth. There is no movement and no sound but the rasp of stagnant breath.

"She isn't here." It is not possible to disguise the relief in my voice as Bess takes my elbow and begins to help me from the room again. But as we reach the door we are brought up short by a high-pitched giggle, a vacant, girlish giggle we both instantly recognise.

Regardless of danger or what I might find, I march across the room and snatch back a curtain. Eve, clad only in her night shift, is sitting on the knee of an individual whom I can only assume is an associate of my brother. He looks every inch a reprobate.

"Eve!" I exclaim, grabbing her wrist and dragging her away. She comes easily, still giggling, her hair hanging loose and her breath reeking of wine. "What in God's name do you think you are doing, Sir?"

His gaze trickles impudently to my swollen belly. "I don't think I have to explain that to you, Miss." He tips his head back and swigs from his wineskin, wipes his mouth on the edge of his sleeve. I cannot believe this foul, arrogant jade has laid hands on my sister. He should be horsewhipped!

Before I can respond, he stands up and begins to stagger toward me, stumbling over his sword as it becomes entangled between his knees.

"Come away, Lady. Come on…" For once ignoring etiquette, Bess grabs my arm and pulls me toward the door. I waste no time in following, and dragging Eve behind me, we head for safety. In our haste we make a great noise, tripping over abandoned clothes and plate while the fellow bellows in indignation behind us and the hounds begin to bark.

At the bottom of the stair we are confronted by half the household who, disturbed by the racket, are descending from the upper floor. We stop and watch them approach. Mother is hurriedly tying her robe and behind her emerges the pale face of my brother, a thunderous look in his eye.

"What goes on here?" Thomas pushes to the front of the crowd and it is obvious he is still very much the worse for wear. His hair is on end and there are dark circles around his eyes. I am drawn to a large red bruise on his throat. He stinks like a doxy.

Very much aware of the need to keep gossip to a minimum, my eyes dart from Thomas to Mother as I search desperately for a credible tale. "Eve has been sleepwalking," I say, snatching the idea from the air. "Bess and I heard a noise and went to find her; that is all. I am so sorry to have woken everyone, we knocked some plate to the floor in the hall …"

The servants are turning sleepily back toward their quarters and Bess begins to lead Eve up the stair. Just as I am beginning to think we will keep the truth to ourselves, the drunken fellow lurches accusingly from the great hall. Heedless of the gathering, he raises his finger and points directly at Eve.

"Hey, I paid good money for her!" he cries. All eyes turn toward my sister, who smiles back at him like a wanton. For the first time, I notice a small bag of coin fastened about her neck and the last thing I hear, as I fall crashing to the floor, is Bess' voice shrieking, "Lady Greywater is going to faint! Somebody catch her!"

I roll in a relentless sea of agony. I have heard gossip of course, and witnessed the labour of cattle in the barnyard, heard the cries of our household women. But nothing, *nothing,* has prepared me for the reality of childbirth.

Everything is wrong, displaced and nightmarish. Mother comes mistily into view, hovering in and out of my reality. "Fetch Jennet from the village ... and hurry," she says, leaning over me. "There is no time to lose."

And then Bess is there, her soothing hands stroking and dabbing my brow with a cooling cloth as she sings soothingly beneath her breath. There is something I must tell her and I try to speak, but my tongue won't work properly and I am taken again by inexorable pain. I twist and writhe on the bed until Jennet arrives and they give me a potion, something to ease the pain. Yet although it dulls the agony in my guts, it does nothing to soothe my mind.

The drug possesses me and twists my reality so cruelly so that I am lost in a nightmare from which I cannot wake.

Katherine! She offers herself up to the blade and I see it falling, feel her blood hot on my face. I should have saved her. Katherine's death is on my hands. She leans toward me, a livid red ring about her little neck, but she is no longer my friend. "Your pain is nothing," she spits, "nothing to what I suffered. Why didn't you stop them?"

"I am sorry," I sob weakly. "There was nothing I could do. I am just a woman."

"You're a whore!" My brother is laughing and the doxy on his arm is laughing too. They are all laughing. His woman looks like Eve, and then she looks like Katherine and then becomes me; a cheap me, raddled with the marks of whoredom. And I am laughing at myself too, for I know myself to be defiled like all the rest.

Father turns away, too shamed to look at me. "Father, forgive me!" I shout but he bows his head, his brow furrowed. "What have I done, Father? I am sorry. I am sorry!"

Anthony, my unloved husband, watches emotionlessly from the foot of the bed, watching my torment, waiting for me to die so he can take another, more affectionate wife. Someone like Eve. She is the pretty one, the happy one, the one everybody wants!

They are all here, the dead mingled with the living, haunting me, hating me. Only Eve is smiling, but now she is turning to leave and she must come back. Eve!

She walks away. I can see her growing smaller; we are separated, the distance increasing until the gulf between us can no longer be breached. I have to stop her. I have to bring her back. "Eve!" I call, twisting on the mattress. "Eve!"

The pain is greater now, they tie ropes upon me and my body is wracked apart. Like a traitor to the King, I am drawn and quartered, and despite my battle, the blood flows and I am rent in two. I scream for Eve.

But she does not hear me. She does not come.

Much later, when the visions have faded, I am sitting up in bed with my hair tamed and tucked beneath a veil. My body is sponged clean and my nether regions wrapped in wadding. When Bess places my son in my arms, my heart fills with joy.

"He is bonny, My Lady. Those bruises will fade soon enough."

"John," I whisper, and kiss his baby hair that smells delightfully of new life and promise. "You shall be John."

Bess is folding my linens and placing them in the clothes press. I look up at her and, my terrors pushed aside, present her with my best smile.

"Where is Eve? Could you bring her to me, Bess?"

She stops what she is doing and looks away toward the hearth. "I can't do that, My Lady."

"Why ever not? What do you mean?"

She comes toward the bed, glances anxiously at the door and her voice drops to a whisper.

"The master has locked her in her chamber and will not let her out, nor me in."

"But who is looking after her? She cannot be left alone."

Bess shrugs. "Your mother has tried to reason with him but … after what happened he says she is not welcome in his household and threatens to send her away."

"Away? Away where?" My voice is almost a shriek and my son stirs in my arms, beginning to fret, searching for and chomping at his own fist as if he will swallow it.

"I don't know, My Lady. Try not to fret or you will upset the babe. I should never have told you."

"Of course you should. Where is my mother?"

"She is with some gentlemen in the hall."

"Gentlemen, what gentlemen? Have they come to take Eve away?"

"I don't know, My Lady, I just saw the carriage, that is all. Oh, no, please stay in your bed. You need to rest …"

She tries to push me back onto the pillow but I slap her hands away. "How can I rest, Bess? I cannot let them take her …" I struggle from the bed, press my child into her arms and look about for my clothes, immediately aware that she is right. I am too weak for this.

The room spins wildly and there is no strength in my legs at all. I sit down again, suddenly. "I will be right enough in a moment, Bess, my head is just a little light but it will clear."

Against her will, she helps me roll up my hose and slip into a loose robe before tucking my hair beneath a French hood. By rights I shouldn't leave my chamber for another month, but Eve's wellbeing takes precedence over social niceties.

The room rocks and sways as I follow a winding path to the door that Bess holds wide. Outside, I cling to the bannister and prepare to tackle the stairs which suddenly appear very steep and very wide. While I stand there, ignoring the rushing sound in my ears and forcing my eyes to focus properly, the door of the lower hall opens and voices waft toward me. I hear the lighter tone of my mother and the deeper voice of a man.

Mother and a gentleman approach the staircase. As they set foot upon the bottom step, they both look up and see me there but, before her companion can speak, Mother is halfway up the stair. "Bella! What on earth are you doing out of bed? Bess, take her back at once."

I ignore her words and fasten my eyes on the man behind her, my heart giving a little leap of joy ... or something. He is paler and thinner than I remember and he seems somehow younger … less sure. His eyes are anxious, belying the flush of pleasure on his cheek. For a moment, I cannot tell if he is pleased or not.

"Bella!" He takes the steps two at a time and I feel his hand warm on mine, his lips moist on my knuckles. I close my eyes and smile as his familiar perfume wafts over me. Somehow, I sense that all is to be well between us.

"Anthony." I choke on the word, my knees trembling. "I have never been so glad to see anyone in my life!"

Seeing that I am about to faint, he scoops me into his arms and bears me back to my chamber, Bess and Mother fussing in our wake.

"What are you doing here? Are you sure you are well enough to travel?"

Anthony sits at my bedside, his face still flushed, clasping our son awkwardly in his arms.

"Possibly not, but I was anxious to see you, although I had no idea I'd be presented with a son so soon."

Bess is lifting my legs back into bed, pulling the cover to my chin again and tucking the sheet down tight.

"He comes a week or two before we expected him. Oh, my Lord, I am glad to see you."

A long silence follows and then he says, "Was it very bad?"

Our eyes meet. "Was what bad, giving you a son or watching the Queen die?"

He looks down at his child. "Both, I suppose. I have been worried for you every minute since she was taken prisoner but there was nothing I could do. I was powerless at first, and then later, I was sick."

"Anthony, once it was happening and she needed me so much, I would not have left her even had you sent for me. She was just a silly girl, caught up in the intrigues of her uncle. I was glad to be there for she had no one else to trust."

213

"I didn't think you liked her."

"I didn't. Not at first. I saw what everyone else saw. She was shallow, greedy, vain, everything I despise. But, Anthony, she was a *child*. A child in torment and when the King turned against her, all her sycophantic friends faded away and she was left with no one."

"Except for you."

"Yes, except for me who had no love for her. But by the time I watched her on the scaffold, I was proud to be her friend. There was more nobility in the way she died than any *Tudor* has ever shown."

He leans forward, covers my hands with his. "Hush, hush, you must not say such things. We will return home and forget about the court. We will sit in the gardens and watch our son flourish."

I smile wistfully. "That sounds lovely, Anthony. Indeed it does. But first, I need you to help me with something else."

Anthony offers the baby a finger and smiles when he feels the strength of his son's grip. "Something else?"

"Thomas means to send Eve away, and I have only just found her."

"Why would your brother do that? Where is he sending her?"

Slowly, as I begin to relate the sorry tale of Eve and all that has befallen her, he comes to understand the import of my words and I gain his full attention. "She is not herself, you say? Is she violent?"

"No, no. Not at all. She is like a child, harmless and affectionate, but Thomas cannot see past her strangeness. Since her, erm, indiscretion with one of his friends the other night, he is refusing to keep her here."

"And he is planning to send her where?"

"That is what you must discover, Anthony. I hope we can change his mind. I was hoping that you might be able to offer her a home with us, in Wales. If that is the case, he may well consent just to be rid of her."

A long silence follows while my husband examines our son's fingers, his wisps of fine hair, his button nose. "And she is not violent, you say?"

"No. Well, a little maybe, but she is troubled, Anthony, and … confused. I think stability and love will keep her calm. We must at least try."

"Must?"

For a long while we stare into each other's eyes, while I remember all the things I could have done that would have made me a better wife to him. Things I neglected to do that could have made him happy. *Is it too late?* I lick my lips and raise my chin.

"Anthony, in the short time we have had together I have not been the best of wives, but I hope to make things better now. I feel we have been given a second chance. I have Eve back and we have our son and perhaps, God willing, more will follow. I would like to make a proper home, in Wales, and, and …well, Eve is my *sister*. To be truly happy I need her with me. I cannot abandon her … I hope you will help me, but I have to tell you. I will protect her with, or without, your help." Defiantly and a little sadly, I stick out my chin.

"Calm down, Bella, and listen to me. Think about this carefully. You are speaking of a woman whom your own brother denounces as a whore."

"Anthony! She is no more a whore than *I* am … or Queen Katherine was! She lived among whores that is all. And besides, women are put on Earth for the use of men, and it seems to me that it is merely a matter of luck whether we serve one man or many!"

215

"Bella! For Heaven's sake; what a thing to say!"

He rises from the low stool with as much dignity as he can muster and hands the child back to Bess. Astounded at my outburst, Bess forces her mouth closed and turns away toward the cradle, leaving my husband and I alone.

I have lost his sympathy and he will refuse my request. Why can I not learn to keep my opinions to myself? Great hot tears wash down my cheeks and fall onto my shift. It isn't like me to weep and I try to dry my eyes, but they quickly fill again.

"I'm sorry, Anthony. I didn't mean that. Please try to understand, I am changed. I have seen some terrible things in the time we've been apart. All I long for is an end to it. I want some peace, time to contemplate and value what we have. I want to be able to count my blessings, but I don't think I can ever consider myself fortunate while Eve is unsafe. She needs me now, more than she ever did."

His breath escapes in a great sigh and he sits on the mattress, takes my chilly hand in his warm one. "I will speak with Thomas and see what can be done."

With great daring I reach out and, placing my hand on his collar, draw his face close to mine.

"Thank you, Anthony." His skin smells warm and fragrant and the touch of his lips on my cheek is as soothing as a blessing.

Of course, Thomas agrees. He doesn't care where Eve goes, just as long as he does not have to put up with her in his home or acknowledge her as his sister. To my shame, he offers us nothing in the way of financial aid, not even at the last minute when Mother asks if there is a place for her with us too. Poor Anthony, would he have offered for my hand had he known of the responsibilities he was taking on?

216

I doubt it very much.

So, on a damp May morning when Mother, Eve, Bess and I are preparing to climb into the carriage and embark on our new life in Wales, a stranger shambles into the yard on a hired hack, and asks to speak to Eve or her guardian.

He is not a gentleman but his appearance is decent; his plain homespun clothes are dyed a dreary shade of green. He pulls off his cap at Anthony's approach and shifts from foot to foot. *What can he want of us?*

I strain my ears to listen but Anthony leads him away to the far corner of the yard, where their words are cloaked by the clanging of the blacksmith's hammer. I watch them, my curiosity rising as my husband appears to listen intently to all the man has to say and I am greatly relieved when Anthony raises a hand and summons me to his side.

"This fellow has ridden from London Town to speak with Eve's guardian. It seems he has some information regarding her ... erm, her adventures across the river." My heart fails a little. I am not sure I want to hear of this.

"We are her guardians now ..." I hear myself say. "What is it that you have to tell us?"

He wets his lips, looks at the sky and back at his shoes again before clearing his throat. "We found your sister, My Lady. She was lost and wandering and, not knowing who she was or where she had come from, a friend of mine took her in, looked after her ... as good as if she were kin. She meant no harm, begging your pardon, Sir ... Madam."

He looks from me to Anthony, unsure which of us he should be addressing. I decide to take control.

"She was filthy, lice-ridden and starving. How can you claim to have looked after her? Why didn't you just bring her home?"

"We couldn't do that, Madam. We didn't know where she come from and besides, when we found her she was covered all in blood and we thought she might be in trouble. We just thought to protect her, like. And Joanie, she who had the main care of her, why she came to love her like she was her own child. There's been days when I've seen her give your sister the food off her own plate so she wouldn't starve."

His words are a blur, all but one of them.

"Joanie?" I say, weakly as everything falls into place. "She was called Joanie? – Oh, my God."

"What is it, my dear? What is the matter?" Anthony takes my elbow and prevents me from stumbling before leading me a short distance away. I put a hand to my head and swallow my repulsion.

"Eve," I whisper. "When Eve is upset, she calls out a word. We hadn't realised it was somebody's name. She cries out over and over for something, a thing, someone it now turns out, that she calls Oanee. It can only be her … the whore, Joanie."

The fellow, who has been eavesdropping, steps a little closer. "Your sister loved Joanie, wouldn't let her out of her sight, and Joanie loved her in return and protected her like she were a queen cat with its kitten."

"Well, Eve is back where she belongs now." Anthony offers him a few coins. "Thank you for your concern and give your friend our thanks."

But the fellow shrugs off the offering, his face reddening with belligerence. "Eve may be safe, Sir, but meanwhile, my *friend*, as you call her, is in The Clink awaiting the hangman's noose. And for what, Sir? For what? For protecting your sister and keepin' her from harm!"

Joanie Toogood – The Clink Prison

I take the proffered stool gingerly, my eyes darting from her to Peter and back again, questions teeming like silver fishes in my mind. After the squalor of my prison the lady is like a Queen, her gown as grand as any I've ever seen at close quarters. She is so clean that I am suddenly aware of the stench of my own body, the raggedy state of my clothes. I lift my chin and try to look down my nose at her while inside the real Joanie is shamed and cringing.

What does she want with me? Peter is nodding at me like a lunatic, trying to tell me something, but I am wary. I cannot trust the likes of her, whoever she is. While we confront each other, the door opens and Sybil slips in, coming to stand beside me.

"Joanie … I can call you Joanie?" The lady is smiling, gracious, like a flaming goddess. I lick my stiff lips, my returning smile more like a snarl.

"It's my name, might as well use it."

Her expression is pained as she looks around for another stool and, in an instant Sybil produces one, her ears perked like a Jack-rabbit's. The lady looks somewhat distastefully at the stool and declines to sit. She smiles again and I can tell she is ill at ease. I sniff and wait for her words.

"My name is Isabella Greywater … I used to be called Bourne …"

I stare back blankly, the name means nothing to me and unless she has the Clink keys secreted about her person, I don't care if she is the Queen of England.

"My sister's name is Evelyn Bourne. On her marriage she became Evelyn Wareham …"

Wareham! Francis! She is talking about M'lady, she is Eve's sister. I stand up, instantly on my guard, the stool skidding backwards across the floor. "I ain't done nothin' to be ashamed of!"

Peter steps forward, places a hand on my arm, his voice soothing as he presses me back into my seat. "It's all right, Joanie. Sit down, I told Lady Greywater what you did … it's all right. She wants to help you."

I raise my eyes to hers. She is many years younger than me, almost young enough to be my daughter, and she is Eve's sister; that gives us a link. Her skin is milky pale and her body firm and upright, but when I look in her eyes there are shadows and doubts, and I can see that life has touched her and she is as afraid as I am.

"How is she?" I whisper reluctantly, wanting to hear she is thrivin' but at the same time wanting her to be missing me as much as I am her. Lady Greywater fiddles with a loose thread on her fine white gloves and doesn't look me in the eye.

"She is physically well now that she is properly fed, but, well, I think we both know she will never be in possession of her mind again." She pauses as her eyes sweep the dim contours of the room; the damp straw, the stench of suffering. And this is one of the better rooms. "Joanie, I need you tell me exactly what happened. I need to know where and how you found her. Was she … injured … when you discovered her?"

I puff out a hefty breath that makes her flinch and raise her kerchief to her nose. She pretends to dab a tear from her eye and I watch her for a little while longer as I gather my thoughts. *Should I trust her? Will she believe me? Can she get me out of here?* If she doesn't have the key to my freedom, she might have the wherewithal to get hold of it. I decide to tell the truth and shame the devil.

"No," I say boldly. "She was as right as ninepence when I found her. She was looking for Francis … I – I knew Francis … He was a friend of mine. I was jealous of her and I told her where he was out of spite … to my shame, Lady."

She drops onto the stool and I lower my eyes to her fingers that are shredding the lace edging of her kerchief.

"And where was he?"

She is looking at me now and I glare back at her, refusing to give in to the shame and remorse that are churning in the pit of me stomach. "In my bed, Lady. Where he often was."

A slight indrawn breath and then she swallows and blinks rapidly, confounded by my honesty. "I said I'd tell it true …" I add belligerently.

"I know, I know, and I thank you for that." She fights to regain her self-possession and slowly her blushes fade. "So - so Eve found Francis in your bed and then … then what happened? Peter here says she had blood on her hands and on her gown ... Do you think she killed him?"

Her voice has dropped to a whisper, her chin trembling, her face pale as parchment. I shift in my seat, rustle the straw underfoot and sense Sybil creeping closer. Her hand slips into mine. "Careful, Joanie," she warns, with an unfriendly leer at the lady.

"I have nothing to hide, Sybil." I look Lady Greywater firmly in the eye. "When she come out of my chamber, there was blood on her gown and she was in a proper state, babbling nonsense and scrabbling at me. I tried to stop her but … but she fell, My Lady. She fell top to bottom down the stair and when she come to again, she was like she is now, sort of … lost- like."

She is weeping freely now, dabbing her cheeks with her shredded scrap of lace, her eyes red. "And do you think she killed him? Was anyone else there?"

"No, my Lady, nobody else but ... Well, at first I thought she done it, there was no one else and what with him being caught with his trousers down, so to speak, I gathered she must've lost her temper and snatched up his dagger. But, as I grew to know and ... and to love her, if you forgive me for saying so, My Lady, I came to realise that Eve could never harm anyone. She is as gentle as a lamb ... as soft as a kitten ..."

"Kittens have claws." Sybil climbs to her feet, brushing muck from her skirts. "Of course she done it. She must've if she was the only one there."

"NO!" Lady Greywater and I speak together, a gentlewoman concurring with a whore. "No," she repeats, "I cannot believe that. My sister was – is – many things but she would never harm Francis. She loved him – probably more than he deserved."

"Didn't we all?" I hear myself say.

Peter is deep in thought, his head down, stirring the rushes with the toe of his boot which is not necessarily a wise thing to do. He looks up suddenly. "Joanie," he says. "Lady Greywater." He bows his head. "I've been thinking about the day we found her. Before now, I had always assumed she must've killed him, it just seemed obvious. But well, I was in your yard that morning, Joanie, and there was another fellow there, a stranger ... not a neighbour."

I look up sharply. "Why've you never said before?"

Surprised, he scratches his head. "I don't know. Nobody ever asked. I've never given it a thought. It isn't as if it's unusual to find gentlemen of the court lurking in your alley, is it?"

222

I give a half-laugh. "Well, I'll give you that. What did he look like?"

Peter comes close, crouches at my side, his goose-turd green tunic linking the undyed homespun of my own skirt and my Lady's rich brocade. "I didn't look close. He was beneath the arch leading from The Cock. Not a great gentleman or anything but a middling sort. He could have been a servant or bondsman. I assumed he was waiting for his master to appear. Did Francis have a servant?"

"Not that I ever heard of. He kept a low profile. As Master Cromwell's spy, the less who knew about his dealings the better. He never told me a thing ..."

"Master Cromwell's spy? What do you mean, Joanie?"

I gape at the lady, worried I have said something I shouldn't, but there is no point starting to dodge the truth now. "That's what he was, Lady. That's how he kept his purse fat. He never told me much about it, but he couldn't help bragging when he first began the work. I told him it would lead to trouble ..."

"Are you certain of this, Joanie?" Lady Greywater leans closer, her narrowed eyes darting about as she fights to digest this piece of news.

"Sure as I'm a Goose, my Lady, yes. He reported weekly to a Nicholas Brennan, who passed his messages and ciphers back to Cromwell."

She straightens up and I can see her mind working as she speaks as if to herself. "Francis and Eve disappeared around the time Cromwell was executed, didn't they? There must be some connection. There must be." She stands up and turns to Peter. "Peter, would you know this man, this servant, again if you saw him?"

Peter rolls his hat into a ball, his face the colour of a cardinal's cap. "I don't know, Lady. Maybe, if he was wearing the same clothes."

I get up too and for a few moments we stand in a circle, Sybil a little apart, watching sulkily. Lady Greywater takes a deep breath. "I think you have been very helpful, Joanie. I – I thank you for the care you gave my sister and I will do all I can to discover the answers to this puzzle and see what I can do to free you from this … this place."

She waves her gloved hand around the dingy cell. I don't know why but I bob a curtsey, it just seems the right thing to do. "Thank you, My Lady," I say, and squeeze Peter's hand as he escorts her out. He smiles and winks at me.

"I will be back, Joanie, with news, just as soon as I can."

Isabella Greywater – May 1542

Anthony is waiting outside, ill at ease in the squalor of the Southwark street. I inhale deep, deep breaths to rid myself of the fetid air of gaol. He takes my elbow. "Come along now, let us hope you haven't contracted gaol fever. I gather you learned nothing to your advantage?"

I pull away, fiddling with the cuff of my glove. The embroidery is beginning to unravel and I will have to send them to be repaired. "On the contrary," I reply briskly as he helps me mount my mare. "I have learned something very interesting indeed but I shall save it until we cannot be overheard."

I toss Peter a coin. "I will send word to you when the time comes, Peter," I say and he makes a clumsy bow and dissolves into the crowd.

Anthony rides ahead and I fasten my eye on his erect back and follow him through the throng. Our servants walk before us, clearing a path through the common folk with the aid of their whips. The crowd regard us sullenly, standing bedraggled and cold on the slick, black cobbles. Soon the shoulders of my cloak are darkened as the rain settles like seed pearls on my sleeves and gloves.

Once safely back at Richmond, Bess helps me strip off my wet clothes and rub my hair dry. She is out of sorts here in the splendour of the palace, and frets about the children succumbing to the summer fevers that beset the city every year. I have promised that it isn't for long, and indeed I too am desperate to escape to the country.

After weeks of mist and drizzle, the summer promises no improvement. Anthony and I shiver

225

before the fire that is roaring up the chimney as if it is a January day while I relate all that I have learned. I pause when a servant brings hot drinks and Anthony sends him away and serves me himself, leaning over me with a steaming jug. "So, we didn't postpone our journey home for nothing?"

"Did you have *any* idea that Francis was … well, that he was a spy?"

He sits down and crosses one leg over the other. "Of course not. I would have thought he was too light-minded to be trusted with secrets … but someone obviously thought otherwise."

"Do you think Eve knew?"

He shrugs and dips his nose into his cup, takes a long pull at his drink. When he looks up, his moustache is white with froth. "I don't think we will ever know the answer to that … or many other things. I say we forget about it and go home, put it all behind us."

"Anthony, we can't! We must at least get Joanie out of gaol, she doesn't deserve to hang."

He raises his eyes slowly. "I am sure she is guilty of something." His words are eloquent although they leave a lot unsaid. I drop my eyes before my husband's antipathy of whoredom but I am determined to fight for her.

"She doesn't deserve to die, Anthony, and I won't hear otherwise. I see her as *unfortunate,* not evil. She is a good sort, deep down, loving and gentle and Peter says …"

"Oh *Peter*, well I am sure a costermonger's opinion is wiser than my own."

I jerk my head and am relieved to find him half in jest. I adjust my attack to pleading. "I need to help her, if I can, Anthony. If it weren't for Joan Toogood there is no telling where Eve may have ended up. Why, she might be at the bottom of the river by now."

Anthony holds up his hands. "All right, all right. I submit, my dear. I shall speak to Gardiner, since the matter is in his jurisdiction, and see what, if anything, we can do."

"Gardiner? A memory stirs of my few encounters with him and I shudder with irrational dislike. I would sooner avoid owing any favours to the smooth-speaking Bishop if I could.

Ten days later we are on our way home. Anthony promises me that Joan will be set free, and since I am so unwilling for her to return to her former life, we make provision for her future. But no matter how I plead, he refuses point blank to let me visit her in gaol again. All I can do is send instructions and a bag of coin to Peter to ensure that she has all that she may require.

As the horses' hooves eat up the arduous miles and the soft contours of the Welsh hills come into focus, I find I can forget London and begin to look to the future. Opposite me in the ladies' litter, Mother's head rolls and nods on her pillow. I don't know how she can sleep, the perpetual jogging and jolting prevents me from closing my eyes for longer than a moment.

Eve and Bess are travelling in the second litter while little John is here with me and his wet nurse. Anthony, of course, rides ahead. Without me and the household he would make much faster progress, but he pretends patience, for which I am grateful.

Most nights we stop at a wayside inn where the staff look askance at Eve, and Anthony on more than one occasion has to speak sharply to the landlord to convince him that she is harmless. People cross themselves and eye her warily as she shuffles up the stairs, her blank eyes wandering over the furnishings, a string of dribble at her lips. Their ignorant cruelty

227

makes me angry but Anthony says I must grow used to it. I comfort myself that once we are home, she will be safe from the eyes of strangers.

She seems content to be with us now and has ceased to cry for Joanie, but sometimes the expression on her face is so sad and lost that my heart could break. In a few short years my poor mother and sister have lost so much. I, in comparison, am steeped in riches.

I have a good husband and a lusty child and the promise of so much more to come. It is the least I can do to try to share my good fortune with them, I just wish that Eve could show me she is aware of my care. Constantly, I tell her I love her, I stroke her hair, hug her when she will allow, but I am never sure she understands. Often, after such a display of affection, she jumps up and runs away, chasing after Bess' daughter and squealing like a child, as if my soft words have never been spoken. At least, at such times I know she is happy ... or I think she is. Who can really say?

We are deep in the Welsh hills now, the road more rutted than ever, the mud claggy and wet. When the horses stop suddenly, I lean forward and lift the curtain to discover the reason for it. Anthony rides up and halts besides me, and I crane my neck to look at him. He holds out a hand. "Come," he says, "ride with me."

Too surprised to argue, I issue some hasty orders to the wet nurse and allow Anthony to haul me into the saddle before him. After I have ensured my legs are decently covered by my skirts, he wraps his arms around me and urges the horse forward.

It is a strange sensation to be in his arms again. His strong body rubs against mine as the horse rocks us back and forth. Above our heads the trees are showing tight green buds and apart from the creak of the horse trappings, all I can hear is birdsong. We leave the rest of the party behind, diverge from the worn track and climb upward, the horse labouring from the unaccustomed additional weight.

"Look," he says, his breath whispering in my ear. I follow the line of his finger to where a grey stone house nestles in a cleft in the hill. The stark walls are softened with flowers and foliage, providing a welcome splash of colour.

"Is that it, Anthony? Is that Greywater Abbey?"

"It is," he says, pride ringing in his voice, "and the alterations to the Abbot's quarters are almost finished. Do you like it?"

"Oh, I love it." It is quite true. I am instantly enamoured of my new home, the afternoon sun is shining on the subtle grey walls, blending it perfectly with the tranquillity of the valley. "It seems to have grown out of the hill." I don't know what else I can say, for my words inadequately convey my emotions and seem contrived somehow, and false.

"I like it too," he says, and I twist a little in the saddle so I can look at him.

"I will make you happy, Anthony." His face reddens and he pulls off his glove, tucks a tendril of hair back beneath my hood, his touch as gentle as thistledown.

"You already have," he whispers and when he kisses me, something turns in my tummy like a small silver fish in a stream. "Come, let us go home." While my mind lingers on the kiss and the strange feelings it evoked in me, he kicks his mount onward and we begin the slow descent to the Abbey. His arms are tight about my waist and I can feel his heart is beating, just as fast as mine.

Joanie Toogood

"Go on, out of 'ere." The turnkey throws open the door, his voice breaking into my early mornin' dreamin'.

"What d'yer mean?"

"You've been let off, someone put in a word for yer with the Bishop." I look about the filthy cell where Sybil and Jack are just emerging from a shabby blanket. She rubs her eyes and blinks up at me.

"What's goin' on, Joanie?"

I stare at the turnkey, suspecting trickery, and it isn't until he grabs me by the hair and drags me from the cell, chucking me and my bundle out onto the road, that I finally believe him. Sybil comes swiftly after. It is plain to see that she too has been wrenched from her bed. I've never 'eard of anyone being thrown out of gaol, 'tis usually the other way about. She clutches her stuff to her chest, her mouth upturned and blubberin'.

"What's the matter now?" I ask, exasperated.

"What about Jack? I can't leave Jack."

"Oh, yes you bloody well can," I say, and grabbing her arm I march her briskly from the prison precinct. "We need to get as far away from 'ere as we can, before they change their blimmin' minds."

I set quite a pace, instinctively heading for the Cock Inn yard, wondering if me rooms are still empty. In the alley we bump into Peter.

"Joanie," he cries, with a great bear hug. "I've been waiting for you. They really let you out? I wasn't sure it would ever happen."

"Well, I'll wager you were surer than I was." With a question in my eye I cock my head toward the stairway that leads to our old rooms, but Peter shakes his head.

"They've been let to someone else, Joanie love, but it's better so. You need a fresh start."

I think of the happy times I've spent in those rooms; childhood days when my mother kept me safe; and prosperous days spent with Francis. Even the recent times of poverty and want seem to have a rosy glow to 'em now I am forbidden to enter.

I sigh. "Well, I don't know where we'll stay then, looks like we're homeless, Sybil."

Peter relieves me of my bundle and takes my hand. "Don't be silly, Joanie, as if anyone around here would see you in want. There's no one in all o' Southwark who hasn't enjoyed your motherin' at some time or other. Come on. Bertha is waiting, she's put on a bit of a spread."

And so she has. There are meat pies, bread and a couple of jugs of ale on the table. Compared to what I've eaten lately, it is fare fit for a Queen. While we gather at her hearth, reminiscing on the larks we had when we were girls, and laugh at the antics of her dead, drunken husband, one by one the neighbours drop by to give me their best wishes.

"Good to have you back, Joanie," they say. "We missed you." "It 'asn't been the same without you." I am so touched by their kindness that I am forced to swallow a soppy, sentimental tear. And when Bertha offers me a bed at hers until I am sorted, it's all I can do not to blub openly like a bairn.

"I must be going." Peter stands up and cocks his head for me to follow. I half expect he is after a favour and it's the least I can do for him, he has been so good to me. But outside, when I reach up to kiss him, he grabs my wrists and presses me away.

"No, Joanie, that isn't what I want. I wanted to give you this."

He presses a purse into my hand, a fat one. "You can't afford this, Peter, it must be a small fortune!"

He laughs. "If I possessed such a sum I'd give it to you, Joanie, but it isn't from me. It's from Lady Greywater, travelling money, she wants you to follow them to Wales to take care of Eve."

I am gaping at him. "Look after Eve? Travel to Wales? What nonsense is this? I've never so much as travelled a mile up-river. I don't even know where Wales is!" I don't know if I should laugh or cry, so I bluster about having a job to do here and needing to look after Sybil.

He shuts me up with a sudden kiss. "This is your chance, Joanie. You can get away from here; go some place where no one knows what you've been. Lady Greywater's only demands are that you stop your whoring, go to church regularly and keep yourself clean. They need you. You want to see Eve again, don't you?"

I remember her wide eyes, the silkiness of her hair, the way her body used to tremble when I rocked her to sleep at night. The way she never took from me more than I was prepared to give.

"'Course I do." My voice is a bit hoarse so I clear my throat and try to make out I am not tempted.

"Well then." He crouches a little so he can see into my lowered face, and a tear drops onto my apron. Gently, he raises my chin and smiles into my eyes and, for the first time, I realise he is a man now. In my own special way, I've raised him from boyhood and there is just a chance he will be a better man for knowing me, not worse, as I have always feared.

"It's a long way," I sniff, wiping my nose on my sleeve. "An' I don't know how to get there."

"Well, I will have to help you to find a way then." He skips away, blows me a kiss. "I have to run,

I will come back tomorrow. You'd better break the news to Sybil."

Sybil is the fly in the ointment. I can't leave her here alone, for she has no idea how to look after herself. But when Peter comes back the next day and I tell him the change of plan, he looks from me to Sybil and back again. "Take her with you then, I'm sure they can find her work in the kitchens."

Sybil gets up and leans over the table. "I'm not a child, Joanie, and if you don't mind, Peter, I'm big enough to look after myself. Work in the kitchens indeed. I ain't going to no far off foreign place just to look after the likes of M'lady Wareham. I've a man to be thinkin' of now."

I had forgotten about Jack but Sybil, it seems, is set on sticking by him, whether they hang him or not. He is the only thing keeping her here, giving her a reason to stay, but I have nothin' to stay for and in the end, after much argument, I agree to go. But before I consent, I open the purse and give her a palmful of coins. With a whoop of joy, she flings her arms around my neck and, for the first time in years, I think that maybe she ain't so bad. She has it in her to be a good person ... if fate allows.

Sybil, Peter and Bertha stand on the quayside and watch me board the ship that is to take me to the port of Caerleon in Wales. It is a heavy day and as the figures of my friends grow smaller, my heart sickens. Part of me wants to leap over the side and swim back to shore but since I have no idea if I can stay afloat, I stay where I am, clinging to the ship's rail to keep them in my sights for as long as I can.

When we hit the open sea and the deck lurches beneath my feet and I discover it isn't only my heart that is sick. I am slumped on the deck with a leather bucket between my knees and it seems I'm not just vomiting up breakfast but my stomach along with it. The crew ignore me, and the few passengers give me a wide berth. I draw my forearm across my mouth, push back my sweat drenched hair and wish I could die of misery. Of all the things that have ever befallen me, this has got to be the worst. By the time the port is in sight, I have sworn never to venture on board again – not as long as I live.

Along with other merchandise on route to Greywater Abbey, I am loaded onto a produce cart where I cling to a barrel of herring and hope that I can sleep for a while. But the jolting and jerking of the cart is as discomforting as the ship. If my head isn't banging on the wooden sides, the ruts in the road are jarring my teeth. Every single bone in my body is aching and I feel as if I am being tortured. When we finally pass beneath the gates of the old abbey, I am too weary to be thankful and just longing for someone to show me where I can lay my head.

"Mistress Toogood?" A dark-haired matron is smiling at me, her cheeks a pretty shade of pink, her eyes not quite reaching mine.

"That's right," I say, hoisting up my bosom and giving her the benefit of my boldest stare. She holds out her hand.

"My name is Bess. I've been looking after Eve. The mistress says you are to come with me."

I trail after her, not to the big house itself but a smaller one that she tells me used to be the gatehouse when the monks were here. "It's where me and my daughter lodge," she says, flushing again, "and you'll be sharing with us."

She must know what I am, or what I was, and I wonder how a decent woman feels to be forced into the company of someone like me. Throwing open the door, she ushers me inside and I look about me.

It is plainly furnished and spotlessly clean. Compared to my old lodgings, or the rooms I have lately shared with Bertha, it is a palace. A proper big fire burns in the grate beneath a smoke blackened pot, and there is even rush matting instead of straw. In the centre stands a well-scrubbed table. It is a simple, decent room with three doors leading off. One must be a chamber, but I know not where the others lead. "Very nice," I say and she smiles at me and pours me a cup of short beer.

"I've water warming so you can bathe before I take you to greet Lady Greywater. She is mightily strict on cleanliness."

"It was a rough crossing," I say, not wanting her to think I am always so grubby.

"Come," she says and I follow her through one of the doorways into a bedchamber where sits a wooden tub, half full of tepid water. "Shall I help you undress, or will you manage?"

"Undress? Why?" I stare at her, full of suspicion.

"So you can bathe. I thought I had explained that."

I point in alarm at the tub. "What? Get in there? Naked-like?" I have never been wet all over. I had thought, when she mentioned 'bathing,' that she meant giving myself the once over with a bit of flannel.

She adds a steaming jugful to the bath. "Come on, it won't hurt you. The mistress is waiting to see you."

I watch her busy about, laying out linen on the bed. I slowly begin to untie my bodice. In Bess' company, for the first time in my life, I feel shamed of my own body. Maybe it's the way she averts her eye that makes me shield my dugs with my arms as I step anxiously into the water.

"Sit down then," Bess orders, and I do as she says, sinking my arse into the warmth. After a moment or so I realise it isn't as bad as I thought it would be. The water is a bit like a caress and almost right away I can feel the aches in my bones begin to ease. But when she tips a great jug of boilin' water over my head, I scream like a pig in the slaughter house and come up splutterin'.

"What did you do that for?" I blink water from my eyes and glare at her as she approaches with a big hunk of lye soap.

"The mistress mislikes vermin," she says firmly, "and your hair is alive with lice. Come on, Joan, be a good girl now."

Bess is fiercely thorough. The soap burns where the little blighters have been feastin' on my scalp and her nails feel as if she is raking great holes in my head. But afterwards, when I am wrapped in a linen sheet before the roaring fire so she can tease the snarls and dead livestock from my hair, I begin to feel more like myself again.

"There," she says, when I am all trigged up in a home dyed woollen skirt and fresh linen. "That is much better." I look down at my clothes, they have never been worn by anyone else. It's a new experience for me. The linen feels prickly on my fresh-scrubbed skin, and with my hair tucked away beneath a modest cap, I am as decent looking as a nun on a holy day. Bess looks pleased with the result of her labours. "There," she says, "I think we are ready to greet Lady Greywater now."

The big house that Bess leads me through is grander than anything I've ever seen. We pause outside Lady Greywater's inner chamber while Bess scratches on the door before taking me inside.

The chamber walls are lined with bright tapestries, the floors are clean and even the air is rich with the fragrance of herbs. When I was a girl and my mother took me to the priest for the first time, he spread me on a rich brocade counterpane. I remember noticing the way the colours of the pattern wove in and out of each other. There were birds and flowers and vines, but it was never so fine as the fabrics I see around me now. This place is fit for a Queen, I think to myself in those first moments. And then a movement takes my attention and I see Lady Greywater seated at the fireside. She is to be my mistress now. Although outside the sun is blazing it is not so warm indoors, but as we draw closer to the fire, the comfort increases. She looks up and smiles at me. "Joan." She beckons me closer to the hearth. "How well you look. Was your journey very tedious?"

I shake my head, for once made speechless by her treatment of me. She is speaking to me as if I am a decent sort, like Bess, and I am touched by it.

Bess bobs a curtsey and nudges me to do the same, but although I try to copy her, I am awkward in comparison. I let my eyes stray about the room again, taking in the rich furnishings, the gleam of the panelling on the wall, the stiff effigy of a man that seems to be painted on a board. "Eve is with my mother, would you like to see her?"

Her words drag me back to her face. I bob again, a better effort this time, I hope. "Oh yes, my Lady, I should indeed." She nods to Bess who, after sending me a silent scowl that warns me to behave myself, departs, leaving us alone. Lady Greywater looks at me quietly for a while before she breaks the silence again. "My sister seems to have loved you."

"That's nice to hear," I reply, not sure what she wants me to say.

"Of course, everything depends on how she receives you now. I'm sure you understand that, if she has forgotten you, we will not require you to care for her. But be assured, I will find you work in the kitchen or dairy but perhaps not in the house."

"I understand," I say, but I don't, not really. Why would she bring me all this way, make me suffer all I've suffered just to keep me in her dairy when she must have skilled workers aplenty? It makes no sense to me.

And then I hear a voice; a loud, childish babble of nonsense that I remember well. I turn to face the door. When it opens and Bess enters, leading Eve by the hand as if she were a child, my heart jumps a little in my chest.

This is an Eve I've never seen before. She is plump and rosy, no longer in rags and craving for food. She is so clean!

I take a step toward her and wait for her to notice me, praying she will recognise me. My mouth is as dry as ashes and I swallow a lump in my throat while she examines me dispassionately from the other side of the room. Her dull eyes rest upon me for a long, long moment and while I whisper a silent prayer, she keeps on looking. I feel as if I am going to sweal away with the waiting.

Then, in a few shuffling steps, she crosses the space between us and, without speaking, lays her head on my breast. I close my eyes as her arms slide around my neck and she begins to rock, back and forward, humming very gently. And all the while, my silly tears are dropping onto her linen cap.

Isabella Greywater – July 1542

There can be no mistaking Eve's fondness for Joanie. She has been calmer and happier these last few hours than I have seen her in a very long time. It may seem foolish for Anthony and I to allow her contact with a woman like Joan Toogood, but it was the only way to ensure my sister any lasting peace.

In fact, the more time I spend with her, and the immodest images that my mind conjures of her unspeakable past begin to fade, I find her company much easier than some of the gentle women I knew at court. She is funny and unpretentious. I do not doubt her when she says she loves Eve like her own child, and that she protected her as far as was possible. Her devotion seems to be returned full measure and although I am sorry to have lost the closeness I once shared with my sister, I can take some comfort from her present happiness.

They are walking before me in the garden now, and Eve's head is resting on Joanie's shoulder. Bess' daughter, Mary, tags along behind them with her fat fists full of daisies. It is so long since I have felt such contentment that I am unsure it can last.

In the Abbey precinct Anthony and his steward are overseeing the unloading of the produce brought by ship from London. When he sees me, he raises a hand in welcome. I alter my direction and cross the grass toward him. Joan and Eve, seeing my departure from the path, follow slowly in my wake. When I reach him, Anthony removes his feathered cap and tinkers with it, casting a doubtful eye in Joan's direction. "So, she has arrived, then?"

"As you see, my Lord, she has, and Eve seems very pleased. Indeed she has scarcely let go her hand since they were reunited." I am determined not to allow his reservations to sway my resolution.

"Well, she is certainly more wholesome looking than I expected."

"She is indeed, and is still very handsome, I think. I begin to see what charm she held for Francis."

Anthony's brow crinkles. "Good Lord, she is not fairer than Eve."

"No, but she has a certain motherliness that some men favour."

He makes no answer but I notice the flush upon his face and know that he is thinking of the intimate hours we have lately both enjoyed in the privacy of our bedchamber.

Joan and Eve are close now and he looks down his nose at Joan and gives her a grudging welcome. "It is good to see you in happier circumstances," he says guardedly.

"Yes, my Lord, and 'tis good to be here among honest folk ..." Her words trail off and her brow furrows as her eye is taken with someone in the yard. "My Lady, what is he doing here? The fellow bearin' the sack of grain? I'm sure I've seen him before, loitering on the Bankside."

Anthony and I turn to where she is pointing and my husband quirks his brow. "Do you mean Perkins? My steward engaged him a week since. His recommendation was good. Do you know him well?"

"Nay," Joan replies, "not well at all, but I know his face, if I can only place just where I have seen it."

"Which fellow do you mean, Joanie? The one stacking the sacks in the barn? Oooh ..." As the man turns, I am at once struck by so great a coincidence that my blood runs quite cold. I too have seen that pale face and those bulbous eyes somewhere before. "Anthony, th – that is Bishop Gardiner's man, I am sure of it! I saw them together at Greenwich, and

240

while I was on progress with the Queen, I saw him speaking to Dereham, the man that died along with Culpepper. Why should he be suddenly working as a servant for us, here in the wilds of Wales?"

"I have no idea, but I mean to discover it." Anthony strides determinedly across the yard and, summoning his steward to follow him, hails the fellow forward. As if I am watching a play, I see the man whip off his cap. Realising he is in some trouble, he cringes beneath the hail of my lord's questions. He nods and then shakes his head, every vestige of colour flooding from his parchment cheeks, and his eyes dart about the precinct as if seeking an escape. Then, quite suddenly, my husband thrusts him bodily against the barn door and whips out his dagger.

"Anthony!" I cry, running toward him and hovering just a short distance away. "Take care, my Lord."

Anthony ignores me. "Why has Gardiner sent you?" he snarls. "What do you hope to find here? Who do you wish to harm?"

The fellow's neck is stretched and the point of the dagger is digging deep into his skin. I see a ruby drop of blood appear, followed by another, the crimson beads forming a chain that dribbles down and soaks into his collar.

"I mean no harm to anyone." He gasps, his eyeballs swivelling from Anthony to the steward and back again. "My instructions are to keep an eye on the girl and ascertain that she is indeed a lunatic."

"What else?"

"I am to seek out what she knows about her husband's last movements."

"Why?" Anthony leans in closer, increasing the pressure of his blade. His usual demeanour is quite abandoned and I am seeing my husband in a whole new light. My heart beats rapidly and beside me I can

241

hear Joanie's breath issuing in short, sharp jerks as she absorbs the scene. The tension hovers in the air around us, making the skin on the back of my neck prickle. "I'm waiting." Anthony's voice is menacing, I feel I scarcely know him.

"Wareham stole some papers detrimental to my master's cause and sold them to his enemies. The Bishop seeks to lay hands on them."

"And," Anthony persists, "presumably he also seeks knowledge of Wareham's whereabouts." The fellow is quiet. We can see his mind feverishly determining how to answer, but before he can make reply, Joan steps forward. Her voice is low and dangerous as she seals the fellow's tomb.

"He ain't interested in Francis. I reckon he knows very well what happened to him for he's the one that killed him. Ain't that right? I'd bet my quaint this is the sly fellow Peter saw in my yard that day, and I'll wager he's been dogging us all ever since."

The villain says nothing, but flinches when Anthony drives his fist into the barn door just inches from the fellow's head. "Answer me, man, before I forget myself and give you what you deserve."

He keeps his eyes closed and decides to neither struggle nor deny his crime.

"It was an honest fight, my Lord. I did but seek the papers he carried but he resisted me and drew his knife. It was him or me. I had no choice."

Joan crosses herself, and we draw in a shared breath of horror while Eve, unaffected by the presence of her husband's murderer, sits on the ground and begins to hum a nursery tune.

No one tells her to get up.

"But you found no paper, did you?" Anthony continues, twisting the tip of his blade, making the blood flow afresh.

"No." Perkins, if that truly is his name, is beaten, his body submissive as my husband persists with his questions. "And you snuck off into the shadows like a cur and left Mistress Wareham to take the blame. Have you any idea how she has suffered since?" When he makes no reply, I can contain myself no longer.

"You should be flogged," I cry, but Anthony turns a stern eye upon me.

"Keep out of this, Bella. Take the women back to the house and stay there. This fellow shall be chained in the dungeon until I can get him back to London. It's the hangman's noose for him, no matter who his master is, for I shall be taking this matter directly to the King himself."

He signals to the steward and as I hurry the women back inside, I turn in time to see them leading him off in chains.

As soon as we reach the fireside I am stricken by a fit of shivering and nothing serves to warm me. I submit willingly as Mother covers me with a blanket and chaffs my hands and arms, while Bess brings me a strong restorative drink.

"Just imagine, Madam; if Joan hadn't recognised him, we might have all been murdered in our beds!"

It is not a thing I care to dwell on but I understand her need. "We may indeed, Bess. I think we are all deeper in Joanie's debt than ever."

Joanie looks up from retying Eve's sleeve. "You owe me nothin', My Lady, nor ever shall. Having the care of Eve is all the thanks I will ever need."

And then she goes back to her task as if she has been doing it all her life.

Isabella Greywater 1543

A year has passed and all is well at Greywater Abbey. We keep as far from London as we can, although Anthony is summoned to attend the wedding of the King and his new bride. Henry chooses another Catherine this time, as if he has some fatal fascination with that name. Knowing what Catherine Parr has in store she has my pity, but I plead sickness and stay away from the wedding.

I have no wish to return to Greenwich, for everything I need is here. I have a warm and happy marriage now and a good husband. Our son is thriving and another child is already on the way. We both hope for a daughter, which is strange, for no one knows better than I that a woman's lot is often hard.

My mother, with old age fast approaching, is comfortable here among the lush hills of Wales. She finds peace among the flowers and if she ever remembers that the garden paths she treads once knew the footsteps of dispossessed monks, she does not mention it. The Abbey maintains a certain monastic peace and I am reminded of them often; how can it be otherwise? We sleep in the Abbot's bedchamber, prepare our food in the monks' kitchens, dine in their refectory and worship in their church. I should, I suppose, feel guilt to have profited by their downfall, but it was the hand of Cromwell and the King that brought them down, not us. The only recompense I can make is to ensure their buildings are maintained and my prayers are added to theirs. I spend many hours on my knees, giving thanks that Eve has been returned to me. For that I am truly grateful.

She thrives as well as she ever will and knowing her days are spent in Joanie's loving hands, I enjoy the kind of peace I thought I'd never know again.

I am enjoying an hour of solitude in my solar when voices floating up from the garden draw me to the window. I peer through the open casement and the scene below teases a smile.

Joanie and Eve are taking air around the gardens.

"Mistress Eve, what 'ave I said? You will get me hung if you keep pluckin' your sister's blooms. Give 'em 'ere."

The girl holds out a fistful of white roses and Joanie sinks her nose into them. "Mmmm," she says, taking them from Eve. "I can't blame you fer pickin' 'em, mind, they smell sweeter than an angel's breath. Did I ever tell you about that time I saw a real angel?"

My sister shakes her head, silently willing Joanie to reply. "No? Well, I was walkin' across London Bridge, mindin' me business, when all of a sudden there she was, lightin' up the world around her …"

Her voice fades as they move together across the garden, and then Bess appears from the house with my son on her hip and calls to them that it's time for the midday meal. Bess' daughter, Mary, toddles into view and I see Joan bend down and scoop her into her arms, swinging her around and making her squeal with glee.

My hand caresses the burgeoning globe of my womb where the babe kicks lustily beneath my ribs. And, riding into this idyllic scene is Anthony, swinging from the saddle, calling for his groom and completing the happy picture.

The End

Author's Note

The Winchester Goose is a work of fiction based upon a foundation of fact. Everyone knows about Henry VIII and his wives, we all know the impact he had on English history. What I wanted to explore was the possible effect his actions had on the wider population, in particular the underbelly of society.

Southwark teemed with the more dissolute section of society, but they were not all of the lower class. Attracted by the sex on sale, visitors to the capital sought the entertainments on offer there and there are reports of night-time trips across the Thames to and from the royal court.

The prostitutes who worked in Southwark did indeed pay their rents to the Bishop of Winchester and before the reformation provided a service to monks and clerics. They were known as The Winchester Geese, but their world was a great deal bleaker than I have painted it. I have only touched upon the likelihood of contracting sexually transmitted disease or the risk of imprisonment or physical abuse.

The incident with the young noblemen firing stone arrows at the girls working on the Bankside is mentioned in the historical record, although it takes place a number of years before the narrative begins. The main culprit in this crime was the young Henry Howard, Earl of Surrey who ended his life on the scaffold for another unrelated offence to the King. The incident with the bear on the Thames barge did indeed take place, but the papers the clerk was carrying were to do with Cranmer's findings on the six articles and not concerned with Katherine Howard at all. I changed the nature of these papers to suit my story because I

246

could not resist the colourful picture the incident evokes. I make no apologies for this.

The women who worked as prostitutes formed an unexplored section of Tudor society. During the course of my studies I became fascinated with what they may have made of the goings on at Henry's court.

Henry, for all his extra-marital and marital escapades, was quite a fastidious man and, offended by the tales of disease and crime, determined to clean up the area. Vice in all its forms thrived and theft and murder were commonplace, but it was not until 1546, a few years after my story ends, that he finally succeeded in closing the brothels down. Of course, it didn't last. The women simply moved on, spreading the contagion and making vice more widespread in London than ever and after Henry's death, his heir Edward VI was still complaining about the widespread Vice in London.

In many ways, most women of the period, particularly the upper classes, were bought and sold. Forbidden the luxury of choosing their own mate, the marriages of gentlewomen were financially or politically motivated, and subject to parental control. Love didn't come into it but politics and power played a large part.

Historians widely agree that Katherine Howard's marriage to Henry was instigated by her uncle, Norfolk, who together with his allies, Stephen Gardiner and Suffolk, desired a return to traditional methods of worship. With Anne of Cleves out of favour with the King they lost no time in promoting their own candidate.

Opposing this was Cromwell, serving both his King and his own preference for church reform and his fall had less to do with disservice to Henry and more to do with the plotting of enemies.

The brief years of Henry's marriages to Anna of Cleves and Katherine Howard contrast and compare very nicely with the role played by Joanie Toogood.

I have tried to be as accurate as possible in telling this story, but some things have to be simplified to make for an engaging read. I did not want to bog my reader down with historical detail and tedious explanations, not because I doubt their ability to understand, but because I wanted them to become more engaged with the characters.

Apart from historical court figures, all characters are fictional and their opinions not necessarily mine.

I do hope you enjoy the journey into Tudor England and despite some of the more unsavoury characters you have met there, join me there again in my next novel *The Kiss of the Concubine.*

Judith Arnopp's other works include:

Peaceweaver: the story of Eadgyth, Queen to Gruffydd ap Llewelyn of Wales and Harold II of England.

The Forest Dwellers: a tale of Norman oppression.

The Song of Heledd: the story of a 7th century princess of Powys.

Dear Henry: Confessions of the Queens: Short Tudor Stories

All available in paperback and on Kindle.